Mafia King
Vi Carter

Copyright © 2021 by Vi Carter

All rights reserved.

No portion of this book may be reproduced in any form without written permission from the publisher or author, except as permitted by U.S. copyright law.

Vi Carter

a man, made of flesh and bones. The moment he hit the ground, I knew the game was over.

I push my nails a little deeper until they bend and threaten to snap.

Right now, as I sob on the floor, the thought that races through my mind is: What have you done, Noel?

What have I done?

My vision blurs, and I close my eyes as I drag another breath in; it hitches on a sob that I can't hold in any longer.

It's their screams and panic that still pierces my mind. Hundreds of people fighting to get over each other, with love flying out the window, protection didn't exist at that moment, as each person fought for their own safety.

Yet, all the while, he had stood at the altar staring at me. Knowing who was behind this.

It's the look of absolute betrayal in Shay's eyes that I will never forget.

Bending my head, I seal my lips together, so the scream doesn't erupt from me. He hadn't run like everyone else; he didn't dive to the ground; instead, he stood before me in his dark suit, looking like a King that had just climbed off his horse, only to find out that there was nothing at all here for him to rule.

Footsteps pound along the wooden corridor, and I tuck my head deeper into my chest. *Keep running, check other rooms. I'm not here.*

My memory is filled with brown eyes widening before narrowing, while guns released countless rounds of ammunition. Hysteria reached its peak as everyone scrambled across church pews. Large golden candle holders collided with marble. The impact rattled the ground, but nothing rattled me like Shay.

Another sob has me slipping from the stool, and my hands touch the dark wooden floor. My polished nails drag along it as my mind grows more frantic as I replay the pain in Shay's eyes. He no longer was a god with a shield around him. No, he became

PROLOGUE

O'REAGAN
AN CHLANN
EMMA

The air is too thin. I can't breathe. It's like a swollen storm that's all caught up inside me—rose-red blood blossoms on my once white wedding dress. My fingers play along the destructive substance as I drag air painfully into my lungs. The dress had been designed just for me. Every inch of the trim was done in lace, each stitch done by hand. It was truly a masterpiece that was smashed to pieces.

The room tilts, and I dig my hands deeper into the soft fabric to keep myself on the small navy stool. I focus on the white piano in front of me, the cover open, the white stool at an angle like it's waiting to be played.

NEWSLETTER

Join my newsletter and never miss a new release or giveaway:

WARNING

This book is a dark romance. This book contains scenes that may be triggering to some readers and should be read by those only 18 or older.

North rises up demanding retribution for a crime that was buried a long time ago.

The clock is ticking as I battle a war around me and within my own walls. Every minute takes us both closer to certain death. I'm unsure of who my true allies are and where my enemies are hiding. There's only one thing I'm certain of.

I will never give up.

I will fight to the end, no matter the cost.

I am a King and I will die on my feet.

He's a savage. She's a willing bride who dreams of freedom; only she gives up one cage to find herself in another.

EMMA

I was a willing sacrifice in an arranged marriage.
Until my father made a new deal and gave me to another.
Now I must marry a savage.
A Northerner- the very thing I had been taught to hate.
I vow to never be his. I will never belong to Shay O'Reagan.
I will defy him every step of the way.
He may lay claim to my body, but he will never own my heart.

SHAY

In order to secure my place in the Irish Mafia, I agree to an arranged marriage.
A marriage with a willing bride, one groomed to be the wife of a mafia king.
What I get is a redheaded beauty hell bent on my destruction.
Turns out, she was meant to be the perfect mafia wife- just not mine.
That treacherous detail doesn't stop me from wanting her.
From needing to taste her ruby red lips.
The fire that blazes in her defiant eyes lights a desire inside of me that demands I claim her as my own.
While she wastes my time defying me with every breath, the

CHAPTER ONE

O'REAGAN
AN CHLANN
EMMA

A wooden ruler brought down heavily on my hand brings me back to the present.

"Are you trying to scare the livestock away?" Breda's pale face tightens as she shakes her head in disapproval. Her Cavan lilt is more pronounced now that I have annoyed her.

I shake out my aching hand while holding the tin whistle in the one that she hasn't assaulted yet.

"You're not concentrating!" She barks. She's strict, but normally not this strict. She steps away from me and circles the red high-back chair that is reserved for her alone. She rarely sits throughout our lessons. I'm not sure if standing makes her feel more powerful. Her standing or sitting doesn't affect me. I've been around Breda far too long for her stern, nun-like face to frighten me anymore. As a child, my reaction was very different.

A slow grin stretches across my lips. "You're as excited as I am." I point the tin whistle at Breda.

Her short legs make quick work of the floor, and the ruler comes down harder on my hand. My body responds, and I jump away until I'm at a safe distance from the offensive weapon while cradling my throbbing hand to my chest.

"From the top." She steps away and walks behind the chair again. Her long piano fingers grip the back of the chair. I bring the tin whistle back to my lips. My knuckles are red, but I know I'm right when I see the smile in Breda's gray eyes. She can keep her face like stone all she wants, but I've been looking at her since I was a child, and I know that the slight tightness around her eyes isn't anger; it's amusement.

I continue to play 'As I Ride Out' by Christy Moore. The notes flow through the room, and I fight the smile as I hope the music reaches Liam O'Reagan's ears. He is in the next room discussing my upcoming wedding to his son.

My excitement sends the notes out too fast, and Breda releases the chair and takes a step towards me, but I reel in my excitement quickly and slow my pace. She nods her head in approval and circles me as I play. I'm watching that ruler as I play the hauntingly beautiful melody.

The day I have been trained for my whole life is finally here. Everything I've been taught was all about being the perfect wife for Jack O'Reagan. I will be free. At last. My mind bubbles and bounces through all the possibilities of what I could do with my freedom. I'm picturing parties, shopping, holidays.

The song ends, and the door opens like they were waiting for me to finish. Breda is alert when James, the second eldest boy in our family, looks directly at me.

"Dad will see you now." James doesn't look like me. He has Dad's features, dark brown eyes, and his skin takes well to the sun. I just blister, peel, and turn back white. It's another enchanting Irish trait that I have inherited.

Nervous butterflies erupt in my stomach as I step towards the small round table and place my tin whistle on it. I pause, not ready to leave all of a sudden, and look back to Breda. She's all I have ever known; now I wonder if I'll ever see her again. Will I be shipped off today? Will I have time to pack?

She gives me a nod of approval, and I see a glimmer of moisture in her eyes before she turns away from me.

The navy swing dress I wear skims my knees and hugs my small waist. I feel pretty as I follow James down the large open hallway. My heels click click on the tiles, and I have this image in my head of being the lady of a grand house, much grander than this, where I will host parties. I keep the smile at bay as James leads me to the large kitchen.

Dad is there and gives me a reassuring smile. My youngest brother is sitting at the table. He averts his gaze from me. The eldest, and the one I thought would be lifting me into the air, already has his back to me; his large frame heaves. The kitchen grows smaller the longer I stand in it. There is no sign of Liam O'Reagan.

Noel's wide back is heaving and has me worried. I want to call out to Noel and ask him what's wrong, but my father speaks.

"The marriage will be in four weeks."

My heart pumps blood so fast around my body that I want to reach out and grip something. I hold still, but I can't stop the smile that consumes my face and showcases my teeth.

"You will be leaving tomorrow."

I'm ready to pass out with excitement, but each time my gaze travels to Noel's back, worry starts to lace its way through my excitement, dismantling the happiness inch by inch.

"We can't." Noel's voice is low.

I'm taking a step towards him.

"She is." My dad's angry voice would normally recapture my attention, but I'm taking another step towards Noel.

"What's happening?" I'm asking him, and once Noel stands to his full six-foot height and turns to me, my stomach swells with all the worries that course through my system.

Noel's dark green eyes pin my dad to the spot. "This goes against everything we stand for, everything you taught us."

"This is a small sacrifice for the greater good." My dad hasn't looked at me. His hands curl into fists. Fists that I've seen do a lot of damage over the years to Noel. He had shaped him into a man with his fists. At least that was his own explanation for each thump.

"I'll take his place." Mark, the youngest, steps up beside me as he speaks to our dad. His sleeves are rolled up to his elbows. Large muscles flex from his hours at the gym.

My father dismisses Mark's words with a slight wave of his fisted hand, and I'm back to looking at Noel.

"What's happening?" I bark loudly.

"Tomorrow, you're leaving, and that's final." My dad's words are heavy with something that leaves me unsettled.

Noel finally looks at me fully, and everything in me stands to attention. I'm proud of the man he has always been. Noel would walk through fire to protect me, he's my best friend, and I know nothing bad will happen with him in my corner. My shoulders automatically relax.

"You're not marrying Jack O'Reagan." Noel's brows drag down, but his gaze never wavers from me.

"Don't say another word, my boy." The warning from my dad has my heart pounding heavier.

I'm shaking my head at Noel to stop. He's pushing Dad too far. I know what happens when our dad is pushed too far.

"You have to marry a Northerner." Noel doesn't stop even as my dad moves closer to him.

My hand reaches out and grips the marble breakfast bar top. "No."

No one hears me as James and Mark move as one and stop my father from touching Noel. My mind reels as I hear the soft footfalls behind me. Breda is in the doorway, and from the sadness in her eyes, I know right then and there that she knows. She knows I've been handed to a savage.

I turn to her because she's like a mother to me. "Did you know?" My voice rises substantially, and the room falls silent.

"Did you know that....?" I trail off as I think of all the nights I've dreamt of Jack O'Reagan. I swallow around the lump in my throat.

"There is no need for such dramatics. It was a last-minute change. You are still marrying an O'Reagan."

I remember my place. I remember that this is my father who is speaking to me. I remember to show respect as I turn to him.

Hate burns deeply in my veins. The severity surprises me, and I lower my lashes so my dad can't see the rage in my eyes.

As I lower my lashes, I glimpse Noel still being held by James and Mark.

"What if it's a setup?"

My gaze jumps to Noel as he questions my father while shrugging off my brothers like they weigh nothing more than paper. That's what Noel was to me, an indestructible giant. A force that no one got through. Right now, seeing him red-faced and questioning my dad is terrifying.

"What if it's not?" My dad fires back.

Another fist tightens around my stomach, I have no idea what they are talking about, but my dad's answer shows that whatever this really is, it's a risk. My mind veers down a dark and deadly path that I pull back from before I sink into a fatal fear that I may not be able to drag myself out of.

"It's not worth the risk."

Pride swells in my chest at Noel's words.

"I say it is." My dad turns to me. His lips are always downturned; they've been that way since Mom died. As he approaches me, they lift ever so slightly, and my body sags a little.

"You are leaving tomorrow, and you will be marrying Shay O'Reagan. You will be his wife." My dad doesn't touch me or embrace me, yet he's close enough to drag me to his large chest, where I rested my head as a child, but I'm not a child anymore.

I want to say no, I want to tell him I don't want to marry a Northerner. We hated them. This made no sense.

"Will he hurt me?" I ask the question that makes him flinch like I had hoped it would.

"Will a dog bite if it's cornered?"

Noel growls behind our dad, and it's answer enough. Be obedient, don't give him a reason to hurt me.

I nod before turning my back on my dad. He doesn't stop me as I expect him to. The stairs are before me. I take the steps quickly as voices rise in the kitchen, and Noel tries to stop this, but there is no stopping my dad. I know that. He knows that.

The minute I enter my room and close the door, I kick off my heels. I want to fire my shoes across the room. I want to unleash the rage that is building up inside me and burning my cheeks, but I don't move.

The door behind me opens.

"Count to ten, remember that the temper of yours will get you into trouble." Breda's voice sounds the same as it always does when I'm ready to lose my head.

My father always said I had my mother's temper. Noel said I was as thick as a mule going backward through a hedge.

"Ten? I don't think counting to a hundred would calm me right now." I spin on Breda as she opens the large wardrobe.

"Then count to a thousand." She has dragged a chair over to the wardrobe and climbs up on it while yanking up her pleated ankle-length skirt.

"Get down, Breda, I'll do it." The last thing I want is her falling.

She ignores me. "Count." She reaches the suitcase and slides it halfway out before stopping and glancing at me.

"One, two, three…" I take a step back as I count and watch Breda pull down the suitcase. She takes it to my bed and opens it before returning to my wardrobe.

I'm still counting as she starts placing my dresses in the suitcase. My counting ceases, but she doesn't.

"He's a Northerner."

Now she stops, holding a bundle of dresses that are still on their hangers.

"You know what they are like," I add.

Conflict clouds Breda's already pale eyes. I notice the change as she stands straighter and grips the hangers tighter. "A man is a man, no matter where he comes from. He's still a man."

Frustration claws at my insides. "I don't understand. They are the enemy."

Breda places my dresses in the suitcase. "It might be a challenge from God. To love thy enemies."

What a crock of shit. I'm moving again.

"God isn't handing me over to the Northerners. God isn't going to rape me."

Breda holds her hands in the air and waves them close to her ears like she can brush away my words. "Don't say such things."

"What? In case I anger God?" My rage is encasing me, and I can't breathe.

"Stop it, Emma." Breda's voice holds the authority that normally shuts me up but not this time.

"What can God do? He took a mother from me. What else can he take?"

"Noel." Breda's one word has dread threading itself through my veins, not Noel.

"Now. Count while I pack." She returns to the wardrobe, and I return to counting as my mind buzzes with a fear that has me vowing one thing. No matter what happens from here on in, I will fight the Northerner with everything in me. My dad says I have my mother's temper; well, I'll use that to my advantage.

"Twenty-four, twenty-five, twenty-six...."

Vi Carter

CHAPTER TWO

O'REAGAN
AN CHLANN
SHAY

There is an electricity in the air that pulses all by itself. Everything in me is tight, ready to snap back into place, but I hold it still as I move through the roaring crowd. Hands reach out and touch my bare back. I'm aware of their hands but don't feel their touch.

"Are you sure about this, King?" Amanda grins as she holds open the cage door. She doesn't give a fuck if I step in and never step out again. Her long, plaited hair swings back and forth as she pushes the crowd back with leather-clad hands.

I don't answer her, and her laughter trails in behind me before the gate is slammed shut. I know the noise of the lock by now. I've heard it too many times before.

The floor is still wet from the last fight. Blood that didn't get washed away in the rushed preparations for my fight still soaks the ground beneath my feet. I hop from foot-to-foot to keep the tightness in my body there. I've wrapped my hands lightly, but not too much that I don't feel the burn of each thump.

My opponent steps into the cage from the opposite door, his head is covered with a leather mask. I continue to hop from side-to-side as the noise swells and squeezes between the small open squares in the cage walls, pouring itself over us and sending the excitement into our veins.

Amanda is roaring into her microphone, but I'm fucking moving. I need to unleash all that burns me up inside. My fist hits the leather of his head, and he shakes from side-to-side before his back collides with the cage. The roars grow wilder, and I don't stop as I pound his face in. My skin splits. My hands beg me to stop at the assault on my flesh, but I can't. I won't. Something in me has taken over. And it's hell-bent on destroying the giant who pushes off the side of the cage and roars.

I grin. *That a boy.*

Gravity doesn't exist, and I'm airborne, but it grips me by the throat and slams me into the ground. The back of my skull bounces off the cement floor, the pain is like ice-cold water flushing through my system, and I'm fucking alive as my teeth slam down on my tongue. I roll, letting the blood pour from my mouth. I have a moment when I look up and see Amanda rolling her eyes at me before the ground shifts, and I'm in the air before the giant slings me across his shoulder.

I'm laughing, and he pauses. I don't want him to pause. I don't want the pain to stop. Joining my hands, I bring them down on his back, aiming for the spine. He releases me, and the air is ripped from my lungs again as I hit the ground.

The fucker stays on his knees, and that pisses me off.

I'm up, and the crowd rattles the cage. The sides threaten to collapse on top of us as I drive my black military boot into his face. He reels back as blood pours from his broken nose, and I can't stop as I drive my foot into his face over and over again. The sound around me ceases, the cage disappears, and the giant under my foot morphs into my brother. My brother's face is coated in vomit and blood. I stumble back and hit the side of the cage; fingers scrape and prod my skin.

"Finish him." The roars have me shaking my head, and the image of my brother disappears. I lean away from the prodding fingers, but the fight leaves me as I walk to the cage door.

Amanda raises a dark brow and doesn't open the gate immediately.

"Open the fucking gate." Everything in me starts to ache, and I spit out a mouthful of blood on the floor.

Amanda jumps down off a wooden crate. She's not impressed as she opens the door. "You're barred, Shay."

I grin as I pass her. Boos and roars for me to return and finish the fight slams against my aching skull. Each set of eyes I meet divert quickly from me as I make my way back out.

The dressing room is a shit hole. The image of me is fractured as I stare into the cracked mirror. My face is coated in blood.

Turning on the taps, I bend and allow the pain that ruptures my sides in. My brother's face springs to my mind, and I force the picture away.

Dragging on my top, I grab my bag and leave the fight club through the side door. The light outside is harsh. The sunglasses that I take out of my bag helps.

I've been avoiding going home. I needed to release the rage before I saw my da. He was the only reason I was allowed to walk into a fight club like this one in Belfast. These were known as free grounds. No one had a stake on the ground, no one controlled it. The respect didn't come from me being a King. The respect came from my da's legacy. He won every fight. He taught Frankie and me how to fight. Only Frankie had a fear in him that got him killed in the end. Since that day, my da has never put his foot inside a ring.

My body aches as I walk the few kilometers to our house. Only five houses take residence in the cul-de-sac. It's a private area. The curtain upstairs shifts, and I would know my ma's profile anywhere. She's been waiting for me. I stuff my bag down along the bushes at the front of our house. I've two guns in it, and that's one rule Ma has—no weapons in the house. Pity, she doesn't know that Da has the house loaded to the gills. The red front door opens, and her smile falters.

"Jesus Christ, Shay." Her small hands grip my face.

"Ma, I'm fine."

She doesn't release my face as she tilts my head back so the light can shine better on it.

"Ma." I take her hands from my face. "I got jumped, but I'm fine."

She takes her hands back and folds them across her chest. "I've patched up your da long enough."

I scratch my forehead before leaning in and kissing her. "Did you make an apple tart?"

She's hiding a smile as she walks up to the house. As we pass the sitting room, I glance in to see if my old man is there. No sign. The remote rests on the sofa, the TV flickers with a horse race, but the sound is muted.

"He's in the kitchen," My ma informs me. The moment she steps in, she puts on the kettle.

"The prodigal son." My da rises stiffly from the table, still nursing a gun wound. He's taller than me, and the child inside me fears him, but the man wants to take a swing.

"Don't start, Connor. He's just home." My ma pulls out a chair. "Sit down, son."

I do, and my da sits back down, picking up his mug.

"You told Liam that my position as King was temporary." I can't keep in the anger any longer.

My da sips slowly. The white shirt is tight along his arms. He might not fight anymore, but he's still in prime shape.

"Why?" I ask when he doesn't answer. "Thanks, Ma." A slice of apple tart and a cup of tea appear in front of me.

My ma stays at my shoulder, and I pick up the fork and take a bite of the apple tart without looking away from my da. "It's perfect, Ma."

Her small hand squeezes my shoulder, and I hold in the hiss.

"Where were you?" Da asks, and my ma releases me with a heavy sigh.

"In County Meath," I answer and take a large bite of the apple tart. It has my ma's signature taste, but my da's face is turning my fucking cream sour.

"Just now." The smugness on his face tells me he knows; Amanda, the mouthpiece, must have rung him.

"At the fight club," I answer.

"Where Frankie died?"

Plates crash in the sink. Ma's head is bent as she stares into the sink. "Please, Connor, don't start."

I turn back to my da, his jaw clenched, and the sorrow is there like a tangible thing in the room, one that I don't want to touch me. I blame my da. He pushed Frankie into fighting, and he wasn't a fighter. No one could bear his soft demeanor, especially my da, who felt men should be men.

But Frankie was different.

"You have them all laughing at me," I tell him as I chew on ma's tart like it's leather in my mouth. My da's fucking spoilt it. I wash it down with tea.

"Laughing at you? You really care what Liam O'Reagan thinks of you?" My da rises, holding the empty mug. Ma doesn't let him get much further as she takes it from his hand. He sits back down after a pleading look from her and with a reluctance in his step.

"I'm King, I deserve respect, and you undermined that."

"I told him it was temporary because you can't kill a temporary King. But you can kill a King, Shay. You have no idea what you're up against with Liam."

"Tell me. I'm not a boy anymore. Tell me why I should fear him."

My da looks away, and frown lines appear on his forehead.

"I'm getting married," I say and clean the plate in front of me. I wouldn't let ma think her apple tart was anything other than perfection.

My da says nothing, and my ma's steps are weary as she walks to the kitchen table. She's clutching the dishcloth as she pulls out a chair and sits down.

"Who is she?" My ma's voice wobbles, and I hate this part. She's always wanted me to settle down, maybe give her grandkids.

"Emma," I say her name and glance at my da, who's watching me.

"That's all you're going to give me is a first name?" My ma lets out a watery smile like she's not sure what's happening.

"It's an arranged marriage, so that's all I know." I can't look at my mother as I break her heart. "It's giving me a place as a King in the East."

"A King in the East," My da repeats.

"Arranged?" My ma's words ring loud beside me.

"Yeah, Ma. But I'm sure she's lovely." I try to take my ma's hand, but she stands still clutching the cloth and leaves the room.

"You just broke your ma's heart again."

The chair hits the kitchen floor as I stand. "Don't fucking say it."

My da rises calmly. But I see the temper flex along the vein in his neck. "Frankie wasn't my fault," he says the words, and I take a step away from the table.

I'm aware of the shadow along the door line. My ma hasn't left. I'm sure she's afraid that we will kill each other. It's come close to happening too many times.

"The wedding is in four weeks." That's the only invitation he's fucking getting.

"What's the girl's full name?"

"Emma Murphy," I say.

My da nods like that makes complete sense. "He's setting you up."

I don't want to hear his conspiracy theories about Liam. He's rambled about them since we were kids, yet he never gave a clear picture of what the fuck he was painting.

"If I marry her, I have a seat on the board in the East."

"What happens to the North?" My da asks, and we are both still standing, both still rigid.

My da tenses, and he tilts his head to the side like he just had a thought. "This was your idea of joining together. You always wanted more. How is being King of the North not enough?"

My da is right. I am always chasing something. Maybe I am trying to fill in the hole that Frankie left behind.

"You're afraid of change."

"You're a pup." My da leaves the end of the table the same time my ma steps into the room. I don't need her to think she has to be a referee between her son and husband.

"I'm staying at the Banistoir. I just came to pack a few things."

I begin to leave the room. "Don't go, son." My da's plea would normally eat away at me. He's a King, a ruthless ruler, but he was also a ruthless teacher and father.

My ma sobs, and I don't brush past her but stop and take her face in my hands like she had done to me outside.

"There's no need for tears. This girl, Emma, is a beauty. She's excited to get married to me, and I know you're going to love her." I lie and smile. "You never know; she could even like me."

Laughter bubbles up my ma's throat. "She'll love you." She touches my hand that still covers her face. "I might even get grandkids."

"Don't push it, Ma." I release her face, and I'm glad that she's still smiling as I place a kiss on her cheek.

"Promise me you'll be careful."

"Yeah." I lie again and head upstairs to get a few belongings. Tomorrow I would leave and return to the East. I had no idea what exactly I was walking into. The wedding to the girl would be the easy part. She was willing and the least of my worries. Keeping an eye on Liam was an entirely different thing.

Vi Carter

CHAPTER THREE

O'REAGAN
AN CHLANN
EMMA

L ady dips her head the moment she sees me, and all my worries leave me, like a second unwanted skin falling off me with each step. The moment I reach her, I touch her head and rub it.

"How is my Lady today?" She neighs as I rub under her chin. Her mouth dips lower, and she nudges my closed palm. I open my hand and laugh as she devours the red apple. I rub behind her ear as she continues to eat and look around at the white fencing that surrounds her arena. Dad always said I could take Lady with me. Now I think she might be safer here. I have no idea what Northerners ate. I wouldn't put it past them to eat a horse. My hand tightens on Lady, and she neighs again while nudging my hand.

"That's all I've got," I say and open my empty hand. Her long pink wet tongue runs the length of my small hand.

"Still feeding her apples?" Noel's voice rings behind me. My trainer had told me to stop feeding her so many apples, but it's the only treat she gets.

I don't answer Noel but push Lady away, and she knows to leave. "I can't take her with me." My throat burns. "He might eat her for all I know."

Noel's chuckle isn't welcomed, and I swing around and face him.

His laughter stops, and he stuffs his fists into his jeans pockets. "He won't eat the horse."

"Can you guarantee that?" I'm not going to take his word for it.

Noel doesn't answer, and that's answer enough for me.

"A Northerner?" I say it again. I must have said it a thousand times in my head. "How could Dad?"

"He's an O'Reagan." Noel bites out the words.

"What do you get in return for this marriage?"

Noel pleads with me before releasing a heavy sigh. "A seat as one of the four Kings of the East."

"Then it's worth it." The air whooshes out of my lungs as I fight back the tears. I look back at the fence line and watch Lady gallop in the distance. "I'll pack my bags. I'll go to him."

Something in me cracks, and I rub my chest as Noel steps up to me.

"Now, come on, drama queen. You know I won't let that happen."

I smile but don't look at him. "I don't think I'm being dramatic. He might hurt me."

"Didn't I teach you how to fight back?"

I lean against the fence. "Yeah." He did. He taught me how to take a man down without using strength. It was to use my wit and attack when I was calm; Never when my temper flared. Noel said my burning cheeks and angry eyes gave away my next move.

"You won't be marrying him, Ems."

The nickname tugs at my heart, and I look up at my brother. I can't stop the burn along my nose. "What if..." My cheeks flame, and I can't hold Noel's eyes. I dip my head and look back out at Lady.

There is an awkward lull in the air. "Dad spoke to Liam. You don't have to do anything until after the wedding."

Noel isn't looking at me. When I glance up at him, his jaw is tinged slightly pink.

I can't stop the smile. "You mean sexually?"

"Yeah." Noel's gaze lands on me briefly, and I see the fear in my big brother's eyes. Fear that he might have to discuss something like sex with his sister. I laugh. I have no experience, but the idea that Noel fears talking about sex with me makes me laugh.

Maybe it's the pent-up fear of leaving behind everything I know. Maybe it's the relief of knowing the savage can't touch me. It won't stop me from fighting him every step of the way. Everything he is is wrong. It won't matter how nice he is to me, even if he tries to woo me. Nothing will make me bend.

Noel snorts before he laughs, too.

My laughter grows before it turns to tears.

"It's okay." Noel stops immediately and drags me into his chest. "I swear to you; you won't have to marry him. No matter what it takes, Ems, I'll get you away from him."

Salty liquid fills my mouth. "You promise me." I cling to Noel. His heart thumps wildly in his chest. "Swear, Noel. Swear on Mom's grave, no crossed fingers or toes." His heart thrashes against my ear, and fear has me tightening my hold on my brother.

"I swear, Ems. I swear on Mom's grave. No fingers or toes."

My tears dry up. That's it. He's not lying. He will do it. I hug my brother a bit tighter and step out of his embrace. I have to crane my neck back to look up at him.

"Now I need you to listen to me." Noel is no longer looking wild and lost. Now he's my brother, ready to bestow knowledge onto me. I'm alert and ready to hear his words.

"You keep quiet, but listen to any conversations you can. Don't let him know you're listening. Pretend to be invisible."

I raise both brows. "You want me to be a spy."

My brother's lip tugs up slightly. "Jesus, Ems, I just want you to stay safe and don't get any wild ideas. I'll get you out, but while you're there, keep the head down."

Noel taps the crown of my head.

I'll trip over my own feet. My being a spy isn't possible.

"If he asks you questions, act dumb." Noel's words are delivered quickly but pique my interests.

"What kind of questions?"

"Any." Noel's voice is stern.

I nod. "Okay. I can do it."

He's ready to reach for me again when a figure on the back porch catches my attention. It's Breda.

"I better go in and help her pack before she breaks a hip."

My brother snorts again. "Try to keep that sense of humor."

The smile I give him doesn't feel real.

It's a moment. It's a moment that I have replayed over and over again in my head. It's a moment that should have been perfect. It ends up just being a moment.

Liam O'Reagan opens the back door of the Range Rover. His formidable stance has me raising my head. My dad, James, and Mark stay at the door, waving me off like I'm going to some fancy college, with soaring high windows arched with gargoyles and secrets.

"Emma." Liam greets me.

"Mr. O'Reagan." I had thought this day would be a pleasure. I had thought wrong. I'm still in awe that I'm in his presence. I've heard stories about him from Noel, from my dad, stories that made me think he couldn't be real. A line from the movie '*Braveheart*' jumps into my mind. 'I thought you would be taller?' Someone had said to William Wallace. It was a funny moment because of the tension before the war. That's what this feels like with Liam; only he is the man I'd imagined: he's as tall as I pictured; as Intimidating as I had imagined.

I pause at the open door and take one final glance back at the house. I skip the three figures in the doorway and scan the windows. Something shaky rocks my body as I meet Breda's gaze. Her thin lips have nearly disappeared, she looks like the ghost of a very unsatisfied nun, but it's her eyes.

Goodbye, I mouth, and she quickly turns away from the window. The one person who I was truly looking for isn't here. Noel.

I get in, and the door closes behind me. I don't look out the window at my family. My bags are already in the trunk. Liam climbs into the front and takes a look at me in the rear-view mirror.

"Are you sure you have everything?"

His question would be considered considerate, but there is no emotion attached to it. Dad said it was a trait that people admired Liam for. You never knew if he liked you or not, you never knew if at that moment he was planning and plotting your slow and painful death.

"Lady." As the Range Rover rolls down the driveway. I think of my horse. "I have a horse, but I'll come back for her at a later date." Once I know the savage won't eat her, that is.

The Range Rover picks up speed. I want to turn in my seat and look out the back window. I'm imagining Noel running after the Range Rover, devastated that he never got to say goodbye to me. I give into temptation, and I turn in my seat.

My breathing grows quicker, and something deeply rooted and frenzied grows bigger and swallows my hope as I stare back at the rising dust. There is no Noel chasing after the Range Rover. I face forward as my breaths grow shallow.

One, Two, Three...

I continue to count as the Range Rover runs smoothly down the main road toward what must be my new home. If I closed my eyes, I would think we weren't moving at all. The scenery around us flickers past quickly, and each time I reach one hundred, I start counting again.

Time passes in a blur of trees and numbers before buildings start to rise and fall away again. as I reach for the window. I stop a hairbreadth away from touching it. Green eyes that are so wide hold my attention, and I look away from my reflection and sit fully back. Gray turns to green, and the small part of me that had dreamt of this moment dies inside of me.

Liam hasn't spoken a word, and I stop counting when it no longer keeps everything inside me at bay. I sense the panic that circles along the edges, waiting for a break in my armor, so it can escape and infiltrate my system.

I take another look at Liam as we drive into a darkened tunnel. He sits rod straight, both hands on the steering wheel, and I find myself analyzing him, looking for a kink in his famous armor. It wouldn't matter how long I looked at him. I truly believed I wouldn't find it.

The orange glow of the tunnel wall lights moves past us, and I start to count them just as the world is lit up with fireworks. The explosion rocks the vehicle, and the fireworks bounce off the Range Rover, becoming something deadly.

"Get down." Liam doesn't shout, he doesn't raise his voice, but his words break through my frozen state, and my fingers fumble with the seatbelt. It takes me three tries before I get myself unclipped. The vehicle swerves, and I grip the back of Liam's seat as glass rains down on me like the aftermath of a sprinkler. A screech fills my ears as I dive to the floor. The sound stops as I bite my cheek.

Closing my eyes, small chunks of glass coat my back. The vehicle swerves, and I swear we are airborne. Gravity shifts and I'm flying backward, my back taking the assault from the floor. The dark ceiling fills my vision, and light pours in, and I think it's the end.

Isn't that what people say when they die, that they see a bright light wash over them. They say it's warm. Mine's not. It's cold and harsh against me. My eyelids flutter closed, protecting me from the onslaught of light after the darkness of the tunnel. The light dances and filters behind my lids as I hold my hands just above the glass-strewn floor, but with each movement of the vehicle, I have to grip the floor to stay in one place. Warm liquid leaks, but I don't dare get up. The vehicle seems to smooth out, and I slowly open my eyes.

Air pours into the space and beats against my clothes. My hair rises on the wind and whips against my face. Trees move past, and I start to count.

"Emma?" Liam's voice breaks my bubble of control.

"Emma, answer me." Liam's voice rises, and I'm rising too, each piece of glass making me hiss as it embeds itself deeper into my flesh.

"Yes." The opposite side of the back seat seems to only have a few shards of glass on it that I brush off. I pull myself up. My limbs wobble, and my ears buzz as I stare out the windowless frame and onto a green world of grass and trees.

"Are you injured?"

Am I injured? A stream of light pours in across me, and I reach out and touch a small steel hole, yet the impact of what it is, has a hand reaching in and clenching my gut. I feel like it pulls all the way up my throat and tries to turn me inside out.

The wind whips my hair wildly around my face, and I close my eyes, keeping my finger on the bullet hole. It wasn't fireworks. It was gunfire. Someone just tried to kill us.

Liam doesn't ask me again if I'm injured, and we don't stop driving. Closing my eyes, a tremble that's from the cold along with the shock has taken its full hold on me, and when the vehicle slows down, I finally open my eyes.

The sun has dipped, and time hasn't moved. Yet, I'm sure a clock would contradict me. The more I look around the vehicle, the more bullet holes I see.

"They were trying to kill us," I whisper as I scan all the broken glass.

"Maybe." Liam sounds thoughtful.

"Maybe?" Did he not see the destruction I just saw?

His dark eyes meet mine in the rear-view mirror, and I can't hold his gaze as he slows down. We move down a narrow road. We pass three large homes before he slows at a set of high black gates. Lights on the pillars are lit, and the gates slowly open.

"Welcome to your new home," Liam says once the gates open fully, and he drives through them.

I had nearly forgotten why I was here. Now, as the large dark structure grows larger, the closer we get, fear and something else strangles me to the point of nearly cutting off my air.

One, two, three...

CHAPTER FOUR

O'REAGAN
AN CHLANN
SHAY

The white covering comes easily away from another piece of furniture. I ball the white material in my fist. Another fucking chair. That's the fourth chair in what was starting to look like the sitting room. A crystal bowl on the top of a large round table acts as an ashtray as I extinguish my cigarette. The sound of a vehicle rolling up the drive tells me it's show-time. I'll play nice, give her a tour of the house, and then I can get back to my business as she plays house.

I open the double front doors, impressed with the house that was given to me as a new king. My thoughts flee as the vehicle that is riddled with bullet holes and no windows stops close to the steps. Liam climbs out and opens the trunk, removing the bags like the vehicle isn't a write-off. The back door opens, and I see a mass of red hair. Liam places a suitcase at my feet.

"You ran into trouble?"

"Yes." Liam returns to the trunk, giving me no more information. As I leave the steps and round the shot-up Range Rover, I'm not sure what I will find, hopefully not a woman full of bullet holes.

Her head snaps up as I approach her; she's halfway out of her seat. I try to smile and reach out to her, but she recoils from me and slides off the seat. She's tiny, like a fucking kid. The green dress reminds me of what Irish dancers might wear. With all the red curls and pale skin, she really resembles a porcelain doll—the creepy ones.

"Is someone going to explain to me what happened?" I take my mind off my child-bride and look to Liam.

My future wife ignores me as much as Liam does. She hobbles to her suitcases, her blood-soaked hands gripping the handle, causing fresh blood to erupt.

For fuck's sake.

I move past Liam as he takes out a final bag and closes the trunk. I reach around the redhead to take the bag out of her hand.

"I got it." Her voice is sharp but feminine. Older than her tiny appearance would suggest it should be.

"Let me help you."

Green eyes that sparkle snap up at me. "I said, I got it." Hate, disgust, rolls off her, leaving me more fucking confused. I let her drag her bags inside. The moment she steps through the door, I'm back to looking at Liam for an explanation on the child-bride or the shot-up Range Rover.

"We were attacked," he says, looking at the Range Rover.

That much was already fucking clear. I take out my cigarettes and light one up. Glancing over my shoulder, the noise the redhead is making with her suitcase has me tempted to help her. But I don't.

Liam reaches into his suit jacket and hands me an envelope. I open it as he circles the vehicle.

I take a few more drags of my cigarette as I read the words on the piece of paper. "The child-bride comes with instructions," I sneer.

It's a CV about my bride-to-be whose name is Emma.

Emma, who plays the tin whistle. Riveting.

"So what's with her hostility? All I've been hearing is how willing she is."

"She nearly died. She's in shock." Liam's explanation doesn't sit right with me. It felt more personal, but it didn't really matter.

"Did you see who attacked you?" I stuff the paper into my back jeans pocket and join Liam at the vehicle.

"Three men, all dressed in black. They were on motorbikes. I couldn't chase them with Emma in the back."

He didn't give two flying fucks about Emma. I throw the cigarette on the ground and stomp on it before picking it up and placing the butt in my jacket pocket.

"Did you just arrive?" Liam faces me now, done with analyzing the vehicle. Now it's my turn to be under the cunt's scrutiny.

"Yeah, I had to take care of a few things up North."

My face still hadn't healed. I had no intentions of voluntarily giving him an explanation of what happened.

"I'm not sure what side the attack came from, but considering your face, did you happen to annoy anyone while up North?" Liam, the cheeky bastard, doesn't hold back.

Cunt.

" I was cage fighting."

"Did you happen to annoy anyone while cage fighting?"

I take a step towards Liam, he doesn't flinch, but I'm sure I see a spark of humor in his soulless eyes. "What would it matter if I pissed someone off? How would that cause a retaliation of this degree on you or the child-bride?"

Liam's lip tugs up. "You sound so worried about your future wife."

"I don't give two flying fucks what she does or what happens to her, as long as she's alive walking down the aisle."

Liam's lips return to their normal resting place, and he nods. "I'll find out who did this." He takes the three steps off the porch and gets into his vehicle. I return to the house to see all the suitcases are no longer in the hall. She's stronger than her tiny frame would suggest. I take out the piece of paper that Liam gave to me and scan for a date of birth. It doesn't give me one; it just says her birthday is in March, and she's a fucking Pisces. *That's the kind of information I wanted on her.*

I close the doors and climb the stairs. I didn't have time to see the upstairs, and that's where Emma has taken all her bags. My da's earlier warning about not marrying her and not trusting Liam replays in my mind. I had no idea who shot at them, but I am just hoping it isn't my da's doing as a means to stop this.

Emma's suitcases are stacked in the first room that is still covered with sheets. I don't see her and knock on the door.

"I didn't get a chance to tidy up before you came." I step into the room when she doesn't reply. There are sheets over everything, and I pull the nearest one off to reveal a large blue wardrobe. The next piece of furniture is a dressing table that has a golden hairbrush and mirror sitting on it. I couldn't imagine anyone using them.

"Emma," I call again as I reach another white door.

There is so much red hair sticking in all directions as she steps out of what I assume is the bathroom. Her hands are wrapped in a white towel. Jesus, she's tiny.

"Let me take a look at your hands, love." I shrug out of my jacket and throw it on the bed that's also covered. Looking back at her, I still can't get over how young she is. She must be only seventeen. I don't like this arrangement at all. She's only a fucking kid. I try to give her a smile that I would reserve for kids, and her lip curls up in a snarl. Not what I expected. But I remember she was nearly shot to death.

I take a step closer to her, and her cheeks flame as she drags her hands to her chest. "I'm fine."

"Clearly, you're not." I nod at the towel that's turning pink from her blood. Why do girls have to be so awkward? I had places to be, and she was burning through my fucking time.

I don't let that level of anger spill, but I let enough seep through so she'll give me her hands. "Just let me take a look."

She doesn't move, and I grip the towel, ready to pull it away.

Her movements are quick as she stumbles away and slams her back into the wall. "Don't touch me."

Her wild green eyes are fueled with disgust. I see it. She can't hide it if she wanted to, but she isn't trying to.

I scratch my beard and exhale loudly. "I have some things to take care of, so you make yourself cushy, love."

"I will never be cushy with the likes of you." She sprays her venom as she shuffles away from the wall. Her small shoulders rise and fall, and I fold my arms across my chest.

The angrier she grows, the redder her face becomes.

"You're a savage." She fires as I stare at her, clearly making her uncomfortable.

I nod my head and take the paper out of my back pocket. I scan it, and she shuts up as I pretend to read it.

"It says here you play the tin whistle. Give us a tune, love." Maybe talking about something she's used to would put out the fire raging inside her. She's too small to showcase this level of anger.

Her blood pressure spikes, and she's as red as her hair as she drops the towel and rips the paper out of my hand. I get a quick glimpse of her hands that are crisscrossed in cuts.

She's a spitfire. This is just what I need.

"Who gave you this?"

I'm considering spanking her so she can calm down, but I'm watching her as she shakes the paper in front of me.

"You have no right to any of this. You're an animal." Her small chest rises and falls quickly as she rants at me.

I had no idea what she was ranting about, but I don't have time for this. Grabbing her arm, she starts squealing and tries to pull away as I drag her to the large blue wardrobe and open the door. The empty hangers rattle as I push her in. The moment I release her, her wild eyes narrow, and I close the doors on her before she can do anything. It takes a second before her screams and bangs start.

While she has a hissy fit that I'm in no mood for, I keep one hand on the doors and reach across to the dressing table. I take the golden handled hairbrush and push it through the handles of the wardrobe. I step back and light a cigarette as the doors rattle violently.

"I wouldn't hit it too hard, little Emma. You might topple the wardrobe."

She curses at me, and I grin as I collect my jacket and leave her to settle down.

CHAPTER FIVE

O'REAGAN
AN CHLANN
EMMA

My hands continue to shake long after the savage has vacated the room. Hope dies as time passes, and he doesn't come back to release me. My heart pitter-patters as his face consumes my dark mind. No light filters into the wardrobe, and I've given up beating the doors. My hands are sore. The wooden surface under me is what I cling to as I drag my fingers across the grains of wood. At first, I had started to count each bump I'd felt, but as the darkness edges closer, panic infiltrates my system and scatters the numbers to the corners of my mind.

Heat fills my cheeks as I think of him. Shame and something deeper has my heart gaining too much speed.

I squeeze my eyes closed, hoping to force the next thought away, but I fail. He was the most handsome man I had ever seen. Handsome isn't correct. He had a wildness to him, not just with his beard and the bruising on his face—a perfectly sculpted face. No, it was his dark eyes. He had spoken gently to me, but there was nothing gentle about him. My body had responded in the worst possible way to him, and I was mortified, so I had lashed out like a child, allowing my darkest thoughts to fire themselves at him.

I dig my hands into the wooden floor as I think of calling him a savage. Stupid. Childish comes to mind, and that's how he had looked at me. Like I was a child. More heat rises along my chest, and I want out of this wardrobe. I want to get away from my thoughts.

I keep replaying that moment of seeing him for the first time, how he had rounded the vehicle like he had just stepped out of one of my magazines. My stomach squirms, and I keep dying all over again. I need to pull myself together. I rise in the large wardrobe that accommodates my full height of five-foot-five inches. Beside *him*, I may as well have been the size of a mouse. I reach up and pull one of the old-fashioned steel hangers off the rod.

I pour my frustration into opening the hanger. Stupid man. My temper flares as I think of how easily he had pushed me into the wardrobe and left me here. A lot of time has passed. I thought he would return, apologize and release me. That hasn't happened, and I don't believe it will. Once I get out of here, I need to restrain myself and show better control.

Using the hanger, I push it out through the small crack in

the door. No light filters in, so it must be night time now. I push the hanger up, and it hits something solid. I needed to get that out of the way so I could open the doors. Using all my strength, I wriggle, push and pull the wire but whatever he lodged in the door isn't moving. I finally give up. Sweat has made a path down my back, and I push my hair out of my face. Small spaces and me sweating do no good to my hair.

I drop the hanger and carefully sit back down. I'm tempted to start counting again, but my mind keeps drifting between the journey here and seeing the savage for the first time.

Savage didn't quite suit him anymore. But I refused to call him by his name. If I did, that allowed an attachment to form, and that was one thing that would never happen.

Noel had once gotten three lambs, and I remember so clearly how he wouldn't allow me to name them. I had tried on that first day in the shed when I had seen the tiny little things. But he had said I could bottle feed them, play with them, but I wasn't allowed to name them. That was the only rule that came with me helping him out. So I had, of course, agreed.

As they grew, I had forgotten the reason Noel had gotten the three lambs. Food. That's why we got them so we would have organic lamb and none of that water-filled meat. That's what my father called any meat that came in plastic. He said they were filled with water and drugs.

One morning I had heated the three milk bottles and made my way to the shed. I had walked in on Noel. My three little lambs lay dead on the floor at his feet.

Fluffy, Speedy, and Rocky.

That's what I had named them. Even now, my heart thumps a little harder when I think of their small, still bodies on the cold cement shed floor.

I never formed an attachment with our food again. I'd learned the hard way. I didn't allow Noel to see my tears. I had left and opened the bottles at the side of the shed, where I emptied the contents down the drain while the tears poured from me.

My mind slows even further, and I start to drift off. The small minute details assault me. The things I hadn't noticed when we were being shot at while in the tunnel. As I replay the scene in my mind, I remember the rumble, the undercurrent that I had heard before. It was the sound of a motorcycle. My father had one. It had been years since he took it out, but I remember the roar of the engine late at night when he returned to us.

I also remember the smell of something burning, something that weighs you right down, like when a drill is powered up, there is a slight smell of burning, maybe it's fragments of steel from the head of the screw, but that's the smell I remember as the bullets tore through the steel of the Range Rover.

How had we survived it? Small things at the moment that I had missed continue to roam across my mind. Like hearing Liam curse. The shift of the vehicle was more severe than I had fully taken in at that moment.

Had Liam returned fire? I think he had. The bangs of the gun would explain the loudness of the shots that weren't at us but from us. The air that brushed my face after we left the tunnel was cold, but I could taste it, the distant taste of silage that I was accustomed to. So, close to where Liam took me, there must be a farm.

My mind continues to drift even further until I'm focused on lush pink lips that hide behind a dark brown beard that's completely untamed. When he removed his jacket, I couldn't look away from his white t-shirt that stretched across broad shoulders. He was like something out of a magazine. I could imagine him in front of a waterfall, water cascading down his bare chest, that was tanned. From the flashes of skin I had already seen, I knew he was tanned. My mind continues to drift even lower when I'm rattled out of my fantasy as movement outside the wardrobe doors has me sitting up. Light streams in between the crack and continues to grow as the doors open. I can't stop the blush that consumes me. It's like fire racing through my body.

It's him, and there is a look of surprise in his dark eyes as he scans me from my flat black patent shoes all the way to the top of my head. I can't even imagine how I must appear. One hand grips the top of the door, allowing me to see his muscular forearm. Today he's wearing a black t-shirt, and it looks better than the white. His other large hand reaches in for me to take. So we are playing a game, that he's a gentleman, after locking me in here.

I glare at his hand like it might strike me before I try to shuffle out of the wardrobe with as much dignity as I can muster. Once my feet touch the ground, I move past him. He releases the wardrobe door. "There's a fresh pot of coffee in the kitchen," are his departing words as I fight not to stare at his broad back. What was wrong with me? He just locked me in a wardrobe for the whole night and didn't even come once to make sure I was okay.

Northerner. They had no compassion. All they thought of was the kill and their land. But like Breda used to say. You can't eat grass.

The morning light filters into the room from two large bay windows. I try to walk off the pins and needles that consume my body. I'm aware of him moving around downstairs, and in the light of day, it hits me. This is my life for the next four weeks.

It's overwhelmingly different from what I thought this would be, how I had pictured being here with Jack O'Reagan. I'd never met him, but I knew what Liam looked like, and a son of Liam would make any woman swoon.

The room grows smaller, the space inside me grows bigger, and I leave the bedroom, not wanting it to consume me. I follow the noise like a starving person following the smell of food. I halt at the kitchen door. He's there, drinking from a mug. His dark eyes are focused on me, and I slow my steps as I walk into the new kitchen. It has that feel, the new smell, even the new look. It hasn't been used. Some appliances still have plastic coverings on them.

It's a pity because it's a beautiful kitchen, with its gray and white undertones. It has the softness of a farm kitchen, but the modern twist makes it stylish. It won't be used; I remind myself when I purposely bring back Noel's promise to the forefront of my mind. He said he would stop the wedding. He promised I wouldn't have to go through with this sham.

"A coffee or maybe a juice?"

I sense humor in his voice, but I don't see any in his eyes as he walks over to the breakfast bar and opens a newspaper.

I don't answer him as I slowly walk to the coffee pot. I open three cupboards before I find a mug. I know he's watching me. I can sense his heavy gaze on my back. I refuse to turn around as I pour a mug of coffee.

"You want to tell me what happened yesterday?" His question is loaded as I pour in a small amount of milk.

No. I don't.

"We were attacked," I speak as I stir my coffee.

I'm remembering the onslaught of bullets and turn to him holding the mug tightly. "Was it you?"

He's standing and moving, and I'm sinking against the counter as he towers over me with angry eyes.

"Let's clear something up, love. You should be careful with your accusations. You might be a kid, but that won't stop me..." He trails off and takes a step backward, giving me back some of my personal space, but it's not enough. My mind is screaming that he's still too close.

The air has lodged itself in my throat, and I'm shriveling up. Won't stop him from what? Killing me? Hurting me? He hadn't finished his sentence. Was that intentional? Did he want my mind to fill in the blanks? Well, that's exactly what it was doing.

He's still too close, and I'm eye-level with his large chest. "I'm not a kid" is the intelligent comeback I have for him. I don't want him to look at me like that, which is silly, considering that he has just left a threat hanging in the air.

"Just watch your mouth." He steps away and returns to the breakfast bar. I don't move as he sits down and opens the paper, and I'm aware he's not reading it. His gaze is trained on the paper, but he's too angry to take in any of the words. His hands curl up either side of the paper, and I'm wondering why he hasn't struck out and hurt me yet.

Give him time. Emma.

His face is still bruised. His bottom lip has a slight cut close to the corner. I bite my bottom lip and quickly look away as he looks up at me. Why do I want to know how he got those bruises? It was probably from robbing someone.

He's a Northerner, Emma. I have to remind myself.

My reaction to him is throwing me off. I hadn't been around a man like this before. If I ever had been, it was with one of my brothers or a cousin. So this was strange.

"Did you get a look at the men who shot at you?" He speaks without looking up, and my stomach quivers from his deep voice.

My face flames, and I turn away so he can't see me.

"No." Noel had said, not to answer questions but to listen and find things out. He had wanted me to be a spy.

"What did Liam say?" I fire back and continue to stir my coffee.

No response.

I turn with the coffee in my hand. My fingers flex and clench around the mug. He's grinning at me, and there is nothing friendly about it. My heart starts to gallop as he stands.

"That's not how this works, love."

Love. It's an insult. I can hear it in his deep voice.

I stand as tall as I can.

"They said you would be willing."

Heat travels from my chest and scorches my face. My fingers tighten around the mug. The mug of hot coffee that I would fire at him if he tried to touch me.

"You seem..." He tilts his head from left to right, the movement intimidating, like he's getting ready to wrestle with me. The thoughts of his large frame on top of me have me taking a step back so the counter can support my weight.

"Hostile." He finishes and places his mug in the sink.

Having his gaze off me allows me to count to ten to try to regain some control.

He throws me a sideways glance. "Go shower and change."

I don't move as he returns to the breakfast bar and folds the newspaper up. Like hell I was going to take off my clothes with him in the house.

"I'm fine."

"Have you looked in a mirror?" His comeback has me wanting the safety of the wardrobe where his smell and size weren't consuming every rational thought.

"Have you?" I fire back, my mouth moving before I can close it.

His lip rises, and I see a flash of white teeth. "Was the wardrobe comfortable?"

I put the mug down on the counter. My hands grow slick. The thought of being dragged back there isn't appealing at all. I don't push the mug too far away in case I need it. "I slept." There goes my mouth again.

I see a spark of amusement in his eyes, but it dies very

quickly as he assesses me. I have no idea what he sees, but he's frightening, and having his full attention makes me want to flee.

"We have to make this work, Emma." He starts, and my name on his lips makes my stomach squirm for all the wrong reasons. It sparks an anger inside me that's reserved for my own stupid thoughts. My only defense is that I've never been around a man before, and not a man that looks like he does.

"Can we agree to try to make this work?" He's nodding at me like the movement will have me agreeing.

I have no intentions of making this work, even if I have to constantly remind myself that he is the enemy. "Of course."

"Then go shower and get changed." His head is higher. He's daring me to say no. I did, after all, just agree that we could make this work. But the stubborn part of me, that's as thick as a mule going backward through a hedge— Noel's words make me grin as they cloud the rational part of my brain and the stubbornness takes control.

"I'm fine."

His lip rises again, and this time, when he grins, I know I've really pissed him off.

My fear heightens as he takes a step toward me.

CHAPTER SIX

O'REAGAN
AN CHLANN
SHAY

She's fiery, and she seems different this morning. I can see interest in her eyes when she looks at me, and that look makes her appear older. She no longer appears so child-like. I'm trying to picture her out of that fucking Irish dancing dress. I can't see her properly with it on. It swallows her, hiding the truth that she is, in fact, a woman. Yet, her green eyes hold an innocence that tempts me. Right behind it, I see intelligence; she's analyzing things. But most of all, right now, she's pissing me off to no end. She needs to learn who's King here.

I grin at her, take a step forward, and her earlier smugness dies as I leave the kitchen and make my way upstairs, taking the steps two at a time. All her luggage is piled up in the middle of the floor where she left it last night. I grab the first one and open the bedroom window.

If she won't get changed, then she has no use for her clothes.

I hear her footfalls on the stairs and lob one of her bags out the window. It sails down two stories and explodes on the front drive. It's a mass of colors and fabric. It gives me some satisfaction as I return and pick up another. She steps into the room cautiously. Her hands grip the door frame as her wide eyes jump from her luggage to the window. I grin at her again as I fire the second one out the window.

She releases the door and marches into the room. "That's my stuff." Her voice rises. My cock grows hard. My reaction to her catches me by surprise. I didn't feel it last night, so why now?

I pause for a second and stare at her, confused by my reaction. It's the fire in her eyes that calls to me. I want to see them blaze. "Really?" I ask as I pick up the third one. She's moving toward me, and I stop my advance to the window. She pauses, looking unsure now. She reads the warning in my eyes and doesn't dare try to stop me as I fire her bag out the window. Her face turns as red as her hair. She folds her arms across her small chest. I walk around her and pick up the final bag. She's moving again but pauses as I stand at the window and hold the bag high in the air. My cock rubs against my jeans, and I don't hide the want as I trail my gaze along her body. "Are you going to get showered and changed?"

Her nostrils flare as confusion widens those green eyes. The fight is back in her, and before she can answer, I let her bag sail towards the pavement, where it explodes. I'm assessing her outfits. Dresses. All dresses. Irish fucking dancing dresses. I close the window and turn to Emma.

"I'm glad I didn't bring Lady with me." If she could breathe fire, I'm sure we would all be charred right now.

"Who's that, your broom?"

"You're not a man."

Her words have a part of me dying inside. I've done a lot of bad shit, but the way she's looking at me now is like she can see it all—all the lives I've taken, all the lives I've allowed to be taken, whether it was personal gain or retaliation.

"How would you know what a man is?" I take a step towards her.

Her face blazes like I knew it would.

"You're a goddamned Northerner." Angry tears brim her green eyes.

"I'm starting to get the feeling you don't like us, Northerner's, love."

"I'm not your love."

I snap and reach for her. The scream that leaves her plump lips should make me stop and rethink what I am about to do. But I can't. I'm ready to make her take her words back; I'm ready to show her what a man really is. As I grip her arms and drag her closer to me, my body responds to her closeness. Her scent is sweet, like vanilla. My fingers dig deeper into her small arms, and fear sparks in her eyes. Before I can talk myself out of really hurting her, I move us both. Her breath comes out harshly. I push her back into the wardrobe and slam the doors. Pressing my back against it, I push my fist into my aching eye; my hard-on slowly dies.

I've drunk up so much fear in my time while cage fighting. It always makes me pause because I used to see it on Frankie's face before every fight. The fear that he couldn't hide. The fear that Da hated to see on his son's face. He made Frankie feel like a fucking disappointment. Like he was less than me, but Frankie was more of a man than I could ever be.

The door shifts under me as she starts to pound and scream hysterically. I used to enjoy watching that fear grow on men's faces, and soon fear had a smell, it was excessive sweat, and sometimes it was accompanied by the scent of piss.

The doors rattle against my back, and I reach over and pick up the gold-handled brush and slide it into the handles again.

"You motherfucker, open this door."

I step away as she pounds on it. I don't warn her to take it easy, or she'll topple the wardrobe. Right now, I don't give two fucks as I head back downstairs.

I need to eat. The hollowness in my stomach is starting to eat me up. I had no idea when I last had food. My mother's apple pie, I think.

Opening the cupboard doors, the basics are here. But nothing to make a meal out of. I take out the bread as Emma continues her onslaught on the wardrobe. I take out a slice and eat it as I walk back into the sitting room, not bothering to put anything on the bread. Pulling off a white cloth, I find a large set of cupboards.

Opening the door, I grin as I drag a bottle of Jack out of the cupboard. I unscrew the lid and make my way back to the kitchen.

Taking the tray of ice-cubes out of the freezer, I drop them all into a cloth and take a swig of Jack before pushing my t-shirt aside. My ribs ache, and I push the cloth filled with ice-cubes against the wound. Lifting all the bags and firing them out the window has brought the pain back full blast.

Upstairs, Emma continues to bang and scream. The quietness of the house allows me to hear her clearly. I take another drink before putting the bottle on the counter.

The ceiling rattles, and I can picture the wardrobe toppling over. I take another drink and drop the cloth before pulling my top back down. My side burns as I make my way back up the stairs. If she has knocked it over, she could fucking stay in it. I was in too much pain to pick it up. I see a flash of red as I clear the landing.

She's broken out. The brush is lying on the floor in front of the open wardrobe doors. I can't see her as I step cautiously into the room.

She appears from the bathroom holding a pair of scissors. Her skin is flushed and sweaty, and I have a moment of regret from locking her in the wardrobe, but it lasts a millisecond as she opens her pretty little mouth.

"I want to speak to my father, now." Her demand is delivered with several jabs of her scissors that she is pointing towards me.

"You want your daddy?" I tease, and I'm questioning why I'm riling her up again? Did I really care if she went to her daddy? Not really.

"Don't say it like that. You're disgusting." More venom spews from her lips.

"You like pissing me off?" I ask, taking a step into the room. She doesn't answer. "I'm highly fucking confused here, Emma. Why was I told you were willing? No one mentioned that you would be wielding scissors."

"I was willing for Jack O'Reagan. Not you."

A hand tightens around my gut, and I try to hide my shock. "Jack?" I say his name before running my tongue along my teeth to try to force back down the onslaught of anger.

"Yes. I had agreed to marry him. Not a savage like you." She's still jabbing those fucking scissors.

I've been lied to by Jack and Liam. They should have known she would tell me, eventually. They must have known she would be angry and pissed off. My da was right. They have set me up. They have fucking set me up.

"I could have been handed to another O'Reagan. Any of them. No, they gave me to you." She's still mouthing off, and the disgust in her eyes, I understand now.

I'm nodding my head at her like I get her disgust, yet my mind can't believe that I bought into Liam's lie. Jack. I didn't expect that. I scratch my brow, trying to ward off the smile. He really got one up on me. I honestly didn't see this coming.

"I want to talk to my father."

Emma's still wielding the scissors, and I'm tempted to force her to use them. I'm tempted to step right up to her so I can feel the fucking burn of their betrayal on my flesh.

"You won't be talking to your father," I say to her calmly as I leave the room and make my way downstairs.

"You can't stop me." Her shouts have me moving faster as I open a door under the stairs. It's a clothes closet.

They fucking lied to me. I slam the door with more force than what is necessary. I open another door that's beside the kitchen door.

The stairs disappear into the darkness below. I switch on the light, and it illuminates the first few steps. It's perfect and exactly what I had been hoping for.

"You can't stop me from speaking to my family." She's coming down the stairs, so that saves me going back up to drag her down. I leave the basement door open and meet her on the last step of the stairs. She seems startled to see me, and I use the moment to grab her arm.

"What are you doing?" I get her close to the basement door when she pulls back with more force than I expected, and I lose my grip. Her gaze darts to the open door, and she's backing away from me. "I'm not going down there." She spins on her heels but not before I see the fear that is back in her eyes.

This time it doesn't stop me as I chase after her. She doesn't get far. Her waist is tiny, and I wrap both hands around it and lift her into the air. Her feet kick out and connect with my legs as she drags her nails along my arms. I get a mouthful of red hair as I carry her screaming form to the basement door. She's fighting with everything she has inside her, and she has a lot. I'd throw her down the stairs; only I didn't want a dead bride. My ribs ache, and I pause at the first step and lower her enough to the ground so I can press her against the wall. Using my chest as a solid wall to her back, she's trapped.

"Calm down," I say and press her harder against the wall. I know there is no way she doesn't feel my raging hard-on. Her cheek presses into the wall, her breath moves locks of red curls, but I can't see her eyes. I reach up and move the hair aside slowly and carefully, not putting it past her to try to bite me.

"You keep calling me a savage, Emma. So this is what a savage would do."

She's looking at me from the corner of her eye. She shifts and rubs up against my cock. "I wouldn't keep doing that if I was you." I move my face closer to hers. "Unless you want to." I want her to want me to.

"Fuck you."

I try to move past the anger I feel that she was Jack's. Now I want to make her mine.

"Say something nice to me, and I'll let you go." I'm trying to take the high road here. I'm not one to fight over any woman, but this time it's very personal.

She draws in a shaky breath, and her gaze diverts back to the wall. "Fuck you." Her two words don't hold the same level of conviction they had earlier, but it's enough to make me want to push her down the fucking stairs. I think I show a tremendous amount of restraint and drag her away from the wall until she's facing me. My arms keep her locked in place, and she's pressed against me so she can't kick out.

The flickering heartbeat in her neck makes me pause. My gaze trails across her face to her plump lips—her small pink tongue flicks out, and she licks her lips. My cock twitches.

"Final chance." I can't look away from her lips.

She juts out her chin, and my gaze skips to her eyes. I can see the answer there. She isn't giving in and fuck me if I don't admire that. But she needs to learn some fucking manners. I start down the stairs, and she doesn't fight me. She isn't so stupid to cause both of us to fall.

There's nothing down here but a washer and dryer. The moment we touch the ground, she gets away from me and tightens her arms around her waist.

I want to offer her one more chance. But I've given her enough. She doesn't stop me as I march back up the stairs and lock the door behind me. I leave the lights on. I'm a cruel bastard, but not that cruel.

CHAPTER SEVEN

O'REAGAN
AN CHLANN
EMMA

My heart won't slow down long after he leaves me. My body keeps reacting to him in the worst way possible. I don't want to keep thinking about his large body pressed against mine or how that made everything in me quiver.

I force my mind away from him, and I think of my horse, Lady. I miss her. I miss the simplicity of my life. I miss my room. I miss my dreams of freedom.

This isn't freedom.

I move around the basement. It's fairly empty, but I know what I am looking for.

It's not about freedom. It's to show him that he can't keep

locking me up. I'm not just going to sit here and take it. I wasn't some docile female.

As I scan the room, I look up and see what I'm looking for. The washing machine and dryer stand free, and I use the door of the washing machine as a step. I climb on top of it. Pushing myself up onto the tip of my toes, I tug on the insulation that's wrapped around the pipes. On top of the yellow itchy stuff, I slowly strip back the aluminum foil. It takes time, and some of the yellow insulation falls onto my face. I have to stop several times and brush all the bits away, but when they do, I smile at my pile of aluminum that I have collected successfully.

A small cabinet is filled with full bottles of cleaning products. I push aside the bleach and take out a bottle of drain cleaner that's tucked away at the back. I scan the rest of the cleaning products but know the drain cleaner is perfect for what I need.

I look around for a clear plastic bottle, but I don't find one. I also needed some water, and there isn't a sink down here either.

Great.

Taking my drain cleaner and aluminum, I stuff them inside the tumble dryer and close the door. I make my way up the stairs. The door at the top, of course, is locked. But I had to try it, anyway.

I want to bang on it and demand he let me out, but that didn't work before. I place my ear against the door, and I'm sure I can hear someone in the kitchen.

My heart thump thumps as I knock softly on the door. "Can I have a drink of water?" I'm tempted to say please, but if I'm too nice, he'll know something is up.

"I haven't had any in nearly two days," I shout at the door when I get no response.

"It's just a bottle of water." I continue.

I hear movement.

"Say please." His voice startles me. He's right on the other side of the door, and now all I can think of is how hard he was against me. He had been aroused as he had pressed me against the wall earlier, and I had liked the feel of his body against mine. My mind had skipped and jumped, wondering what it would really feel like to have a man.

I press my legs firmly together as if I can stop the thoughts. Heat quickly makes a path up my neck. It was the worst thing about having red hair and pale skin; I couldn't hide my burning cheeks. I was like a beacon.

"I'm really thirsty." The word please lodges itself in my throat.

His footsteps move away from the door, and I clench my fist. I need to say please.

I'm ready to go back down the steps and find an alternative when I freeze on the third step.

"Go back down, and I'll give you water."

I'm grinning at how stupid he is and walk back down the steps. I stand still and place my hands behind my back. I look too suspicious, so I fold them across my chest. Now I look guarded.

I drop my hands on either side of me as the basement door opens. There is an energy of anticipation at seeing his face again. His legs appear, and he stops his descent.

"Are you going to say please?" He asks, and I can't see his face, but his voice holds no humor.

I won't say it.

He bends, and I meet his dark eyes, my stomach squirms. He takes a quick look around me before he throws the bottle of water down the flight of stairs. I'm rushing forward and jumping. I just barely catch it in mid-air.

I can't wait to wipe the grin off his face as he heads back up the stairs. I don't move until the door closes before I open the bottle of water. I wasn't lying about being thirsty. I empty nearly three-quarters of the bottle before I set it on the top of the washing machine and get to work on the aluminum. I roll it into small balls and drop them into the water bottle. Each one brings a memory of Noel teaching me how to build homemade bombs. It's what my family did. My dad was known for his bomb-making. He had built a lot for the RA. He was a respected member.

The likes of the Northerner upstairs was the enemy. I'm still confused why I was handed over, but right now, all that mattered was staying strong and remembering what they did to us. They killed innocent women and children. They took our land. That's all they cared about, land and killing.

Once I have enough aluminum balls in, I take the drain cleaner out of the tumble dryer and pour it into the water bottle. I place the lid on and make my way up the stairs. The impact wouldn't blow down the door or anything, but it would be enough to cause a loud explosion. I shake the bottle and place it at the door before racing back down the steps. I'm waiting, and the excitement that bubbles up inside me starts to dispel. It was silly of me to build a bomb. I'm ready to take a step towards the stairs when the explosion roars down the stairs. The plastic bottle shoots past me like a missile, and I duck as it rolls to the ground close to my feet.

The door opens, and his feet clear the fifth step before he comes into view holding a black 9 mm pistol. He glances at me but looks around the room with the gun raised. He's looking for the threat. It takes him a moment to see there isn't one, and I'm the only one down here.

His gaze darts to the torn bottle close to my feet; he frowns but doesn't put the gun away as his gaze dances between me and the bottle.

"What's that?" He's pointing at the bottle with the gun. "What's that smell?"

I don't answer. Pride swells inside me, and for a moment, I can picture Noel grinning at my antics.

That slowly dissolves as the gun is pointed at me. "What the fuck did you do?"

I'm not stupid. I have a gun pointed at me, and I have no idea if he will pull the trigger. It's the first time in my life someone has pointed a gun in my face.

"I made a bomb," I answer.

He lowers the gun and glances at the bottle before pushing it into the back of his jeans.

"You made a bomb?" He's looking at me from the corner of his eye.

"You can't keep locking me up," I counteract.

"You're right. I can't." He steps aside, and I don't trust him, so I don't move.

"You can go, Emma."

I know I haven't won. It can't be that easy, but I also know not to look a gift horse in the mouth. So I step around him. I'm still ready and waiting for him to grab my arm, but that doesn't happen. Each step I take makes me think maybe that's all I needed to do. I just needed to rebel. The steps behind me creak, and I glance over my shoulder—my stomach squirms as my gaze clashes with his.

I have no idea what he's thinking, but I could go as far as saying that he's angry. It's the set of his eyes, the tightness of his jaw. The smell at the top of the stairs reeks of drain cleaner. I don't see any aluminum anywhere. As I pass the threshold, I'm tempted to turn and slam the door in his face, but he's quicker and stronger. Once I'm in the hallway, I look back at him. He closes the door with a calmness that has me wary.

His black t-shirt is slightly raised, the handle of the gun peeking out. Taking it flitters through my mind, but he leaves.

"We should talk." He enters the kitchen, and this time I follow him.

"I think you're right, but first, I want all my belongings brought back inside."

He nods. "You're right. I shouldn't have thrown them out the window."

I want to smile at the victory, but I don't want him thinking we will ever be friends. Once I get my stuff back, and he stops locking me up, I can try to spend the next four weeks away from him and maybe explore the outside world a bit more.

"I'll go get them." He takes a pack of cigarettes out of his pocket and a lighter. I don't want the smell of smoke on my clothes, but I don't push my luck either. As he leaves, my stomach rumbles, and I realize it's been over thirty-six hours since I ate.

The front door opens, and while he's gone, I start to look through the cupboards. There's not much in them, but I manage to find a tin of tuna and crackers. Placing them on the counter, I turn towards the fridge and get some butter.

"Why don't you sit down."

I spin, startled by his voice. I hadn't heard him come back in. I can't look away from the blue rope in his hands. I reach behind me, my hand lands on the tin of tuna. Before he can react, I throw it, but he moves his head to the side and races towards me.

He's pissed.

His cologne and the smell of cigarettes assault me as he lifts me easily and pushes me into a chair that he kicks out. A hand presses heavily on my chest, and I freeze. The warmth seeps through my dress, and I feel it race along my skin like electricity.

My moment costs me as he swings the rope around my torso and pulls, tying me to the chair.

"Let me up, now." I push against it, but he makes it tighter. Once he has me firmly tied to the chair, he stands back and admires his handy work while lighting another cigarette.

He hasn't taken his dark gaze off me as he holds the lit cigarette between his lips and takes a phone out of his pocket. Once he dials a number, he removes the cigarette from his mouth.

I struggle against the restraints, knowing it's useless, but sitting here and doing nothing doesn't feel natural.

"Did your father tell you that he dropped off my bride-to-be?"

I freeze in my seat.

He nods and blows smoke into the air; a grin plays on his lips. "She came with a CV." He inhales again, and this time he blows the smoke into my face.

"It says she plays the fucking tin whistle. Doesn't say anything about her bomb-making skills."

I can't hear what is being said on the other side of the phone, but I already know my mistake. It was reckless and stupid of me to make that bomb.

"I want a fucking explanation, Jack." When he says Jack, he watches me closely for a reaction, and he gets one. I die a little more inside.

He walks away and closes the phone. I have no idea why the conversation ended.

"You can't keep me tied up," I say and wriggle again.

He opens a drawer and comes back to me with a piece of cloth.

"What are you doing?" I close my mouth and try to stop him from stuffing it inside, but his strong fingers pry my mouth open, and he stuffs the piece of cloth in.

He doesn't step away from me, and I fight to breathe through my nose as he kneels down. His face is masked for a moment as he releases a long stream of smoke from his mouth. I didn't like the smell but watching his mouth was sending my heart skyrocketing.

"Me and you are going to have a little chat. Tell me how you know how to make bombs." He pulls out the gag, and I swallow.

"It was a guess," I respond, and he roughly pushes the gag back into my mouth before getting up.

"You're lying." He tilts his head, but there is a calmness to his posture that terrifies me. I'm also very aware that he has a gun in the back of his jeans. If I didn't speak, would he use it?

I remember Noel saying not to tell them anything. I mumble around the gag, and he steps forward and pulls it out.

"Are we ready to talk now?" He inhales another drag of his cigarette.

"I'm thirsty," I say.

He kneels back down in front of me, and the smile he gives me chills me right to the bone.

"You will be more than thirsty when I'm done with you, love."

Vi Carter

CHAPTER EIGHT

O'REAGAN
AN CHLANN
SHAY

She hasn't spat out her gag, but she easily could. I keep looking at her, wondering why I was set up. Picking up the tin of tuna off the floor, I toss it in the air before catching it again. She had a very accurate throw for a girl.

A bomb maker.

A Murphy.

My gut tightens when I think of that name. There couldn't be a connection. The crackers she had left on the counter, I rattle and look back at her over my shoulder. She's watching me, and I see the same interest in her eyes I had seen before. She turns her head away as I open the tin of tuna and spread some on the crackers.

I take one over to her; she's watching it like it's a gun. I remove the gag, and she swallows several times before licking her dry lips. I push the cracker to her lips that she seals shut. "I'd eat it if I were you."

I'm surprised when she takes a bite. I didn't really expect her to take it from me. As she chews, I light a cigarette. This might take a long time. She swallows, and I push the cracker back to her lips. Her cheeks turn red, but she eats more.

As I wait for Jack to arrive, I feed her three crackers and give her some water.

"I can't even leave you with the bottle." I wiggle the empty bottle at her, and she looks away, but not before I grab her chin and force her to look at me. I have no idea what I'm searching for? Someone to be honest with me?

I will get my answer soon. I stuff the gag back in her mouth as I return to the sink and extinguish the cigarette.

Jack said he was coming over, so he knew what the fuck was going on and didn't want to tell me over the phone.

The buzzing noise in the hall has me leaving the sink. I glance at Emma as I pass. She's sitting very fucking still. She won't have enough time to do anything. Lifting the phone in the hall, I don't say anything as I buzz Jack in through the gates.

Emma is where I left her, which surprises me. She seems to have a way of getting out of very tricky situations. Like the wardrobe upstairs. How did she manage to get the brush out of the door? She's clever, and her innocent, pretty face would really trick a man.

The front door opens, and I kneel down in front of Emma. She sinks further into the chair like she can get away from me. Fear starts to trickle into her big green eyes for the first time, and that has me rising. I light another cigarette. Tying her up was the only comfort I had that she couldn't do anything else. I had no idea what to do with her, but until I understood what I had walked myself into, she was staying in the fucking chair.

"Meet my future wife," I say as Jack steps into the kitchen. I'm watching Emma as her gaze drinks him in. "Or should I say your future wife?" I look at him for the first time and grin, hoping to keep the depth of his betrayal out of my features. I'm not entirely sure if I succeed.

Jack places his keys on the counter. "Does she have to be tied up?" The first thing out of his mouth has me getting angrier. He doesn't deny she was meant for him.

"You want a bomb maker loose?" I hold the cigarette between my lips and walk toward Emma, grabbing the rope more roughly than I need to. She groans around the gag.

"Leave her." Jack's response has me standing up and looking at him while taking the cigarette out of my mouth. For the first time, I see his guilt. But he can take it and shove it up his ass.

"You didn't really think you could blackmail father and me and expect things would run smoothly, did you?"

His confession has me stepping away from Emma and towards him.

I won't remind him that I saved Maeve's life and that it still rested in my hands. He didn't need the reminder. He knew the stakes here.

"So it's all a lie?"

Jack glances at Emma, and I move right up and block him. Like fuck he can look at her.

"You are a King of the North; you have your place on the panel. That wasn't a lie." Jack grits his teeth as he speaks.

The gun in my jeans is begging to be used. But if I kill Jack, I'll have to shoot Emma too, so I hold off. That thought alone makes me feel itchy.

Jack tries to look past me at Emma again, and I move until we are toe to toe. "You're trying to make a cunt of me, Jack." I let a grin grace my face. "I don't like anyone making a cunt of me."

I take a step back and allow my words to sink in.

Jack steps away from the counter, and this time I can't stop him from looking at Emma. Blood roars through my system, and I stay where I am so I don't react.

"The deal was real. I honestly didn't know until after of the implications of you marrying her."

I turn and face Jack. I can't help but take a look at Emma, whose nostrils are flared as she drags in air. She has no idea what the fuck is going on, either. Does she look at Jack and hate this situation even more? I throw my cigarette in the sink and turn on the tap, watching the amber light go out.

"She's Red Murphy's daughter. He's a bomb maker for the RA."

I bite my lip and re-open an earlier cut. *Fuck*. "Your father just fucked me up the ass." Jack doesn't respond because he fucking can't.

"He was responsible for the bombing in 2015." Jack continues, and I'm moving. I don't give a fuck who he is. My hands wrap around his throat as I slam his body against the wall.

"I swear, I didn't know." Jack wraps his hands around my neck too but doesn't squeeze.

I tighten my hold on his neck. "Thirty-two children!" I roar at him before letting him go. His hands fall away easily as he rubs his own neck.

"Thirty-two," I repeat. I'll never forget that day. It was an Orange March, and a bomb had been planted in the crowd, killing one hundred and thirteen innocent people.

Emma's mumbles have me swinging around to her. Her eyes are wide, and she's shaking her head.

"Your father is a fucking animal that will be slaughtered soon." My anger has my mouth moving; Jack pushes off the wall.

"You still have your crown; my father placed you in this predicament to keep a tight leash on you."

Tight? He was fucking choking me.

"What's going to happen when the people up north find out I'm marrying her?" I point at Emma, who has started to rock in the chair.

Jack takes a step towards her, and I grip his arm. His jaw tightens, and he looks from my hand all the way up to my eyes.

"She's mine. Don't fucking touch her." I release him.

"I was going to take her gag out."

"I said, don't touch her."

Jack looks at Emma again. "If her family thought for one second that she was tied up, you would be a dead man."

"Were you hoping I'd hurt her, so you and your father can get rid of me?"

Jack tilts his head. "Shay, this can work. It's a bit more complicated, but that's my father. He complicates everything."

My own da had warned me, but I hadn't listened. Staying here in the south with so much at stake wasn't an option. Emma is still rocking but has stopped her wailing. Her cheeks are bright red, her green eyes wild.

I can't show any weakness in front of Jack. I can't trust him, not after this.

"The attack yesterday, who was it?"

"My father has a man in to question." Another lie.

"Really?" My hands tighten around the lighter and cigarettes that I extract from my pocket.

Jack takes a step back to me. "Shay. I don't want to see you get hurt, but you need to understand what you are up against."

I light the cigarette and shrug. "I know exactly what I'm up against."

Not just one cunt, but two cunts.

"Shay…." Jack trails off and frowns. "It's different down here."

Yeah, loyalty wasn't a word they would ever understand. Money, that was the motivation in the south. For us, it was freedom. It was taking back what was rightfully ours. It is taking back the land under our feet. It was a hundred-year-old battle. Down here, it was drugs, women, and too much fucking money.

"You can leave now." I turn my back on him.

Silence follows, and I know he hasn't left. "Why would your father have you marry her?"

"Her father is a legend here in the South." Jack's voice is flat.

I turn to him. "A kid killer?" No wonder my da hated Liam. I think all the brothers did deep down, no matter what they said. I think he was a poison within his family.

Jack doesn't answer, and Emma stops rocking in the chair.

He still hasn't left, and I have no idea what is keeping him here, but something is.

"The man that my father's security captured after the shooting had a marking on his neck."

I don't ask what. I'm sure he'll tell me.

"It was a skull with the Irish flag painted on it."

I don't react initially. "Any clown can paint an Irish flag on a skull."

It's there in his eyes, and my gut tightens again.

"The skull's mouth has a shamrock in it."

There it was—one of our own men. Now all I can think of is, did my father send them? Was it to kill Emma or Liam, or both? I'm ready to tap my thigh where my own tattoo is.

Had word gotten around about who Emma was?

"Your da must have pissed off a lot of people."

"Shay, he's my father. If he's harmed, I'll go to war."

I nod, expecting no less from Jack. I'd do the same if it were my da. Where this left us... I had no idea. But none of this was good.

"What does your da want?" Liam did this all for a reason.

"I don't know." Jack looks me in the eye, and I don't see a lie.

"What am I expected to do now?"

"In four weeks, you marry Emma and take your place on the panel with my father and me."

I snort. "As a King?"

"Yes."

But I would no longer be King of the North. Was that Liam's plan all along to take the kingdom from my father's hand by using me? My father's only living son.

"How many security men do you have here?" Jack's question has me on high alert, and I take a quick glance out the window to see if Bernard is still there. He is.

"Two."

"I'd up that number."

I want to ask if that's another threat? but if they wanted me dead, I'd be dead. Liam needed me alive for whatever sick fucking plan he was slowly unfolding.

"I'd also untie her and be careful what they see."

I grin again, but it holds no fucking humor at all. "The security that your da supplied for me, I couldn't imagine them betraying me," I say sarcastically.

"I'm trying to help you, Shay," Jack says, but he's taking a final look at Emma before he nods. I don't take my eyes off him as he leaves my home. The moment the door closes, I throw the cigarette on the tiled floor and stamp on it. I'm still staring at the door before I bend down and pick it up.

"We are leaving." I don't move until Jack's vehicle disappears out the front gates.

Time is ticking.

Vi Carter

CHAPTER NINE

O'REAGAN
AN CHLANN
EMMA

Leaving? I spit the gag out; it takes a few tries, but it finally tumbles down and lands in my lap. His name is on my lips, but I remember the lambs that Noel told me not to name.

"My dad would never kill children." I knew my dad was a bomb maker. The thought of him killing anyone makes me uncomfortable, but it was part of our family. But, children? NO.

He looks at me, and shame courses through my system. The way Shay and Jack had spoken about my family and me made me feel nothing but shame. I had to remind myself that it wasn't true. My father would never kill children.

"I'm not debating this with you, Emma." His mind doesn't

seem present. His words are there, but there is no emotion behind them.

My nose burns as I stare at his large back. I hate the thoughts that consume me. When he had said Jack was coming, I couldn't wait to finally see who I was supposed to marry. But the moment he had stepped into the room, I had felt proud that I was Shay's. My cheeks flame even at the thought. Jack couldn't hold a candle to Shay in the looks department, but if I hadn't seen Shay first, I suppose Jack could grow on me.

"I'm going to untie you."

My thoughts rattle around in my head like loose change, and I try to focus as Shay's cologne surrounds me.

"My dad would never hurt children." I'm trying to catch his eye. I need him to believe me, but he unties the rope, and I wiggle my arm immediately.

I get up off the chair as Shay looks out the window. The betrayal is huge to him. I had no idea how all this worked, but Shay was coming out the worst from the conversation I had just heard. Where I fell into all this, I wasn't sure.

"Did your people try to kill me?" I ask.

He really looks at me this time. "I don't know."

"Comforting," I reply and fold my arms across my chest.

"I'm not here to comfort you, Emma."

I want to correct him. He would be my husband, so he should be trying to comfort me, but we both knew that wasn't going to happen. He was leaving, and that was for the best. I could go back to my family. If it was, why was I still standing here watching him stare out the window? I could run.

I glance at the front door.

"We aren't safe here."

Shay is back to looking at me. "You mean you aren't." After what I heard from Jack, Shay is at risk from my family. Especially if Liam's men relay how I've been treated, I shouldn't feel bad for what might happen to him, but I do.

"I'll tell them that it wasn't so bad," I say and look away from him.

His laughter has me looking back.

"You are coming with me, love." His grin is cold and calculating.

"Why?" What the hell would he want me for?

Shay takes a large step towards me, and the space shrinks while a want inside me grows.

"I'm not leaving behind my 'Cash Cow.'"

My body temperature spikes along with my temper. 'Cash Cow'? So I would be used as a ransom?

"My people want you dead. Your people want me dead. So logic tells me we are better together."

"Your logic is screwed." I'm ready to walk away. His fingers curl around my forearm.

"You won't make it home if you leave this house. That's not an idle threat, Emma. The people who attacked you and Liam won't stop until blood is spilled."

Shay's words are like a breeze that slides in under the door and creeps up on you, making you shiver.

His dark eyes grow darker when I glance at him over my shoulder.

"My dad will protect me."

Shay releases me and looks at me like I'm nothing. Once again, a fresh wave of shame burns my cheeks.

"He didn't kill any children." I know that's what he's thinking.

"You're coming with me, and that's it."

That wasn't going to happen. "Where are we going? To hide out in the mountains?" The thoughts of being alone with Shay in some cabin have too many satisfying fantasies growing and swirling in my mind.

"Up north."

It's my turn to laugh at his stupidity. "If these people are trying to kill me…" I trail off as he stares at me.

"Let me just pack." I lie, and his hand circles my arm again, stopping me.

"You won't need anything."

I yank my arm out of his as panic starts to grow and morph into a strangling panic that I can't get away from.

"I'm not going."

Shay's hand grows tighter. "We can do this the easy way or the hard way."

My mind clouds with darkness, and panic takes over, and I focus on one small snippet that Noel taught me. That lesson becomes clearer, and my panic dissolves as I grow slack in Shay's hand. His hold on me loosens, and I hang my head and pretend to weep. He releases me, and I react. I was aiming for in-between his legs. I'm waiting for him to crumble but find that I'm hopping on one leg as he holds my foot.

"Predictable." He releases my foot, and I nearly lose my balance. This time when he reaches for me, I know his fingers are going to leave marks on my arm.

"I'd advise you to shut your mouth when we leave the house. I don't want to be cleaning your brains off my t-shirt."

I glance at his t-shirt and back up to his to see if he is messing with me. He isn't.

"I like this t-shirt," he says.

So do I.

I don't stop the struggle and find myself pinned against the wall in the hall. His body presses heavier against me, and my stomach squirms. He's turned on. My gaze trails up to his dark eyes. A sudden explosion of want erupts behind his eyes that set my own want for him on overdrive.

His black eyes dart to my lips, they sometimes look lifeless, almost like glass, but now they are filled with a hunger that makes my heart hammer heavily in my chest.

His name is on the tip of my tongue. I want to try it out. If I do, I know there will be no return. I push against him again instead.

"Let me go."

His lips slam down on mine, and I freeze at the impact, but I'm moving under his warm, plump lips. The taste of alcohol and cigarettes fills my mouth. His body is warm; his cock grows harder against me. My body buzzes, and I'm panting, breaking the kiss, not understanding what's wrong with me. I shouldn't want this. Is this how girls feel? Like they have no control over their bodies?

His lips find mine again, and this time I'm sucked further

down the rabbit hole. His hands release my arms, and I reach up and touch his wide shoulders. They feel more solid than I had imagined they would be. Every part of my body is responding by robbing the air from my lungs. I'm trying to focus on the tingle of his mouth on my lips, the heaviness of my breasts in my bra, but I'm drawn to the wetness between my legs.

I groan as my whole body seems to jump towards him. His large hand slides down my side, leaving a path of fire behind it. One I don't believe I will ever be able to put out. The deeper he kisses me, a new taste fills my mouth. It's iron. It's heavy. It's blood. It's his blood, from the wound on his lip, and that has my body bursting with sparks that burn and bubble under my skin.

My clothes feel heavy, my hair feels heavy, my breasts feel heavy. His hand runs lower, and I don't stop him as he grips the material of my dress and pulls it up. He's dragging it up quickly, the tips of his fingers grazing my leg, sending everything inside me spinning. The moment his hand touches my pussy, my eyes spring open.

I'm terrified. I'm brave. I'm not me.

His tongue dips deeper into my mouth, and I mimic his movements for a millisecond before his finger slides inside me, and I groan so loud that I think it's not me. His fingers slide out easily before re-entering. My nails dig into his wide shoulders as he continues pushing his fingers inside me. Another joins the first, and I feel stretched, but I want more.

I break the kiss again as too much spins and yearns inside me, wanting more. More of what? More of him? I had no idea if my reaction was normal, but I couldn't focus on one feeling without another overtaking it. My breasts ache, and each brush of his chest against mine is painful but also sends a throbbing between my legs where he's still fingering. Three large fingers fill me, and I spread my legs a little further. Each stroke grows faster, and I break the kiss again as I cling to him. Something dies before it bursts to life, and I'm crying out, my nails digging into him. I feel the gush of liquid as I cum all over his fingers.

I can't breathe.

I can't stop my body from shuddering.

I can't stop the hammering of my heart that this is what it really feels like.

I'm choking on emotions that make no sense to me. I don't feel vulnerable or ashamed; I want more.

Shay extracts his fingers, and when his gaze swallows me up, I see confusion deep in his dark eyes. He's leaning away like this is over. But I don't work that way.

I'm nervous.

I'm a little afraid, but above all, I won't take and not give. I reach out and touch his hard cock. His hands press into the wall behind my head as he groans at the slight contact. I run my hand along his full length. My juices drip down the inside of my leg. I don't let all the issues swarm my mind as I move down the length of his body. Once I'm on my knees, I look back up at him, and he's watching me, with a trickle of fear in his eyes.

I can't stop the grin as I open his trousers. "I won't bite."

He's hesitating, I don't blame him, but he can't take something from me and not allow me to take from him. I didn't like things unbalanced. I didn't like owing anyone.

Dragging down his trousers, he still holds onto the wall as I push down his white boxers. His cock is in my face, and it's like I've discovered something new. I touch the tip, and it jumps. I touch it again, and it reacts the same way. Veins bulge, I look up one final time, but his eyes are closed. My lips touch the head before I pull back. This time he's looking at me. The hunger in his eyes has me licking it before I take the tip in my mouth again.

Shay reaches down and takes his cock in his hand. He gives it a stroke, and I run my tongue along the top. My fingers trail up his thighs, and I hold them as I push more of his cock in my mouth, and he stops stroking. I have seen enough movies to guess what to do, but I've never done it before. His cock tastes salty, and when I release him from my mouth, I lick my lips, and he takes back over, running his hand up and down his cock. I can't take my eyes off his cock, the head swells, and his pumps grow faster. I lick it again, and his groans cut off. White semen flows from the head, and I taste him. It's salty. Most of his cum drips onto my chin and down the front of my dress. His strokes slow, and his breathing grows harsher as he closes his eyes.

He's watching me as my tongue darts out and tastes a bit more of him. I don't like how tasting him awakens an old feeling in me, one that never was fulfilled. The want to be wanted and the want to want someone else. A sharp band tightens around my chest as he continues to stare down at me like we aren't in the most intimate stance. His lids flutter closed as he reaches down and pulls up his boxers.

I have no idea what to do, but what I don't expect is for him to remove his t-shirt and kneel down in front of me.

Being this close to him hurts, and something carves itself into my chest as I look at all his tattoos. His body is a painting, and I want to follow each story. Yet, it's there, the sense that I am betraying everything I am meant to fight for.

Lines have grown blurred in seconds since Jack's arrival, and I see Shay.

Breda's words that a man is a man haven't left my mind either.

"What are you doing?" I ask as Shay reaches around me and unzips my dress. What we did was huge and was something I didn't think I would ever do with him, but sex, I couldn't go there.

"I'm not having sex with you." My hands slam against his chest, but he's a solid wall of muscle as he pulls the zipper down on my dress.

"Shay." I use his name, and it's like a slap. He sits back, his dark eyes searching my face.

"I won't have sex with you," I repeat.

"Your dress needs to be changed. It's covered in my cum." His confidence is staggering.

My cheeks flame as I look down at the spoils of our fun.

"Oh."

His lip tugs up, and I don't stop him this time as he pulls my dress off over my head. I feel more exposed than I ever have been, but I don't stop him from taking me in.

When he's drunk his fill, he takes the black t-shirt and drags it over my head. It smells like him, and my core tightens.

"I have more dresses," I say.

"I can't look at them." His response isn't what I expect.

"Put your hand through."

I push my arm through the sleeve. His face is still black and blue, and once again, I want to know what happened.

Once his t-shirt is on me, he starts to rise and pulls up his jeans. They hug his slim hips. "I'm going to go and get some fresh clothes. Can I trust you not to run?" He asks the question, but I think he knows the answer.

I nod, and he leaves me kneeling in the hall. I'm not ready to stand up. My legs will run; they know no different, only what I've been taught.

But Jack's words about my father and his comments about how they set Shay up, by using my family's dealings to trap him, makes me not want to rise.

Shame burns deep in my heart.

My dad would never kill children. That's one thing I knew, and I needed to prove. I'm rising as Shay comes down the stairs, fully clothed. His t-shirt brushes the top of my knees.

"Let's go." He drags a jacket over his wide shoulders before lighting up a cigarette.

My instincts want to fight and run.

But something that seeks freedom has me following Shay out into the garage. I stop as I look at the rising door, it screams to me: Freedom.

CHAPTER TEN

O'REAGAN
AN CHLANN
SHAY

She had paused before getting into the car and I had thought I would have to force her into the vehicle but thankfully she had gotten in.

Each time I take a peek at Emma, my gut twists. Taking her up north is a risk. One I shouldn't be taking, but staying here will only result in my death. Having her will give me something to bargain with when they follow us, and they will.

She's removed her shoes and socks. Her wild, red, curly hair covers her face as she lies back in the seat. Why the fuck does she have to look so beautiful, and why had I touched her? I shouldn't have done it knowing what I was leading her into, but at the moment, I wanted to claim her, taste her and make her mine. I needed the reminder that she wasn't fucking Jack O'Reagan's. Her response still shocks me. I look at her again, and my cock grows hard thinking about her licking it. The way she had looked up at me and told me she wouldn't bite had turned me on so fucking much.

Who the fuck would have thought.

"You can't use your name," I speak before turning on the wipers as the rain starts to fall fast and hard. The road in front of us gleams from the recent downpour.

"What about Emily?" She's looking at me, and I've never seen her green eyes so alive.

"You're taking this very well, Emily."

Her smile widens, and I quickly focus back on the road before I take another kiss from her ruby red lips.

"I've come to realize that I don't have much of a choice," is her answer, and I'm not buying it.

"So if I let you go now, you wouldn't go home?"

There is a lull in the conversation, and I glance at her. She's focused on her nails. Her lips are tugged down. "I would go home. I miss my horse and my brother."

She doesn't mention a ma or a da.

"But I want answers." She continues. "Answers to why Jack said those things about my dad."

I pull over as my stomach clenches painfully. Dropping her on the side of the road all of a sudden seems appealing. Taking her up north just doesn't seem as wise if she even considers asking fucking questions like that.

"Emma." I put the car into park.

"Emily." She corrects me.

Her long legs are white and creamy, and I'm imagining what it would be like to bury myself deep in-between them. My cock instantly grows hard, and I let my gaze wander up my t-shirt that looks so fucking good on her.

She's older-looking since she has shed her air of hostility. I don't know if she's a good actress or what she's up to, but nothing here is adding up.

"You can't ask those types of questions up north. If you do, you're dead."

"I wouldn't dare. But, you can. Jack said you're King of the North."

I nod and tighten my hands on the steering wheel, not liking the word Jack in her mouth where my cock had just been.

"No one told me you were King of the North."

Now her sudden interest makes sense.

"Are you a gold digger?"

"No, Shay."

There she goes again, using my name.

"I'm a 'Cash Cow', and now you're my highly valued bull." She isn't smiling.

I face the road before she sees the amusement in my eyes and continue to drive. That's a first—a highly valued bull. I think I might like the sound of that.

The rain eases off, and the night creeps in. Emma is quiet, but she's not asleep. I've kept the heater on. She hasn't complained about the cold, but she can't be warm in just a t-shirt. Once we cross the border, I'd take her to a friend who would help us.

"This is the first time I've ever been in a car shoeless." Her voice sounds soft, but it carries weight, grabbing my attention.

I'm thinking she's had a lot of firsts lately.

"It's over-rated." She speaks while dragging a finger along the window that's slightly fogged up.

I could drop her off, let her go home, and keep whatever innocence she has left. I have no idea what the North will bring to her, but deep down, I know it won't be good. Each mile that goes by brings her closer to her death. If anyone finds out who she is, it's game over, and they could already know.

I glance at her, and she's watching me now.

"What we did wasn't over-rated." Her cheeks are pink, not her normal burning red.

I should tell her that won't happen again, but if she's willing, I'm not going to stop her. Anyway, I liked how she looked on my cock.

"I think maybe it was under-rated."

"Are you trying to give me a compliment?" I'd prefer if she didn't.

"No. I'm just saying that it's more than any book or movie could show you."

I take another glance at Emma. She's chewing on her lip; her brows dragged down.

"You like porn?"

Now her cheeks blaze, and I suppress a smile.

"I like chemistry."

That she fucking did. It reminded me that she knew how to make bombs, just like her da. She turns away from me, and I wonder if she is remembering the exact same thing I am. The rest of the drive moves by silently until we are consumed by the darkness.

The small farmhouse has a red light in the window. She's here.

"Where are we?" Emma is sitting forward, and for the first time since she willingly came, she sounds uncertain.

"What's your name?" I ask as I unbuckle my belt.

"Emily." She responds, sitting forward and staring out the window like she might be able to see through the walls.

"Second name."

"Emily Larry?" She looks at me.

It will do. "You're my friend," I inform her.

"Girlfriend?" She tugs at my t-shirt before bending down and slipping her feet into her shoes.

"No, Michelle wouldn't believe that."

I was a lone rider to them all. I had my fill of women but never took them to places like Michelle's. This was a safe house, and if Michelle ever knew who Emma was, I'm sure she'd cut my balls off.

"Michelle? A lover?" Emma sits up, and I like the note of jealousy I hear in her voice.

I don't answer her question. "Let me do the talking." I climb out, and Emma gets out too.

The front door cracks open as I reach back into the back seat and take out my rucksack.

The door continues to open the closer we get. I don't check to see if Emma is following. Her heels are crunching away on the driveaway behind me.

I step in, and Michelle nods at me as she waits until Emma has passed before closing the door.

"Come in." She doesn't ask why we are here in the dead of the night, why I'm bruised, or who Emma is, and why she's only wearing a t-shirt. Michelle has seen a lot more in her sixty-five years on this earth than most.

She goes to the Stanley cooker and stirs—what smells like soup. Emma is taking in the space, and I let her. Keeping my focus on Michelle.

"I just need to lie low for a day," I say when she returns to the table with the soup. Michelle studies my features for the first time.

"Do you need any wounds cleaned?"

I shake my head and pick up the spoon.

Emma sits down, and Michelle returns with a bowl of soup. "Have you any wounds?" She asks.

"No, I don't. I'm Emily." Emma reaches out her hand, and Michelle looks at it before she takes it.

"She's a runaway I picked up," I explain to Michelle as I devour her soup.

Michelle doesn't say anything but refills my soup and brings it back to the table with some of her brown bread.

"I only have one spare bed."

I dip the brown bread into the soup. "You have a drifter?"

"You know these walls don't talk." Michelle leans in and places a hand on my cheek. "I've missed you, son."

"I've missed your soup." I smile back at Michelle, and she half laughs as she removes her hand from my face. She returns to the stove, and Emma leans in.

"You took me to your mom's?"

That would never happen.

"He's not my son. But he may as well be," Michelle answers, and Emma's face turns red at being caught whispering.

"It's just you said, son."

Michelle half faces Emma. "It's an endearment we use here. Where are you from?"

"She's from the south. Near Wicklow." I keep somewhat to the truth. Michelle returns to the stove. "So, are you going to tell me who else is staying here?"

I drain the second bowl of soup as Michelle returns to the table, but she doesn't sit down.

She won't say. "Do I need to avoid anyone?" I ask instead.

Her smile softens her features. Lines gather around the corner of her eyes from years of laughing and smiling. Michelle's safehouse was one I used the most, even if I wasn't hiding. She never asks what we are running from, only glad that we ran to her.

"You're always avoiding someone, Shay. But no, she isn't here."

"She?"

Michelle doesn't bite, and I drop it. "Now, let me show you

to your room." Michelle leans in on the table as her attention goes to Emma.

"I'm sorry, but you will have to share. I'm all filled up."

"That's okay." Emma's voice is small, and I'm tempted to look at her, but I don't. I rise from the table, and Emma does too. Her bowl is empty, and that makes me happier than it should.

We follow Michelle to the back of the small house. This is the smallest room—a single bed with a storage box at the end. The wardrobe holds hand-me-downs and leftovers. I know if I move it and lift three floorboards, I'll find a bag of guns, fresh passports, and money.

"I'll get more blankets and pillows."

I shrug out of my jacket. Emma folds her arms across her chest. Her eyes grow round with uncertainty. Dark circles under her eyes have me wanting to lift her onto the bed.

"I'll sleep on the floor," I say.

She nods without looking at me and walks over to the bed, and sits down. "Yeah, that sounds like a good plan."

A grin tugs at my lips at how easily she put me on the floor. I did let her sleep in a wardrobe.

"Now, I'll just leave these here." Michelle places a duvet and two pillows on the bed.

"I'll just grab Emily some clothes, and then I'll be out of your hair."

Emma doesn't move from the bed as she takes in the room around her. I'm sure she's not used to a room so small and under-furnished.

"It's only for the night," I say as I open the wardrobe and take out fresh clothes for myself.

"And then what happens tomorrow?"

"I'm not sure yet." I hadn't really thought that far ahead. I knew staying here would give me time to think about what I was doing, and no one would look for us here. I'm sure by now they were already searching. I just wish I was there to see the look on Liam's face. All of Emma's clothes were still scattered across the front lawn, and after Jack seeing Emma tied up, they would think the worst.

"Now, here's a few bits that should fit your tiny frame." Michelle hands a bundle of clothes to Emma.

"Thanks, Michelle." I close the wardrobe expecting her to leave, but she's holding the door in her hands; it's slightly ajar. "The other visitor is back a bit earlier than I thought; I'd advise you to stay in your room."

"Is that so?" I ask, dragging a dark navy jumper on.

"Yeah, it is so. I knew it was you. Just from the smell."

The mouthy blonde steps around Michelle and into my room. I want to tell Siobhan to fuck off, but I'm very aware of Emma in the room.

"Ah, Siobhan. If I had known you were staying here, I would have brought you something."

"Go fuck yourself, Shay." Siobhan slams a hand on her hip. So she was still pissed.

"I like your hair." I lie. She has it cropped to her head like a fucking choir boy. She's still stunning to look at, but under all that, there really isn't much.

"What are you doing here?" Siobhan questions.

"My house, my rules," Michelle reminds her, and Siobhan's defensive stance drops. Her hand slips from her hip, but she doesn't leave.

"A word, please, Shay?" she says with a bittersweet smile.

"I'm Emily." Emma appears beside me with an outstretched hand towards Siobhan. I wish she had stayed quiet. Standing beside me in my t-shirt didn't leave much to the imagination.

Siobhan's gaze digs into Emma before her bright blue eyes fire back to me. "Outside." Siobhan leaves, and Emma drops her hand along her side.

Michelle departs with no words. "That went well," I tell no one as I get my cigarettes and lighter out of my jacket pocket before leaving it on the chest at the end of the bed.

"Is she an ex?" Emma's trying to hold back emotions that find their way into her words and brighten her cheeks.

"I don't have ex's."

"But you were something?"

I don't have to explain myself to anyone. "Not to me," I answer. "Get some rest." I close the door behind me and meet Siobhan's sharp eye. She's not going to give me a second before she starts.

"You're a fucking wanker, Shay." She starts.

I light a cigarette and lean against the wall. I'll give her until I finish my cigarette to get it all off her very perky chest. After that, she can fuck right off like the rest of them.

CHAPTER ELEVEN

O'REAGAN
AN CHLANN
EMMA

The clothes Michelle left for me look a bit tight, but I'm not fussy. I'm ready to change into the black jeans when Siobhan's loud voice has me stepping towards the door. My heart won't slow down the closer I get, and my blood starts to slowly boil at the words she is firing at Shay like he is hers and not mine.

"You could have called. You could have gotten word to me that you were okay."

I step closer to the door, expecting Shay's response to explain to me what she was talking about.

"I could have done a lot of things. I do what I want, Siobhan.

I don't answer to you or any other woman." It sounds like he's smoking.

"Who's she? Another victim?" Siobhan's closer to the door, and I'm picturing her getting close to Shay. My hands tighten into fists, and I hate the reaction I'm having.

Siobhan is beautiful in the most natural way. She's tall and far more suited to Shay than me. Standing beside Siobhan, I'd look a mess. Everything about her is neat and put together.

"She's a friend I'm helping out," Shay answers.

Siobhan's laughter fills the hall. "You don't have any friends."

It sounds like Shay is smoking again. His voice is further away this time, but I hear his words very clearly. They sink deep inside me, and I'm ready to open the door.

"What do you want, Siobhan. You want to suck my cock?"

"I hope it fucking falls off." Siobhan's words are still angry but grow distant.

"Don't be like that." Laughter in Shay's voice would piss me off, but I don't hear a response from Siobhan, so she must have left. She's a far stronger person than I would have been.

I return to the bed and put on the clean clothes that Michelle left for me. The black running shoes are a bit big, but it feels good not to be standing in just a t-shirt. I fold and place the shirt under my pillow. I straighten the green jumper and lie on the bed. I don't get under the covers. It's weird being in someone else's bed beside my own, but anything is better than the hard wooden wardrobe floor that I had spent last night on.

After a lot of tossing and turning, I get up. I had expected

Shay to return, but he still hadn't. I convince myself that I'm only getting up because I can't sleep. It's not the thought of him with Siobhan that drives me out of the room.

The hall is cast in shadows, and the slates under the runners have recently been swept. Light from the kitchen draws me in. Michelle is still there.

"Don't you sleep?" I ask.

She gives me a half-smile. "You should be sleeping." She returns to a large beige bowl. Her hands sink into the dough as she kneads the brown bread mix over and over.

My stomach tightens as I think of Breda.

"I'm not tired," I answer as I sit down at the table that's been cleaned off. I drag the sleeves of the jumper across my knuckles. Michelle continues to knead the brown bread. She takes the large bowl over to the table before leaving and returning with flour that she sprinkles on the table.

"He's outside. Having a bath." She doesn't look at me.

I'm ready to say that I'm not looking for him.

Michelle's gaze rises to me as she shapes the brown bread.

"He's alone." That's it, she returns to baking, and I rise. I pause, knowing I should say something.

"Thanks for letting me stay."

A nod of her head is all I get.

I leave through the back door. The sky is black, but the moon lights up the outside world. I'm ready to call his name, but I don't as the moonlight washes over him.

It's bizarre. He's lying in a bathtub in the middle of the

back garden, smoking, with the moon shining down on him. I continue to walk towards him, trying to figure out why he was in a bath outside.

"Fuck off." His words have me freezing. He turns his head towards me. Those eyes are filled with darkness that slowly lightens.

"I thought it was someone else." He sinks back down in the bath.

"Who, Siobhan?" I ask, knowing I sound jealous.

"Go on to bed, love." His voice is soft, and I can't stop the smile that tugs at my lips.

"Why are you bathing outside?" I ask as I reach the bathtub. I'm trying to keep my eyes above his waistline, but it's very hard. One leg hangs over the edge. I dip my hand in; the water is warm.

"I've always loved this, and Michelle had it ready for me." He throws the cigarette out onto the grass, and I can't stop staring at him. He's gorgeous, and even more so, lying in a bathtub under the moonlight.

"I've never had a bath outside."

Shay's heavy gaze swings to me. "Is that right?"

I'm not sure if his voice holds humor.

"Yeah." My stomach squirms, and I'm questioning who I am as I kick off my runners and remove my socks and jeans. Shay doesn't say a word as I pull my jumper over my head, leaving my bra and panties on.

He still says nothing as I step into the tub. He moves, giving me more space. This time I can't avoid looking at his large cock that's hard. He's sitting up, water dripping down his defined chest. He's exactly like I had imagined he would be with water on his chest.

I can't meet his eyes, and I focus on filling my hands with water and pouring it across my shoulders.

"So, how did this come about?" I ask. My fingers push some of the bubbles aside. There aren't many of them, but I use it to not look at him. I'm not feeling as brave now. He moves, and the water sloshes across the edge.

My heart stills when my gaze meets his. He's looking at me, his dark eyes darker than I've ever seen them before.

"What do you want, Emma?" The way he asks the question has me sitting back slightly. What do I want? Right here and now, I wanted to touch Shay.

I move forward and reach under the water. My hand grips his cock, and he moves abruptly at the contact. More water splashes over the side of the tub.

"Easy, love."

I can't stop the grin as I touch him again. This time he's more prepared. His cock feels huge in my hand. The texture feels odd under the water. I stroke up and down, and Shay rests back with a groan that he releases to the moon. I pause, momentarily captured by the angles and shadows of his face.

"Don't tease," he says without looking at me.

I return to my gentle strokes. I feel like a goddess as he groans and moans. My heart trips and speeds at an alarming rate as I increase my strokes.

"Tell me when you are going to come," I whisper, but I don't look away from his cock that grows and shifts under the water. I'm too taken with the power that touching him gives me.

This is a moment—a moment like no other as I speed up. Shay shifts, and water sloshes over the edge of the bathtub. "I'm going to come."

I don't pause but dip my head under the water and capture his cock in my mouth as I stroke. I can taste the salt on my lips before he fills my mouth. His body shudders and jerks, and I stay as long as I can under the water before coming up.

I swallow, and like I'm at some fine dining establishment., I savor the taste. I release Shay's cock to push the hair out of my eyes and rub water away from my face.

Licking my lips, I finally look at Shay, feeling pretty proud of myself. My stomach quivers with the look on his face. I have no idea if he's mad or shocked.

"I like the taste." It's easy, to be honest, sitting in a bathtub, in a field, under the moon, with a man who looks like a God. It's easy because it's a moment that will stay with me forever. It might shatter when we leave here, or when he says something I don't want to hear, or a thought I shouldn't have pops up. But right now, it's a moment.

"You sure do."

I exhale a shaky breath at his response. He shifts again and reaches out along the side of the tub. I watch as he lights a cigarette.

"Can I have one?" I've never smoked before.

He's eyeing me before he hands me his cigarette and lights another one for himself.

Bringing it to my lips, I inhale. It burns my throat, and I start to cough. When I settle, he's grinning at me.

"First time smoking too?"

"No. I'm a chain smoker. Can't you tell?"

His laughter dances across my bare skin and raises goosebumps in its wake. It's deep, dark, and delightful, and I want to make him laugh again.

I inhale more smoke and cough a bit less. I flick the ashes over the side of the bathtub. I use my time to watch Shay as he lies back with his head thrown up to the moon as he smokes.

"The first time I took a bath out here, I was pissed out of my head. The water was freezing, and I ended up sick in bed for days." He blows smoke into the sky.

"Poor thing." I inhale more smoke and decide I don't really like smoking, so I just hang the cigarette over the side of the tub and focus on the burning ember.

"Why did you come out here?" Shay's question has me knowing this is when the moment will shatter.

I drop the cigarette out onto the grass. "I couldn't sleep." I lie.

"You should go back in and try."

I don't look at Shay, but I agree with him. I've had my moment with him, and everything after this feels forced.

"Goodnight, Shay." I climb out of the bath. The slight breeze is sharp against my damp skin. I gather all my clothes off the ground, and without looking back, I make my way back to the house.

I keep waiting for a sense of shame or disgust to come from my actions, but it doesn't come, even as I enter the room and take off my wet panties and bra. I smell Shay's t-shirt before dragging it over my head and climbing into bed.

I redress the next morning. Shay's not in the room. The pillows and blanket are on the floor, so he was here at some stage.

A soft knock at the door has me turning as Michelle steps in. "How did you sleep?" She asks as she bends down and picks up the pillows.

I step forward and gather the blanket. "Good, thank you."

"I brought you some hair ties. Shay thought you might want it tied up." She meant Shay said to come in here and tell me to tie it up. Having my hair out of my face would be welcomed.

"Thank you." I fold the blanket and place it at the end of the made bed.

"The bathroom is down the hall. If you want to wash up." I take the ties that she holds out to me.

"Breakfast is nearly ready." Michelle leaves the door open, and the smell of rashers and sausages has my stomach grumbling.

I find the bathroom easily and wash up before plaiting my hair down my back. It rolls all the way down my spine.

I don't expect to find anyone in the kitchen with the silence, but the tension is an entirely different thing that I step into. Siobhan has parked herself right beside Shay. She must have dragged her chair as close as possible. Neither of them looks up as I step in. Michelle speaks to me over her shoulder as she moves around the stove.

"Sit down, Emily. Your food is ready."

I'm tempted to sit on the other side of Shay, but instead, I sit at the head of the table away from them but where I can watch them. I drag my chair out, and Shay pauses in running his bread around his plate to gather the yolk of the egg, the remaining beans, and some red sauce.

"How did everyone sleep?" I direct the question at Shay as Michelle puts a plate in front of me. "Thank you."

Her eyes soften, and she nudges my shoulder gently. "Eat. If I had you for a week, I'd put some meat on those bones."

"Delightful. How did you sleep?" Siobhan answers, and I'm glad she bit.

"It was a tight fit; the bed is small. But I managed." I smile as I take a bite of the sausage on the plate. I can't help but look at Shay.

Is that amusement I see in his dark eyes?

"It won't always be so tight, Emily." Siobhan smiles just as sweetly back at me. Shay picks up his mug and drinks from it like this isn't bothering him at all. If anything, he seems entertained.

"One morning, you'll have all the space you want."

We hold each other's stare, and I get it. He left her high and dry. She's hurt. I drop her gaze and focus on my food instead of annoying her.

A ringing phone breaks the silence. We all look to Shay as he starts to pat pockets in his red checkered shirt. He looks like a wood-cutter this morning. My mind springs to him in the bathtub under the moonlight. I snap out of my memory as he pulls a phone from the front pockets of his jeans and leaves the table.

"If I were you, I wouldn't let him out of my sight," Siobhan speaks while staring into a fire that's been recently lit. The dust from cleaning out the ashes still rests on the black marble of the large open fireplace. The wood has only started to burn. I wonder if Michelle ever sleeps.

"Same happened to me. I was sitting here ready to go, and poof, he disappeared." Siobhan looks at me, and my stomach squeezes. I'm tempted to turn and look at the door, but I don't want her to see that her words are getting to me.

I'm straining to hear his voice, any sound, but there is silence. I cut up my sausage as worry starts to grow. What would happen if he just left me? He wouldn't.

"Something must have come up," I tell my plate.

"Yeah. You keep telling yourself that when he disappears on you. It makes it easier." Siobhan moves past me with her plate and mug in hand and places them in the sink.

Michelle has been busy wiping down counters and tidying up. Her pace slows.

"He won't leave me behind," I say more to the room than anyone else.

But the longer I sit here, the longer the silence stretches.

Fuck. He's left me.

CHAPTER TWELVE

O'REAGAN
AN CHLANN
EMMA

"You've been quiet since we left Michelle's." Shay's words cut off my thoughts.

He had returned to the kitchen after I had thought he had left me. It was a stark reminder that I had no idea who he was. Or what he wanted with me now.

I had really thrown myself in at the deep end, and I didn't want to start to sink.

"Just thinking." I shrug but don't look at him, not even sure if he saw the gesture.

"Having a go at Siobhan wasn't wise."

He has my attention. His beard has grown longer, making him look more dangerous, and I kind of like that.

"Will I be seeing her again?"

This time Shay glances at me. "I don't know."

"Will we be returning to Michelle's?" I ask, already missing the warmth and food. How easily a place can grow on you.

"I don't know." Shay turns back to the road.

"Where are you going? Oh, hold on, you don't know," I answer my own question.

"No need to get all funny, love. We are going to a fight."

My spine straightens, and I'm trying to shuffle forward, but the seatbelt keeps me in place. "Like a real fight?"

Shay's dark gaze narrows, and I reel in my excitement.

"It's dangerous, Emma. So no matter what, stay with me. It's uncharted ground. If anything happens, I can't protect you."

I sit back in my seat, but his words don't douse my excitement. "What do you mean uncharted?"

"It's ruled by no one. It's a no-man's-land. Everything goes."

I'm nodding like I get it, but my mind is picturing two men in a ring, with large red gloves on them. I've always been taken with watching them on TV. I hated the violence, but it was the roar of the crowd. If I closed my eyes, I could imagine all the hairs rising on my body at the noise. That many people screaming at once must be amazing.

"So, is someone you know fighting?" I'm facing Shay and notice how his shoulders rise a bit higher, and his arms grow tenser. His jaw ticks a few times as he works a muscle.

"I don't know," His reply has me looking away from him. "The important thing is that you stay with me, keep your mouth closed, and if anyone asks questions, I'll do the talking."

"No problem," I say to the window as I run my hand along the door handle.

"It might get a bit messy."

I stop touching the handle and glance at Shay. What isn't he telling me?

"I'm barred, so they might try to kick us out."

"I thought it was uncharted territory?"

Shay glances at me, and his shoulders aren't so high now. "It is. Just Amanda, the ring woman, doesn't like me."

"What did you do to her? Sleep with her and run?"

He doesn't answer me, and I hate the tug on my guts that sends heat to my face.

"Maybe I should just ask for a list of who you haven't slept with." I hate the words the moment they leave my lips. I sound just how I feel—jealous.

We drive in silence, and I count three cigarettes that Shay lights. When he lights another one an hour later, I ask for one and enjoy it a little more than last night. We stop for takeaway food before we continue on. A sign flashes past us. Welcome to Belfast.

Fear tightens my throat, and I want Shay to tell me that I'll be okay. A southerner up North. I'm picturing all kinds of things happening to me.

"Maybe we should say I'm from the North." The fear doesn't leave my voice.

"That wouldn't work. You have a southern accent." That's all Shay says. No comforting telling me that I had nothing to worry about. His silence on the matter makes my fears grow. We take a side road off the motorway, and I'm sure we are moving away from the city.

Shay keeps driving until we enter a small town. He parks in front of a stone building with large arches that are gated. I think it's a lot of apartments. I stay in the car as Shay gets out and opens his rucksack that's in the backseat. I'm tempted to look at what's in it. He takes something out that is small enough to fit in his pocket.

"Let's go." He closes the back door, and I get out, meeting him on the sidewalk. He towers over me, and I'm tempted to touch his hands, but I tuck my hands under my sweater. I'm excited to see a fight, but I also want some sort of confirmation that I'm going to be okay. I take a peek at Shay as he lights another cigarette. I wasn't going to get confirmation from him.

Shay turns down an alleyway that dips like a ramp into an underground carpark. There's lots of graffiti on the walls, and I pause as an image of a soldier holding a gun fills one wall. Behind him is a tattered and bloody Irish flag.

Freedom is written under the image. But above all, what captures my attention the most, is the soldier's eyes. It's like if you step closer, you might see a war reflected in his gaze. It's the anger, the sorrow, the hate that halts my steps.

"I told you to stay close," Shay calls over his shoulder.

I leave the damaged soldier and catch up to Shay as he drags open a large, red, steel door. The smell of urine hits me first.

"Don't touch the railing." Shay stuffs his hands in his pockets.

I do as he says. "Why?" My voice bounces around the space.

"Some stupid cunts think it's fun to piss on them."

I move further away from the railing and skip down the steps after Shay. Four flights down, he stops at the door and takes his hands out of his pockets. He pauses and takes a final look at me.

"Stay with me."

I nod as a rush flushes fast through my body; if he doesn't move, I'm going to have to shuffle to release some of the energy.

The door opens, and the sound spills out. It's another carpark, but instead of cars, it's filled with people and jutting up like some dark tower; there's a cage in the center that everyone is staring at.

Shay glances at me one final time before he moves through the crowd. There is no pushing or trying to get through; they separate in front of him. He had said this was uncharted territory, but clearly, they know him. Gazes trail over me, and I pray to God that I don't look southern. I keep my chin high as I follow Shay, but I can't stop looking around me. The large pillars that hold the ceiling up are either covered in graffiti of just random words or images of maybe fights that occurred. I pause at one girl with a Mohawk. She's wearing a pair of tight red shorts, and the artist has her breasts pouring out of her top. A hand swallows mine.

I turn, already knowing who it is. My gaze rises, and my heart trips over itself as Shay pulls me along with him and away from all the artwork.

The roars are electrifying as we make a path toward the cage. Once again, my attention gets consumed with all the different people. Large cans hold fire that people gather around. The flames rise high in one of the cans, and the people jump back. The crowd shifts and rattles. My hand slips out of Shay's as a sense of panic infiltrates the space. I can't see Shay, but I keep my focus on the cage in the center of the room and work towards it. It's harder this time as I have to push and shove my way through the crowd—no one parts for me.

I reach the front, and it's like a swelling storm that I'm caught up in as I'm forced closer to the cage that has two girls fighting in. It's a lot of hair-pulling. One with purple hair rakes her nails down the face of her opponent. The cheers are verbal, but another bodily swell comes like a wave, and I'm forced closer. I dig my hands into the cage to keep steady. The purple-haired girl is stronger as she throws the brunette on the ground. All the voices become one, and the crowd declares her a winner. The gates on either side open and both step out as another two girls enter. This time when they start to fight, it's a bit more deadly. One of them roars before she charges, giving away her move.

The other girl is ready, anyone would be, and I'm already thinking of what I would do. Adrenaline anchors itself to me, and I'm on a high like never before. My voice rises with the crowd, and this is it — this is freedom.

I wince at each punch, but something in me grows, and I'm moving down the cage, my fingers clinging to the steel. I can't take my eyes off the fight.

I reach the gate. A tall woman stands near the door. She has a scowl on her face that makes the men around her look feminine.

"I want in." My voice is low, but her head swings around to me. She eyes me up and down. The assessment is over in a few seconds.

I'm ready to say it again, but my bravery dwindles when the girls slam against the cage. It rattles my bones, and I release the cage only to be pushed up against it again. I can smell their sweat, their blood, and I'm pushing back against the crowd.

The fight ends abruptly as one girl lies on her back, not moving. The gates open, and the winner walks out while two men carry the other.

"You're up."

My stomach stirs, and my palms grow sweaty. "Me?" I point at myself.

The woman doesn't wear a scowl; it's like a smile that is carved from jagged glass.

"Yeah, you."

The jeers erupt again and move closer to the cage door. "Will my opponent be the same size?"

A laugh falls from the woman's mouth, and she points at the gate. I'm moving. I'm walking through it, and the gate slams behind me. I'm meeting all the eyes of the people who are geared up for a fight. The gate across from me closes, and I turn to my opponent.

I frown and turn to the laughing woman. "He's a man."

"That's debatable. Fight!" Her roar engulfs the crowd, and I face the man. He isn't well built, but he's grinning as he walks towards me like this might be a casual dance.

I swallow bile, but I'm here now. I take two steps back and cower. Laughter rings out along the cage. I hold out both my hands.

"Please. I made a mistake coming here."

The guy runs his hands through his shoulder-length hair that shines better than any woman's. He hasn't even bothered to shed his brown leather jacket. He's already won this fight.

"Please," I beg again. He's only a foot away from me. I wait until his hands reach out before I react. I think of everything that Noel taught me. I imagine the danger I could be in. I drive my foot between his legs. He's not like Shay. He doesn't foresee my action like Noel said they wouldn't if I acted the victim.

The sound is sucked from the room as he grabs himself before tumbling to the ground. The moment his knees touch the cement, the un-mute button is hit, and all the hairs rise on my body as the crowd roars. I breathe with adrenaline, and I can't stop smiling as I face the screaming crowd. I remember the next move and turn. A part of me feels it's wrong, but I imagine that danger is real and kick out, connecting with his nose perfectly. My foot connects, but I lose my shoe that was too big on me; blood dribbles from the man's mouth. He hasn't fallen down but wipes the blood from his mouth with the sleeve of his jacket.

His narrowed green eyes promise me pain as he rises and stiffly strips out of his jacket.

My heart rate rises, and I quickly move behind him. I had to aim for the ribs next, just like Noel taught me, but I see Shay moving along the cage, screaming, but not at me. He's looking at the man I'm fighting, and I've never seen such savagery in anyone's eyes. I'm ready to witness a man tear through a cage with his bare hands. Veins pop out of his neck, and he's jumping as he walks.

I'm too busy watching Shay. The impact of the slap drives me back further and further before I trip and slam into the cage wall. The roars feel different this time. I want to cover my ears as the air is stolen from my lungs.

He's advancing on me again, and this time, when I cower, it's real, but he doesn't pause. The crowd takes on a different type of beat; it's like the crescendo on a song, the last step of a ladder, or the moment fireworks explode. It's there, it's everything, and I see the shadow in the cage with us.

The man disappears as Shay drags him away. I pull myself up off the ground, the gate door is still open, and the woman who had let me in fills it. She mouths the word 'fuck' as Shay grabs the man by the neck and drives his fist into his nose. I don't have to hear the crunch, but it's there in my mind as blood sprays from the man's face.

Shay's fist moves quicker than what should be humanly possible. He drives it back into the man's face, and blood pours on the man's clothes.

Shay doesn't stop, and the crowd is living for each vicious second as he continues to drive his fist into the man's face.

Horror hijacks my system as the man grows slack, but Shay doesn't stop, even as the man's cheek caves in. Bile claws up my throat, and I can't understand why someone isn't stopping this. I look for the woman who had stepped into the cage, but she's gone.

CHAPTER THIRTEEN

O'REAGAN
AN CHLANN
SHAY

My fist keeps moving. I don't feel the burn that I normally would. I don't hear the crowd. I don't sense the blood that's splashing on my forearms.

All I see is what I came here for. I had gotten the call from an old fighter that he was here. The person who had taken my brother's life had finally shown up. Word had spread. I was down south, so the snake had come out of hiding.

I slow my pace, not because Emma is screaming at me—she's another problem I would have to deal with—I slow my pace because I don't want him to die quickly. The sound slams back into me, and it's different. Everyone is shouting and rambling around, like ants stuck in a bottle.

Emma's gate opens, and I meet her wide-eyed gaze. "Get out of here." The cops pour into the room. This is a first and doesn't make sense. They leave this area alone, so that could only mean one thing, someone called them, someone who had influence over them.

The guy under my foot stirs, and I lift my foot, but he doesn't move. Emma is still standing there, still staring at me like she doesn't know me.

She's right. She doesn't.

People slam into the cage in their bid to outrace each other. I see a flash of navy and black. A copper is close.

"I said get out." I grip her arm, and like a rag doll, I drag her from the cage and push her outside. She stumbles into the crowd, and I slam the gate closed on her. "Go."

I don't stay to see if she does leave. I return to the bleeding body on the ground. Blocking out the chaos behind me, I kneel down beside him.

"Do you know who I am?" He can't answer.

"I'm Shay O'Reagan. You remember Frankie? You remember how you danced on his head?" Anger laces through me. He blinks but doesn't speak.

"What did it feel like when his skull caved in?" I push a thumb into his forehead before knocking on it. I want to smash it. I want to make him pay.

"Open the gate." The bark of the copper behind me doesn't stop me from speaking to the man who took Frankie and destroyed my family.

A baton hits the gate several times.

"Did you feel like a big man? Could you smell his piss?" Frankie had been terrified.

His silence I had wanted, but now I don't. Gripping him by the collar, I shake him. "You answer me."

Hinges screech, and several hands grab my arms, dragging me back. I don't resist, I let them pull me away, but I never take my eyes off the man who took Frankie away. I'm pulled to my feet and spun around to face a pistol in my face.

"Shay O'Reagan, you are under arrest for illegal fighting."

I grin at the copper with his combed over hair and small dick. I'm released.

"Put your hands behind your back."

The copper puts his pistol away and removes his handcuffs from his band. He's hoping I resist. He's hoping he can use the baton that his left hand keeps reaching for.

I don't let the grin leave my face as he circles me slowly. I'm tempted to move when gargling sounds from behind me have me half looking over my shoulder.

"Don't let him die. Get him to a hospital," I speak to a young copper who looks to the guy who's handcuffing me.

The handcuffs clip down hard on my flesh. "I make the orders, not you," he whispers in my ear, more confident now that I'm restrained.

"Ring an ambulance," he orders the young guy, who pulls out a radio and makes the call.

For the first time, I look up and outside the cage. A few

people are being arrested, but most have fled. I'm scanning the crowd looking for red hair but don't see any.

A hard hand on my back shoves me outside the gate, and I'm taken through the room. I leave happily with them as I listen to the radio call.

"An ambulance is on the way."

There is only one hospital in the area, so I'll be able to find him. They can keep him alive for me, like a drink on ice.

"I heard your da got shot." A new copper arrives to help escort me outside. His large frame and dark hair make him stand out from the other two. He doesn't carry the same authority as the one who handcuffed me, but I can tell he's fairly new.

He chews gum as he tucks his fingers into the band of his bullet-proof vest.

"I heard you take it hard up the ass," I say.

He stops chewing, and the snickers close by have the gum nearly falling out of his mouth. He releases his jacket, his ego bruised, but nothing close to what I want to do to his face.

"Leave it, Jackson." The one who cuffed me barks, and Jackson veers off.

"Use Vaseline. It will help." More sniggers follow my words, but the boy doesn't react.

I'm brought down to a squad car and pushed into the back. I take my time searching the sidewalk for a flash of red, but I don't see her.

I get a cell to myself after they take my belongings, and I go through the booking ritual. I always get my own cell as I'm considered high risk. The cuffs are removed from my wrists, and I rub them. "I want a cup of tea before I make my phone call."

The copper stares at me, and his fingers dance along his baton again. I had been sitting on the steel bench, but now I rise. "It looks like you want to break that baton in." I shrug out of my jacket.

"You need to learn to keep your mouth shut." He doesn't bite like I thought he would. The large steel door slams behind him. He has more willpower than I had given him credit for.

I've too much violence still roaring through my veins that needs to be unleashed. Picking a fight with a copper wasn't wise, but right now, all I saw was Frankie's smashed-in skull.

I have to bang on the steel door for a solid minute before the small shutter is opened.

"What?" The gum circles inside his smiling mouth.

"I was going to ask for my phone call, but right now, I'd like it if you stepped in here so I can wipe that grin off your face." I slam both fists against the door, and he moves back.

There is more movement in the hall, and Paul appears.

"Pipe down, O'Reagan." He flexes his muscles. "I'll take care of this, Jackson."

Jackson's smile widens. "Yes, sir." He's grinning at me like I'm in for an ass beating. Paul waits until he's gone before opening the door. I sit back down on the seat as he hands me my cigarettes and lighter.

"The man you beat nearly to death is in St. James hospital." Paul starts as I light up a cigarette.

"I never touched anyone."

"Well, he isn't exactly talking, Shay." Paul seems irritated as he keeps glancing at the door.

"I want his name and address."

Paul nods. "I've rung, Leo. He'll be here soon."

I inhale deeply and blow smoke out. Leo, my lawyer, would get me out of this with a few words. He was that good.

"There's a red-headed girl hanging out in the alleyway of the station. From CCTV, I see she entered the underground carpark with you, so I've been keeping an eye."

I get off the bench, and Paul shrinks slightly. "Thanks." I inhale deeply. "Yeah, keep an eye on her."

"I'll do that." Paul is ready to close the door.

"Any idea who rang it in?"

I'm watching him carefully. "No, but I'll find out." He closes the door behind him, and I sit down and finish my cigarette.

After that, it moves smoothly. Leo arrives, talks the talk, and yep, I walk. It's cold outside, and the full impact of the fight roars to life in my broken and damaged fists.

I walk along the front of the station and pause at the alleyway. I take the cigarettes and lighter out of my pocket.

"Come on, Emma." I don't turn but start to walk again. A block away, she falls into step beside me.

Neither of us speaks as we make our way to the car. The minute she's in, she puts on her seatbelt, I don't.

"You want to explain to me why you entered that cage?" I can't look at her. What she did was reckless and downright fucking stupid. "Now, Emma!" I bark. When she doesn't answer me, I finally look at her.

She shrugs. "I just wanted to experience it."

"You wanted to experience someone hitting you? I mean, you want a man to slap you around?"

She tuts and folds her arms across her chest.

I drag myself closer to her. "I mean, I could go a few rounds with you, Emma. Is that what you want?"

"Of course not. I thought I would be fighting a girl," her words are hissed.

Her reasoning was fucking pitiful. I start the engine. "I mean, I could still go a few rounds."

Her snort is loud in the car. "You look like you've had enough."

"Do I?" I slam my foot down on the accelerator. She had no idea what she had walked into. The odds that the person she ended up fighting was the same animal that killed Frankie still hasn't fully registered. The image flickers from Frankie's smashed-in skull to Emma's smashed-in skull.

"I've half a mind to leave you here on the side of the road."

"Calm down, Shay."

I jam on the brakes and stop in the middle of the road. Cars blow their horns, but I don't give a fuck as Emma slams her palms against the dash before she's catapulted back into her seat. Her face pales.

"The fucking animal wouldn't have stopped. He would have killed you if I didn't intervene."

She's sinking into the seat, but it's not enough.

"Do. You. Understand?!" My roar fills the car and steals all the oxygen from Emma's lungs.

Another car honks his horn behind me, and I'm reaching for my bag in the back that holds my gun. I'll drag the fucker out of his car and put a bullet in his head.

"I understand. I'm sorry." Emma's words spill quickly from her lips. "Shay, I'm sorry. It was stupid of me. I knew that the minute I did it."

Her words have me leaving the gun where it is. She doesn't know it, but she just saved some driver from dying today. I continue to drive to my home. I have nowhere else to go right now. Someone rang the coppers, someone who had a pull with them. Any place up here I thought was safe—isn't.

The car idles outside as I stare up at the house. I didn't want to bring this shit to my ma's doorstep, and if my da had put a hit on Emma's head, I was taking her right to him. He wouldn't harm her while she was with me, but once we left, she was fair game.

My fists ache. I reach across Emma, who hasn't moved a muscle, and take out a pair of leather gloves that I slip my torn-up hands into.

"Don't mention the fight in here," I say without looking at Emma. I get out and take my bag out of the back. She's still sitting in her seat. She hasn't removed her seatbelt.

My hand slams down on the roof of the car, and she jumps. "Now, Emma!" Her fingers fumble over the seat belt. I'm aware that she's wiping her eyes as she climbs out of the car.

My gut tightens, but I ignore it as I stop at the bushes and stuff my bag down the side before walking up to the door. My ma opens it with a smile on her face. Her smile doesn't disappear but lessens as she peeks at Emma, who's behind me.

"Is this her?" There is so much hope in my ma's voice. I nod, still too pissed off to speak. I kiss my ma on either cheek, and we step into the house.

"You are a true beauty," My ma starts as I enter the kitchen.

"Thank you." Emma's small voice has me tempted to look over my shoulder as I take a carton of milk out of the fridge and start to drink deeply.

"Shay, don't drink out of the carton." I stop when my ma reprimands me.

"Sorry, Ma."

"He normally wouldn't do that," My ma is back to speaking to Emma.

I put the milk back in the fridge. "Where's Da?" Closing the door, I come eye to eye with my ma. She's searching my face.

"At a meeting."

"Are you hungry?" My ma asks Emma but doesn't give her a second to answer as she starts to take food out of the fridge.

Red, swollen eyes meet mine, and I curse Emma. She has been crying. She must have cried in the car. My stomach tightens, but I blink and step away from her.

"If you have any apple pie, I'll take it." I sit down at the table and take out my phone. Four missed calls from Jack and even one from Liam. I grin. Fuck them.

A chair is pulled out beside me. The smell of vanilla is sweet as Emma sits down. She's dragged her top over her hands. A red mark on her jaw is stark. I know that wouldn't have gone unnoticed with my ma.

"Take your hair down," I speak quietly to Emma. She doesn't question me but lets her hair fall like a curtain around her face.

My ma's worried gaze clashes with mine as she places a salad in front of Emma. She better not come near me with that fucking rabbit food.

"Thank you." Emma tucks some hair behind her ear. Her movement causes her thighs to brush against mine, and I hate how aware I am of her. I'm still fucking pissed. She could have gotten herself killed.

My ma returns with a cup of tea and a large slice of pie. The moment she places it in front of me, she presses a kiss to my head. She's ready to walk away when I capture her hand in my gloved one. I bring it to my lips and kiss her soft hand.

I can't imagine what she felt the day Frankie died, but for me, it's right there at the surface, and I want to feel her level of pain. I want to take it all away. I want to tell her I'm fucking sorry. I should have told Frankie he didn't have to fight. I should have told them he was soft and hated hurting anyone. I should have told them that their son was gay.

I release my ma's hand. "Whatever has gotten into you is nice." Her smile wobbles, and I see the strain and worry in her eyes.

I can't look away from her. My da fucking adored her, and so he should. She was the best ma anyone could ask for. She didn't deserve the losses she kept receiving. I swallow my pain and grin at her before turning to my pie.

"I'm just feeling sentimental."

That pulls a laugh from deep in my ma's belly. It's a sweet sound that numbs the pain for a moment. Frankie was her favorite. He would help around the house, and he was just there for her when Da was out fighting. He would keep her mind busy; he helped her escape the worrying thoughts.

As for me, I was wild and borderline psychotic while growing up. I did stupid shit.

"Eat, Emma." She's been too busy watching the exchange, but she starts to eat her rabbit food.

I didn't like that I was getting used to her being at my side.

"Have you picked a venue or dress?" My ma slides in across from Emma, and this is another blow she won't be fit to take.

"I have a few ideas for my dress." Emma cuts in, saving me from telling my ma this isn't going ahead. If it makes her happy for now, I let Emma talk.

"Okay, that's a lie. I know exactly what I want." The smile in Emma's voice has me glancing at her. She looks up at me, and I see fear in her eyes, along with something deeper.

"I always wanted a long veil that covered my face." Emma is speaking to me like I fucking asked.

The fear is carried away as hope steps forward. "I wanted my groom to lift the veil, and I wanted to see that look…" Emma turns to my ma, who's smiling with her head tilted to the side like she knows exactly what Emma is talking about.

"That look that says he's at peace. You know?"

My ma reaches across and takes Emma's hand. "That you

are the reason for his peace." Emma's voice trails off. I finish my pie as Emma lies through her teeth about certain flowers, how the tables will be set up. She's a very good fucking liar. If I sit here long enough, I think I might believe we are getting married.

My phone beeps, and I check it. It's from Paul.

Michael Philips

145 Side View Terrace,

Longwalk Road.

He's in bad shape, but he's discharging himself.

That address wasn't far from here. The killer has been close to our doorstep the whole time.

Stay at the hospital and let me know the minute he leaves. I send the text back and put my phone away.

I would finally have my vengeance for Frankie. My ma is engrossed in the lies that Emma is telling. Emma keeps tucking her hair behind her ear, leaving the mark on her face visible. I reach across and push it forward. She flinches at the small bit of contact. Her shoulders stiffen.

"I like your hair fully down." I press a kiss to the crown of her head, and she shrinks a little on the chair.

Emma regains some of her earlier chatter, but she's rattled. She's afraid.

That isn't a bad thing. It might stop her from being so reckless. My mind spins back to Michael Philips. I smile into the mug. I'm so close I can almost taste it.

CHAPTER FOURTEEN

O'REAGAN
AN CHLANN
SHAY

"Stop touching my things." I shrug out of my jacket and put it on the bed. Emma immediately replaces the bottle of aftershave on the top of the cabinet.

Taking off the gloves is like pouring vinegar into an open wound. Sweat and blood mix and burn as I enter the ensuite and turn on the taps. I check to see what Emma's doing; she's still walking around my room, taking it all in. It irritates the fuck out of me. I jam my hands under the running water and clench my jaw as razor blades scrape along my knuckles.

Each punch had been worth it. A buzz races through me. In a matter of hours, Michael Philips will be dead, and I will have my vengeance for my brother.

"Can I help?"

"No." I don't turn to Emma as she hovers in the doorway. "I'm going out for a few hours, so I want you to stay here in my room."

Emma steps into the bathroom. Her smell circles me as she picks up a fresh navy towel. "Where are you going?"

"To kill someone." I expect her to look at me with disbelief, but her eyes swim with a new kind of pain—a pain that tells me she believes me.

A weight on my shoulders from her gaze has me turning off the tap. She holds out the towel, and I take it, dabbing my hands as gently as possible. Fresh blood oozes from the wounds. I place the towel along the hand basin and meet my gaze in the mirror.

"I don't want to stay here. Can't I come with you?"

I meet Emma's green eyes in the mirror. "You want to help me kill someone?" Before she can answer, I turn back on the taps and splash water on my face. My hands burn again.

"The man in the cage…" Emma's words trail off.

The warning in my eyes is enough to make her stop. Pulling the shirt over my head, I let it fall to the floor. When I look up, Emma's cheeks are pink. The mark along her jawline is stark.

"Sit down." I point to the toilet.

She sits while placing her joined hands in between her legs. I run the towel under the cold tap before kneeling down in front of her. This close, I can see gold flecks swimming in her emerald green eyes. Taking her chin in my hand, I tilt her head so I can press the cold towel to her face. She doesn't move a bunched-up muscle.

"My brother, Frankie, used to fight in the cage."

Emma tries to move her head to look at me, but I gently move it back, so she's facing the bathroom door. I push the towel back against her face.

"He wasn't built like Da or me. He wasn't a fighter. He died in the cage."

Emma moves again, and this time when I try to tilt her head away, she stops me by grabbing my hand. Her green eyes glaze over. "I'm so sorry."

I kneel further back. Her sincerity and the way she still holds my hand have me wanting to move away from her. Her fingers are warm, yet she's being careful not to hurt me.

"I couldn't get to Frankie. I couldn't stop the fight."

"Oh, Shay." Emma bites her bottom lip like she can hold back the wave of emotion that swims in her eyes. "Why did no one else stop it?"

"You can fight to the death in the cage. There are no rules."

Reality sweeps in and carries all Emma's guilt. "I'm sorry…" She starts and trails off again. "How old was Frankie?" Her brows draw together as she speaks.

"Twenty-two." I take my hand from Emma's and rise slowly. "Keep this pressed to your face." I hand her the towel.

"Is this who you are going to kill?" She doesn't take the towel from me. I release it, so it falls into her lap and leave the bathroom. "Revenge won't bring Frankie back."

Emma's words send fire exploding through my system. I move, I don't think, and she's against the wall in a second. My hand around her throat, wanting nothing more than to cut off her fucking words.

"Don't say his name." I squeeze.

Emma's frozen for a fraction of a second before she starts to claw at my damaged hands.

I close my eyes and squeeze tighter as she tears more skin from my hands—the pain burns and sizzles before fracturing the pain of losing Frankie. When Emma goes slack, I release her, and she slowly sinks to the floor.

Her head dips onto her chest, and I'm staring at the crown of her head. She gulps loudly, and I move back away from her. I don't stand there long enough to meet her eyes.

Taking a fresh shirt from the wardrobe, I get dressed. Gathering my jacket and placing my hands back in the gloves, I leave her on the floor with all my guilt and all her pain.

Turning the key in the door, I pocket it before making my way downstairs.

"Are you going out?" My ma calls from the kitchen.

I enter and smile at her. "Emma's sleeping. It's been a rough day for her. I'm going to go out and get a takeaway for us."

My ma's smile stretches wider. "I'll keep the noise down so she can rest."

I kiss my ma on the forehead so she can't read the guilt in my eyes.

"See you later." I leave and gather my bag out of the bushes before running across the road to my car. Before I start it, something makes me look up at my bedroom window. I'm expecting to see Emma standing there with all the judgment in her eyes, but no one is there.

I drive to the address that Paul gave me and sit across the road. Lighting a smoke, I watch as a blonde woman gets out of the car with a young boy and girl. They might have been five or slightly more. I wasn't good with judging kids' ages. The front door opens, and Michael's battered face appears. The kids race past him, and the blonde woman takes bags of groceries out of the trunk of the car before walking up to the doorstep. Once she's in, Michael closes the door.

The cigarette bounces off the road as I throw it out the window and roll the window up. The gun is in my hand, and I don't feel its normal coldness as the gloves restrict it. I tuck it in my jacket pocket before opening the glove compartment and taking out a black cap.

No cars are around as I pick up the crushed cigarette before I cross the road while dragging the cap down over my eyes. I move around to the side gate and put my hand through the small gap to open it.

Closing the gate behind me, I move around the back garden, jumping over a small red bike before walking up to the back door. Voices in the kitchen had me pausing. The kids are asking for Smarties while their ma unloads the shopping.

A bucket filled with cigarette butts sits outside the sliding door. That was fucking perfect. I light my own cigarette. I don't have long to wait until the door slides open.

"Close the door, Michael. Don't let the heat out." The woman's voice follows Michael out the door.

He's halfway out when he sees me. "Come out, or I'm coming in."

"I won't be long," he calls back into the house and pulls the door behind him.

His hands tremble as he lights a cigarette.

"Let's talk in the shed," I suggest while crushing the cigarette between my fingers and pocketing the butt.

"The cops are watching the house." Michael's voice quivers. Trepidation drips like a broken tap as he continues to plead silently with me.

I grin and walk to the shed. Gardening tools could become weapons that could make him suffer.

"I have two kids." He stumbles in the door, and I close it.

"Frankie had six." I lie and grip him by the collar to drag him deeper into the shed.

"I didn't know."

My hand connects with his face. I keep my hand open but let the force of my arm fill the slap. "I don't give two fucks what you know and don't know. I'm telling you now." I grin and slap his opposite cheek.

I exhale loudly as excitement has me moving my shoulders in a circular motion. This is the moment I had dreamed of, and I will savor every second of it.

"How old is your boy?" I remove my jacket and fold it neatly on the lawnmower.

Ashes drip from his cigarette. "Hmmm, six, I think."

I laugh. "What a fuck up you are. Don't you know the boy's age? I would have said five." I nod and walk into his personal space. I slap him again, and it feels so fucking good. "He looks strong enough to be a rag boy."

More ashes fall, and I take the cigarette from his hand.

"That's my boy." His voice shakes.

I cover his mouth and push the cigarette into the side of his face. The smell of burning flesh accompanies his screams. It's a sickening smell, but one that tells me the fucker is suffering. I remove it and throw it on the ground.

"Frankie was my brother."

I remove my hand as saliva pours from his mouth. His hand hovers over the burning flesh while he bends at the knees trying not to throw up.

I move back and give him a moment. "How old is your daughter?"

He looks up at me as he spits onto the floor. He still is half-bent, only half a man. To think this is what took my brother's life.

"She'd make a few pennies on the market."

He stands to his full height. I remove my gloves and flex my hands, allowing the burn to slice through me.

"I want you to picture her being passed around a room full of men. As they rape her, she'd cry for her da. She'd beg them to stop."

He spits again on the ground. "Please."

I grin at him and step closer. I slap the side of his face that I just burned.

He roars and jumps away while a string of curses falls from his lips.

"Michael." His wife's voice has him turning gray as he races for the door that I block.

"I'll cut her fucking head off if you don't get rid of her."

I step back, hoping he doesn't force my hand.

"Go inside, Liz. I'll be there in a minute."

"What are you doing in the shed?"

"Go inside now!" His words are harsh. I open the door slightly as she goes back inside, but I know my time is even more limited now.

Pulling down a rag that is stained with oil, I shove it into his mouth.

He's shaking his head and screaming. His fingers manage to get some of the fabric out before I grab them and bend them back.

"Frankie." My brother's name on his lips has me wanting to hear his fucking screams.

"They paid me." The words leave his lips the moment I take the rag out. "They paid me three grand to kill him."

His breaths are harsh, the information doing a number on my system.

"Who paid you?" I keep calm.

He sobs, and I grab his hair while yanking his head back. "This is it, Michael. You tell me now, or I'll beat you to death in the fucking shed."

"If I tell you, will you let me live?"

"No. But your son and daughter won't disappear into the black market."

I'm expecting him to sob some more, but he doesn't. "My wife?"

"She'll be left alone."

I hated that he would protect them. I wanted him to be the

coward that beat Frankie to death and would throw anyone under the bus to save his own skin.

"Amanda, who runs the cage, paid me three grand to beat Frankie to death. She never said why." His sobs grow louder. "Please."

I push the rag back into his mouth and let the knowledge that Frankie's life was worth three grand to someone sink in. Three grand.

I want to roar as I beat Michael into an unrecognizable lump of flesh. I stay quiet as I lose myself in the violence. I don't stop until he no longer moves, and from his caved-in skull, I know he's dead. Staring down at his body doesn't give me the satisfaction that I honestly thought I would feel. Instead, the burn inside me seems to grow. I grab my jacket and leave the shed covered in blood. I keep the cap pulled down as I exit the side of the house and get into my car.

I drive to Woodview Industrial Park that had closed a long time ago. Taking my bag out of the car, I strip down naked and put everything into the car before changing into fresh clothes. I douse it in petrol and stay for a while as I watch it go up in flames. I stay until it's half-burnt out before walking home with my bag on my back.

Amanda had set Frankie up. No doubt she had also rung the cops when I had stepped into the cage with Michael. She must have feared he might confess to stop me.

Taking out my phone, I remove the chip and snap it in half before throwing it into the river that ran alongside the walkway.

Taking a fresh one out of my bag, I place it in the phone and set it up before sending a text to Paul.

New Number. S

A squad car speeds past me, and I want to turn back and watch the horror unfold. The sick part of me wants to watch his family fall apart at his feet. I keep walking, each step bringing me closer to my home and also closer to Amanda.

Why would she want Frankie dead? It wasn't a lovers quarrel. She swung for the other team too. It made no sense. Had he gotten into some bad shit? He must have.

The fresh gloves are filling with blood as I clench my fists. Drops seep through the stitching and leave a trail like bread crumbs behind me. I push my hands into my jacket pockets and walk faster as a fire engine roars past me. That didn't take them long to find the car. It would be well burnt out by now. Most of it was damaged before I left.

Stuffing my bag along the bushes, I glance at the windows of the house. I'm not sure if it's my ma or Emma I'm looking for, but I see neither.

Stepping into the house, my ma normally greets me, but this time I come face to face with my da.

CHAPTER FIFTEEN

O'REAGAN
AN CHLANN
EMMA

I'm counting.

I'm holding back the tears.

I'm holding back my shattered dreams.

My throat burns, and it's the snap of a branch, the opening of a dam, the horror that I'm living a life I feared.

He put his hands on me. He did it to cut off my words. Tears run down my cheeks, and I sniffle as I fight with myself. I want to get up, break down the door and return home.

Home to what? A dad who handed me to Shay? A brother who might not fulfill his promise? A mom who was six feet under?

I cover my burning face as more tears pour down my face. I

swallow the pain that keeps pulsing in my neck. I can still feel his hands on me.

I push myself off the floor and stand. It feels like a lifetime that I stand there facing his window. I'm caged, trapped.

I enter the bathroom; blood still stains the white basin as I slowly strip off my clothes. Would I really go home?

No. I won't let them see me like this. They gave me away, so they won't get me back. But staying with Shay was terrifying. What happens when I annoy him again? Will he strangle me to death the next time? I could never fight him off.

I re-enter his room naked and wipe my eyes with the back of my hand before I start rummaging through his drawers. I'm careful putting everything back. I pause when I find what I am looking for. I open the pen-knife that has been sharpened.

I take the knife into the bathroom and lock the door behind me. I refuse to be a victim. More tears fall. Closing my eyes, I count in an attempt to slow my heart down. A weakness spreads through me, and a tiredness threatens to pull me under.

The water is warm as I step into the shower; I let the water wash over my skin. A sob escapes my lips as my hand touches my bruised neck. My face has started to ache from my earlier fight. I don't want these dark memories.

I bring back a memory. I'm on Lady racing through the field. The wind tears at my hair and clothes. I've no saddle on her, and I know the line of where our land ends is coming close, but I don't slow down. A road separates our land from next door's. I cling tighter to Lady, and I want out at that moment. I seek freedom in running. The hedge line comes into view, and I know if I don't slow down now, there will be no turning back.

I don't stop, and I'm screaming, not in fear, in pure exhilaration. Lady's hooves hit the road, the ground harder underneath her hooves, and then we are bursting into the next field. My heart is wild in my chest, but it was a moment—a moment like only a few moments we experience in life.

I push against the shower tiles as Shay lying in the bathtub under the moonlight reminds me of another moment.

But that's all they are—moments.

I focus on washing quickly and getting out of the shower. The mirror has fogged up, and I don't clear it as I start to get dressed. I don't want to see the marks that still burn on my neck.

The knife in my pocket gives me some reassurance as I step back into Shay's room. A gun would give me even more peace. I return to the drawers and start to look. The rattle of the door handle has heat rushing through my body. I pause before sliding the drawer closed and shuffling back towards the bed. The door handle continues to rattle, and someone knocks.

"Emma?" A male voice penetrates the door. It's not Shay, and that knowledge has me rising to my feet and taking a step towards the door.

"Connor, please, leave her." Shay's mom is out there.

A door slams, and movement at the bedroom door moves away.

"Connor." I hear the pleading tone in Shay's mom's voice. My stomach twists, and I'm walking to the door.

"I want her out of my home. You had no right bringing her here."

My heart pulses, and blood roars in my ears. My hand moves to the knife in my trousers and stays there holding it. I don't take it out of my pocket, but I don't release it either.

"Did you send men to kill her?" Shay's voice is loud, and the stairs creak.

"Connor." Shay's mom pleads again.

I place my other hand over my heart, willing it to stay in my chest.

"If I sent men to kill her, she'd be dead."

They are speaking about me. I'm a sitting duck being here in Shay's home. Waves of panic keep washing over me, and I'm losing the conversation. It's moving closer as Shay climbs the stairs, but the words are getting more muffled as blood roars and thrash in my ears. My vision wavers, and my face is scorched with heat.

"I don't believe you." Shay's words are closer now.

I close my eyes and count while tightening my hold on the knife.

"Get her out of my home." His dad was right outside.

The door handle rattles, and the door opens. I want to withdraw the knife, I want to stand taller, but I can't even manage to breathe. Shay and his dad fill the doorway, both looking at me. Numbers float and disappear, and I've never felt more naked.

Connor steps closer, and I think this is where I'm going to die. Shay's gloved hand lands on his dad's chest, stopping him from entering the room.

"We'll leave." Shay's words allow some air to re-enter my burning lungs, but it's sucked back out as he steps into the room and closes the door behind him. Sweat pools in my hand, making the knife slick as I cling to it.

Shay turns a key in the door before walking over to his curtains and drawing them closed. I can't seem to move as he starts to strip off his clothes. He doesn't drop them on the ground but folds each piece and stacks them on his bed. I move, trying my legs out and getting away from Shay's large form as he moves around to my side. He's only wearing boxers as he pulls off his socks.

His hands are a bloody mess, and red droplets fall onto his strong thighs. He drags his boxers down his legs, and the reaction I have at seeing him naked is shameful for the first time. I shouldn't feel this way after he hurt me.

His dark gaze lands on me and steals all the air, not just from my lungs but from the room. It hurts to breathe. It hurts to hold his stare. He hurt me.

His gaze drops to my neck; I don't see regret or shame. All I see is indifference as he walks away from me.

I don't breathe until I hear water running in the bathroom. I should hurt him back. The want to use the knife has me extracting it from my pocket. I'm imagining the look in Noel's eyes when he hears I slayed the Northerner.

I don't know how long I stand there staring at the knife when I notice the water isn't running anymore. I slip the knife back in my pocket as Shay comes out of the bathroom with a towel around his waist.

He sits on his bed and opens a drawer in his bedside table. Taking out rolls of white bandages, he starts to bandage his hands.

He needs help. He's struggling, and from the strain on his face, he's in a lot of pain. He doesn't look to me like I want him to. I want him to ask for help so I can say no.

I hope each touch of the bandage is like salt in the wounds.

Once he has them bound, he finishes getting dressed and takes a bag from the top of the wardrobe. He stuffs the clothes he had folded neatly on the bed in it.

"Let's go." He still won't meet my eye, and I'm not sure who is stupider here, him for assuming I'll be a good girl, or me, for being the good girl and following him out the door.

We make our way downstairs, but his dad blocks our exit. My instincts are to reach out and touch Shay for comfort. Instead, I reach for the knife in my pocket.

"I already told you we are leaving." Shay had paused and now continues down the stairs.

"Leo had to bail you out of jail again."

My gaze dances to Shay's mom, who watches the exchange between her husband and son; fear and pain are etched into her face.

"You were in the cage again?" Connor continues. Shay's cleared the stairs. I'm on the last step. He and his father are shoulder to shoulder, and my gut twists when neither of them moves.

"Do you want to get yourself killed?" Connor has maybe thirty years on his son, but I couldn't say who would win in a fight. I'd seen Shay fight, and it was savage, but I heard about Connor O'Reagan, the fighter who was undisputed.

"You want to know why I keep going back?" Shay hits his shoulder off his dad's, my stomach curls, and I'm gripping the banister like it might keep me upright.

"I've waited ever since the day Frankie died to find the person responsible, and I did." Shay's breathing heavy, and it's like he's lost.

"I found Michael Phillips." He shoves his shoulder into his dad's again. "I danced on that motherfucker's head."

Shay's mom moves away until she's resting against the wall. A wail leaves her mouth, but Shay and his dad are too caught up in their own rage.

"I gave my brother peace." Shay thumps his chest, and the noise of it would rattle your bones. Blood starts to seep through his bandages.

"I gave my brother his vengeance." Shay's voice rises, and his mom's wails grow.

Connor's gaze wavers for the first time, and when they land on me, I swallow bile. All that rage has to go somewhere, and I'm a target.

"It won't bring Frankie back."

I feel the slap in Shay's dad's words. I cringe and wish for this one moment; he might just say, 'Well Done.'

"No, it won't. You put him in that cage."

Connor reacts and shoves Shay, who snaps back and catches himself before falling.

"You want to have a go at me?" Shay's bouncing, and once again, I've never seen anyone so lost in a tornado of rage and self-destruction.

"Stop it!"

My hands start to tremble, my body cannot take much

more as Shay's mom stands in between them with tears pouring down her face.

"YOU WILL NOT PUT YOUR HANDS ON EACH OTHER!" She's screaming each word. Each word is so filled with pain.

"Okay." Connor steps away from his son and drags his wife into his side. His fisted hand tightens around her as he hugs her to his body. Her sobs wrack her body. Connor stares at Shay, but it's broken as Shay steps around him, opening me up to the floor. I'm moving without thinking. With hunched shoulders, I scurry past Connor and his sobbing wife and follow Shay outside.

Laughter gathers itself inside my chest, and I want to laugh and say, "that was intense." Shay stops at the bushes and pulls up a bag that he slings across his shoulder.

I'm following behind him, and I don't think he even knows I'm here. The laughter comes out in spurts like some broken faucet until my lips drag down and my chest tightens. I have to stop. I can't breathe. More laughter comes out along with tears as I cling to a pillar that no one bothered to paint. It's as neglected as I am.

Something that had a purpose, but no one bothered to give it its final touches.

"Emma." Shay's voice pulls me out of my turmoil, but I don't face him. I can't. I drag in the air. His hand touches my arm, and I move back away from him.

"Don't put your fucking hands on me." I know the knife is there, but right now, if I draw it, I'll use it.

I'll regret it.

Shay's jaw clenches, and he looks beyond me and nods.

"We need to go." He turns and starts to walk. What choice do I have but to follow him? Each step sends me into murky waters. I'm angry. Angry at him, angry at my dad for handing me over. I'm angry at Noel for not stopping this sooner.

"Where are we going?" My voice is low as I catch up to Shay. I count to five before he answers me.

"To a friend of mine."

We're going to another place that might be hostile and with more hostile people. I'm walking down a sidewalk with a murderer at my side. I take a peek at Shay, but he's focused on what's in front of him.

"Will I be safe there?" I ask the stupid question because I won't be safe anywhere. I'm not safe with Shay.

"There's no place that's safe." His answer irritates the fuck out of me.

Shay's pace quickens like he's hoping he'll leave me behind. I tighten my arms around my waist as we continue to walk until the houses fall away and the warehouses pop up. The deeper we walk into the industrial estate, the more run-down the buildings become. Shay makes a beeline for a red steel door at the side of one of the buildings. It's abandoned, and I think this is where he finally kills me.

The door screeches on the hinges as Shay opens the door. I don't follow him but look around for signs of life.

"Emily." The false name drags me closer to Shay. The fact he's using it means we aren't alone.

The door closes loudly behind me as it takes a moment for my eyes to adjust to the red light that fills the hallway.

Shay hasn't moved, and neither do I. I'm not going down there first.

"These are my friends, but they aren't yours." His words are low and far closer to my ear than I expect.

I shiver and wrap my arms around my center.

"Just… don't say anything." I nod my head, not sure if he sees me, but I had no intentions of drawing attention to myself ever again.

He steps into the red-lit hallway, and I follow him to what? I have no idea.

CHAPTER SIXTEEN

O'REAGAN
AN CHLANN
EMMA

Shay stops walking, and my hand automatically goes to the knife in my pocket. I have a moment when he half turns to me—with the red light cast across his features--I think he hasn't come here to meet friends. He's going to kill me.

That's why I'm standing in an abandoned warehouse with a murderer.

I won't die in some run-down building. How long would my body lie here rotting before my family found out where I was? Would they ever find out?

A shiver climbs along my veins, and I can't stop it from erupting along my skin. If I was ever going to plead for my life, now is the time.

Shay turns fully and takes two steps back towards me. Each step sends my heart pounding; it's like my heart is in sync with his steps for just a split second before it bursts from my chest and races ahead.

Shay takes a pack of cigarettes from his pocket and lights one. "You want one?"

I can't talk. My throat is being crushed with my future death. I shake my head, and he steps closer, blowing smoke around him. My mind is conjuring up a skeleton face amongst the billowing of smoke, but each time it's just Shay.

You will fight, Emma.

His gaze skips to my neck, and his hand moves. My body reacts instantly, and I move back from him.

For the first time, I see a flash of something that makes me unsteady—guilt.

It's like my body turns to mush, like I know this Shay and this Shay won't hurt me. The wall is rough against my skin, paint flakes away at the contact.

"I've never put my hands on a woman before." He inhales deeply after speaking.

I don't believe you. I shake my head, not caring for his excuse. If he was telling the truth, did it make it worse that I was the first woman he ever put his hands on?

"I shouldn't have hurt you." He's half shaking his head as he takes the step that has him in my personal space.

My heart bounces and rattles in my chest, and the swell of anger has me pulling the knife out. I'm quick, quicker than

I ever thought I could be—the blade presses against his throat. The cigarette falls from his raised hand, and I press the knife a little closer.

"Love, you don't want to do that."

"I'm not your love." More anger seeps and slips through the cracks, and I press a little harder, nearly getting carried away as the first bead of blood spills.

"You hurt me." My vision blurs, and I curse myself for such a useless fucking emotion. I grit my teeth. "You hurt me," I repeat. I'm telling myself how much he hurt me, and my hand shakes. "You hurt me." My words are lower, but they carry more impact. It's like a punch in the stomach when I realize why. I don't want Shay to hurt me. I don't want Shay to dislike me. I want him to want me.

I want him.

The shake in my hand has the blade rattling against his throat. His raised hands are steady; his jaw relaxed as he stares down at me, towering over me like a dark and dangerous figure. He could disarm me. He could kill me with his large hands.

I'm focused on his hand, that he lowers slowly. I'm watching it like a snake that might strike at any second. His fingers are feather-light along my bruised neck. I don't remove the knife as his fingers dance over my bruises like he might be able to take it back. I want him to take it back. He shifts closer, and the blade releases more beads of blood.

"I'm sorry, Emma." His words are low, his breath fans across my cheek.

His apology blurs my vision, and it almost breaks me.

"I'll never hurt you again."

I'm staring into dark, heavy eyes that still swirl with violence and hurt from earlier, and now I see something moving faster than all the rest, a want.

I tighten my hold on the knife. "You won't hurt me again because if you do, I'll slice your throat." The threat should make him laugh. It tastes dirty in my mouth, but I want him to know I won't stand for it.

"That's fair. I would expect no less." Shay's body boxes me in, and flakes of paint press into my back. His free hand covers my shaking one, and he slowly removes the knife from his throat. I'm expecting him to snap back to the savageness I've seen in him, but he doesn't. Once the knife is away from his throat, his face comes down to mine.

His lips are so close to mine, and all I want at this moment is for him to kiss me. His hot breath sends waves of excitement through my body. He makes me feel like I'm on a ledge. Shay makes me feel alive.

His lips brush mine, and I sink against him, but he holds me back slightly. "The next time you have a knife at my neck, you use it." He releases me and steps away.

No more blood leaves the small slice on his throat, but he is still smeared from the earlier droplets. "Don't ever hesitate." His words are stronger, louder, and angrier. "You run that blade across the throat and put as much pressure as you can behind it."

The knife is still in my hand. My lids blink rapidly. It's like my brain is trying to process what the hell he is talking about. Did he not just almost kiss me?

Shay steps closer to me again with a heartbreaking smile playing on his lips. "Then, you run." His hand touches my cheek, and he leans in again. "You run, Emma." He releases me like I burnt him, and I'm watching his wide back as he makes his way down the hall.

I don't follow. My body trembles, and I close my eyes and count as I wait for my heart to fall into a normal rhythm that won't have it threatening to punch through my chest.

When I get my heart under control, I put the knife back into my pocket. It's a useless instrument against Shay. It's as good as a spoon. I start to walk as light pours in from the open door at the end of the hall. Shay holds it open until I reach it.

As I search Shay's face, I know a knife is worthless. I needed to find myself a gun.

We move across a large open space. Water drips from so many holes in the ceiling that I can't focus on just one.

Shay's focus is on a door that looks more suited to a bank. The only thing that's missing is the big bars that you twist to open them. He knocks in a pattern, and the door opens. Before he walks through, Shay pauses, his attention back on me. I can't read what he's thinking or feeling as he turns away, and I follow him into a hive of activity.

I'm ready to bolt when the door slams behind me. I turn, expecting to see someone there, but I'm faced with the large steel door.

On either side of me people are seated, either counting money or on phones. It's bizarre, and I get that sense again that I've walked in on something that should make me hold my breath. I shouldn't be here; I shouldn't be seeing this. What this was exactly, I didn't know, but I knew things were changing far too quickly between Shay and me. Bringing me here either meant I was going to be disposed of, or he trusted me.

At the far end of the room, a man in a suit stands. His smile is wide as Shay approaches him. A cigar burns away on a desk table that looks more suited to some skyscraper in a billion-dollar building.

I smell coffee and fresh baking. I'm tempted to glance around me, but I can't look away from the man who pulls Shay into a half embrace.

"I didn't expect you here until next month." The man's light blue eyes flicker to me, but it's brief, yet I want to wrap my arms around my waist and protect myself from him.

Blonde hair is brushed back off his face. His suit, his shoes, his desk, even his presence don't belong here.

"Chief Commandant." Shay greets him as he releases the man.

My insides churn as the Chief Commandant's gaze rests on me again. I know who he is; I've never seen him before. A giggle rushes up my throat and threatens to spill, but I swallow it back down.

I was standing in front of the leader of the Irish Republican Army. I repeat that sentence over and over again in my head until Shay takes a step toward me, and the sound of the ding of calculators and the rustle of money comes rushing back.

"Emily," Shay speaks again.

I swallow. "Sorry, yes."

"This is Lucian." Lucian approaches me and reaches out his hand. I take it. Of course, I do. I expect it to be soft and manicured, but calluses brush against my palm.

Lucian Sheahan. I was holding Lucian Sheahan's hand. Awe over-rides everything.

Amusement twinkles in his light blue eyes before he releases my hand and turns back to Shay.

"Tell me what you need." Lucian moves behind his desk as he addresses Shay, who lights up a cigarette.

"The square, I want full control of it." I have no idea what Shay is asking for, but I use the moment to look around me. Everyone is watching; they don't look away from me when I meet their eyes. My hand automatically goes to the knife in my pocket and rests there.

"That, my friend, isn't possible. You know this." Lucian's voice rolls and tumbles around the room, and gazes flicker to him before returning to me.

That is power.

A woman with deep brown eyes and long brown hair hasn't as much as blinked as she continues to stare at me.

"My brother, Frankie, died in the cages of that square."

My attention returns to Shay as he crushes out the cigarette in the large crystal ashtray that sits on the desk.

"I know Shay, and we have all given our deepest condolences to your father." Lucian waves across the room. "And your family."

"Someone paid three thousand to have my brother killed that day."

I glance at the room again. Everyone is working but listening. Shay's voice carries across the space as his temper flares, and I don't want that to happen.

Anyone who went up against Lucian would get their kneecaps blown off. I take a step toward Shay, attracting Lucian's attention. He tilts his head slightly and gives me a curious stare.

"Maybe he annoyed someone, Shay." Lucian steps away and sits behind his desk.

Shay has forgotten his place; I can see that. All the lessons that my father drilled into my head were about respect for the Chief Commandant if you wanted to live. Disrespect in the RA ranks wasn't tolerated.

Shay's fists tighten as he leans on the desk. I'm aware the calculator's noise has ceased. There is no ruffle of paper or low chatter on the phones.

"Amanda, the ring lady, paid Michael Phillips three grand to kill my brother." Shay pushes off the desk. "I want to know why and if I go down there, no one will give me answers." Shay leans back in, his voice low, but I can still hear him. "But if I control the area, I will get my answers."

Lucian sits back deeply in his seat. His gaze flashes to the room before it diverts back to Shay. The noise behind me resumes.

"Leave it with me, Shay. I'll dig around, see what I hear, and let you know."

Shay stands straight, towering over Lucian.

"In the meantime, stay here." Lucian's smile is quick, and his eyes flash with something that I can't decipher.

I'm not sure if staying here is an invitation or a command.

"Chief Commandant." Shay spins on his heels with fire in his eyes. I haven't looked away from Lucian, who's watching me.

A hand circles my wrist, the thumb so close to my pulse. Shay's touch is gentle, and I know he's making an effort from the fiery flashes in his gaze.

We leave the room through the same door we came through. Shay doesn't release me as he walks down another hall that looks as run down as the rest of the building. He knocks three times on a door that has the number 317 on it.

The door opens, and Shay enters, pulling me along with him. The man who opened the door gives us a nod, and it's like I've stepped into a different world. The grandeur of the room makes me think if I touch something, it will disappear like a mirage.

How could this exist in a place like this?

"Mr. O'Reagan. We weren't expecting you until next month."

"A change of plans, Keeper." Shay's voice holds the level of respect that it had for Lucian, and so it should. I'm fighting a smile—the Keeper. The actual keeper was in front of me. He isn't near as impressive as Lucian, but his power, his knowledge and his age shines in his blue eyes.

The keeper glances at me. He's clocked Shay holding my wrist. I wonder what he makes of that. It's not my hand, so it's not intimate, yet Shay is guiding me like I might be a prisoner. Yet, there is no power behind his hold. Now I'm questioning why he hasn't let me go.

I hold out my other hand. "I'm Emily."

He takes it. His long fingers wrap around mine, and I'm tempted to withdraw my hand, but I hold steady until he releases me.

"Your quarters have been prepared."

Shay continues his walk through the grand room with me in tow. It's the low-hanging chandeliers that don't fit here or the lush red and gold rug under our feet. Maybe it's the towering marble pillars or the fact that every painting I pass belongs in a museum. I stop at one. I wasn't into art, but this one I know.

Shay stops too and faces the painting. "Martin gave it to us as a gift."

"Martin, as in Martin, the art thief." I'm repeating what I already know. More laughter bubbles up my throat, but with it comes an onslaught of confusion.

"None of this is making sense, Shay." I'm still staring at the painting of the elf, stroking a cat while the world burns down behind him. The elf is a mockery of our president, but this painting is everything.

"If you're so high up with the RA, why has your name been associated with the other side?"

Shay's hand is gentle as he leads me away from the stolen painting. An heirloom to our Irish history, and I know where it was hanging.

Why was Shay O'Reagan, branded a Northerner--an enemy of the state—if he was rubbing shoulders with Lucian Sheahan and the Keeper? It didn't get any higher than that. Not even my father would have met these people. They were stories, fables even, sometimes myths to us. But here, they were breathing the very same air as I was.

CHAPTER SEVENTEEN

O'REAGAN
AN CHLANN
SHAY

Emma keeps looking around her, repeating the same words. "I don't understand."

She follows me into the bar. I take down a bottle of brandy and pour myself a glass as I watch her take in the space. It's impressive, but it's long lost its appeal to me.

The brandy burns as I drink down the full glass and refill it. This once was my playground—the women, the wealth, the power. The power that had really belonged to my da at the time, but I had lapped it up. That was until Frankie.

"Are you going to tell me what's going on?" Emma runs her

hand down the large snooker table. The balls click off each other as she mindlessly rolls them around the table.

"You've been branded a Northerner."

I take down another glass, and half fill it. Picking up both glasses, I walk over to Emma. The marks on her neck will be a reminder of the madness that stirs in me. I should send her home.

I hand her the drink.

"I am a Northerner," I answer.

Emma takes the drink and sips it. "But I just met Lucian Sheahan."

Bringing her here wasn't wise. None of this was.

"My grandfather was deep in with Lucian's grandfather. He was the Commandant."

Emma's drink stops just at her lips. "But that would make you…" She trails off.

"It's complicated." Everything was, since Frankie.

I finish my glass.

"When I was told I was marrying you, they called you a Northerner."

I return to the bar.

"Because I betrayed my people." I can't explain it all to Emma. The more she knows, the more dangerous this is for her.

"I was branded a traitor." I turn to her paling face.

"But you're here?" Her brows drag down.

"I'm going for a shower. Make yourself at home."

Emma places her nearly untouched glass on the snooker table and starts to follow me from the room.

"I need to understand this, Shay. I've been raised to believe that every Northerner is as responsible as the next for our divided country. That Northerners are the enemy…"

I stop walking and spin on Emma. Fear dilates her eyes quickly, and I fucking hate it.

"That's the problem with you Southerners. That's why I betrayed my own. You can't brand everyone up North as an enemy. There are innocent good people. People who died for a cause they weren't fighting. Your family has educated you with their own version of the truth, and your da…" I'm looking at her again, the daughter of the most famous bomb maker. I shake my head, holding back the flames that fan my anger.

"What about him?" Emma's cheeks turn red, yet she holds her head high. Madness dances in her eyes.

"He killed children, Emma. He took a command, and he didn't question it. If they killed one bad person but took out 100 innocent people, to them, it was worth it."

"My father makes bombs. I know that." Her gaze glazes over. "But children?" She's shaking her head, but I see it deep behind her wide green eyes, the doubt.

"Who gave the order? Hmmm, Lucian?" Fire flickers in her eyes, and it re-ignites my own.

"He did it without thinking. He just took an order to stay in their good graces." I'm pointing at the wall like I can pinpoint where Lucian is— like he is the one to blame for all this.

Emma spins on her heel and marches down the hall.

"What are you doing?" I don't move.

"I'm getting answers, Shay. I can't live like this."

I'm speeding after her, my feet pounding on the marble flooring. The moment my hands tighten on her waist, I lift her off the ground to make sure there is no way she can escape me. Panic has me tightening my hold on her small frame.

"Let me go." She's struggling to get out of my arms. She's trying to reach into her pocket, the one that holds her knife. She gets it out as I give her some wriggle room, and she swings back easily.

I release her, her feet touch the ground. She swings the knife again; I grab it, allowing it to dig into my open palm. Pain pulsates up my arm, and blood drips onto the floor.

Emma releases the knife, her gaze darting between the blood droplets and my hand. She's breathing heavy, tears pouring down her face. She's looking at me like I just hurt her again. I have no idea what she's going to do, but I don't expect the scream that's dragged from deep inside her. It barrels through the hall, filling up every available space with her pain. The knife clangs to the ground, and I think the worst. Did she get hurt during our struggle?

"Are you hurt?" I'm checking her over, but I don't see any cuts or blood.

Her scream ceases, and tears continue to pour. "I'm not him." She covers her mouth with her hands. "I'm not my father." Her lips tremble as she stares at me.

Is this why she was placed in my care? To taunt me? To destroy the last piece of me I've managed to keep together?

"I didn't hurt those children." She's sobbing, and I can't even comfort her.

"I didn't do it. I didn't hurt them. I didn't plant that bomb. I didn't give the order."

The air is thin, but with it is a release, like if it all goes, I'm free of the burden I carry. "No, you didn't, Emma. I did."

Her tears slow, and she's staring at me like I'm the monster I am.

I bend down and pick up the knife from the ground. "I gave the order," I say for the first time.

She's shaking her head. Confusion fills her face. She has no idea what Liam O'Reagan dragged her into.

"I gave your father that order." I make it crystal clear before leaving her on the hall floor.

Drugs, drink, women, and fighting; that's what made me whole. When my da brought me into the Republican Army, all that power went straight to my head. I didn't think. I didn't care. If the order was given to pull the trigger, I did it without question.

I wanted to fly. I wanted to feel like I could control the uncontrollable. Lucian's da was in charge at the time and took me under his wing. My existence in the Republican Army was kept quiet.

I step into the gold bathroom that costs too much fucking money. The shower takes up half the bathroom, and it doesn't give me the comfort it used to. Turning on the water, I let it pour down my back, seeking freedom from a never-ending cycle of guilt.

That day I gave that order like it was for a fucking coffee. I knew there would be children and women at that march. They weren't mine, so it didn't matter.

I press my hand against the tile, and blood flows down the sleek surface.

A movement behind me drags me out of my thoughts. I don't turn fully but look at Emma over my shoulder.

She's fucking with my head. Like a ghost, I don't need to see.

"I don't know what to do." Her confession comes out in half a laugh and half a sob as she wraps her arms around her waist.

I didn't know what to do with her either. I was only sure that I didn't want to give up my seat with the South. This could change everything. I could right all the wrongs to have control in both parts. I could stop the senseless violence. I hated Liam O'Reagan, but he was as powerful as Lucian.

She looks like she's in pain. I can't help but look at the bruises on her fragile neck. I exhale loudly. "You can choose to be different, Emma. You can choose to stop the cycle."

She blinks, and tears spill. "How?"

"Don't ever follow an order without questioning it. Never be in a position where you can't question it."

Emma's gaze trails lower, like she's just realized I'm naked. "What about you?"

Guilt still churns heavily in my gut. "I'm trying to fix things."

"That man, Michael?"

I turn away from Emma; that's not something I want to talk about. "That's different." I start to wash myself, letting her know this conversation is over.

The silence makes me think she's left. She hasn't. She's still standing in the bathroom. She's looking around her with a look of pure despair on her features.

I turn off the water, and she looks at me. Why do I feel like I owe her?

"Michael took my brother from me for three grand. Frankie was…" I'm trying, but the words fail me.

I pass Emma and get a towel off the rack.

"You really miss him," Emma states.

I close my eyes, just wanting her to leave.

"My brother Noel. He's my best friend." A small shaky laugh has me opening my eyes. "I can't imagine if anything happened to him. I think it would …"

I turn, running the towel across my face. Emma's bottom lip trembles, and she sucks it in between her teeth. The innocent act causes my cock to harden.

I continue to dry myself but don't hide my growing erection. The moment she spots it, her cheeks redden.

"I'm just saying…"

I turn away from Emma. "Just leave it."

"I think you're better than this."

Her words should anger me, but they don't. I want to cling to them. I want to believe what she's saying because Frankie always said I was better than the rest. Better than even Da.

"You are so delusional, love." I turn and grin at Emma. "I won't stop until every single person who was involved in my brother's death is eradicated from this earth. I don't care how long it takes or the cost. Every single person will die."

"You will destroy yourself," Emma pleads.

I laugh at the naïve beauty in my bathroom. There is nothing left in me to destroy. I just want to avenge my brother and stop destroying others.

That included Emma, but I needed to keep her to keep Liam happy.

I wasn't doing a very good job at winning her over. Her gaze darts lower, and I take a step towards her. One part of me says leave her alone, and the other wants to bury myself in between her legs and just get lost in her.

It's selfish.

It's wrong.

It's winning.

I clear the distance between us and kiss her. She's frozen under me for a millisecond when she responds, her kisses are frantic and drive the lust in me to a new height.

Her clothes are the only thing in the way. I'm not gentle as I pull her top off. I can't be. Her flesh is warm, and I press quick kisses along her shoulder and up towards her neck. She bends her head and allows me access.

"Take off your clothes," I command.

She hasn't been shy about getting naked with me so far, and she doesn't disappoint this time either. As she takes down her trousers, I meet my gaze in the mirror. Emma's red head of hair moves back up, and I bury my hands in it as I crane her neck back.

She's panting as hard as I am, her ruby red lips parted, waiting. She's too good for me.

My lips crush hers, and I know I can't stop now. I fill her warm mouth with my tongue while pushing my raging hard cock against her.

She's a virgin. I can't just fuck her hard. I move back to give my hand space to dip a finger inside her. She groans instantly, her hands pressed against my chest. She's wet. I slip in a second finger, and her groans grow louder. She's soaking wet.

I remove my fingers and tip the head of my cock into her opening. She doesn't freeze like I thought she might. Gripping her legs, I drag her up my body, so her entrance is level with the head of my cock. Using the counter space behind us, I place her on it and don't break the kiss. Her nipples brush against my chest, and I can't hold back as I push myself inside her.

A squeal of surprise from her lips doesn't slow me down as I bury my full cock inside her. I meet my gaze again in the mirror as I drag myself out of her before pushing back in. She isn't groaning, and her pussy tenses around me.

I push back in, wanting to move faster and harder. I keep looking at myself so I don't hurt her, so I don't take her with the need that swirls and grows inside me. Her pussy loosens slightly, and it's a green light for me to pull out and push in quicker. A squeal mixed with a groan has me closing my eyes and gripping her waist. I drag her onto my cock where I start to fuck her like I want to. I want to get lost in the act, and I do. The sting of my flesh against hers encourages me to go faster and harder. Her pussy clenches again, and it feels so good as I rock my body into hers. I hold her waist with one hand and allow the other to get tangled in her hair. I drag her face away from my mouth and into my chest as I continue to lose myself in Emma.

Her moans grow louder and faster. My hand digs into her

waist, dragging her small frame onto me until I'm fully in her filling her up with all my anger and lust.

Each pound takes me further away. Her nails dig into my chest, and I loosen my hold on her hair, allowing her to breathe as I fuck her hard, driving her back on the counter.

I fuck her until I can feel my release so close. My own groans are filling the bathroom until I release myself inside her tight pussy. My release comes with Emma's. I want to see her. Yanking her head back, I don't slow as I watch her face twist and contract in ecstasy. Her lids fly open, and her green eyes sing her release as I pound into her pussy. I slow when I see the light dwindle in her gaze. My fingers untangle from her hair, and I slow down fully to a stop. I don't pull out of her as she clings to me, panting.

I meet my gaze again in the mirror, and I hate the person I see.

I think I always have.

CHAPTER EIGHTEEN

O'REAGAN
AN CHLANN
EMMA

Shay eases out of me. His gaze is downcast as he steps away from the counter and picks up a towel. I'm still struggling to catch my breath while I watch him, thinking he's coming back to allow me to clean up. Instead, he walks past me.

"There's plenty of warm water," He speaks as he leaves me in the bathroom alone. My fingers tighten on the counter, and I'm wondering if that just happened. Did he just have sex with me for the first time and just walk away?

I close my legs, and an ache throbs in between them. Sliding off the counter is hard, but facing what we just did and how it ended is harder.

What did I expect him to do, hold me and cradle me? Heat races along my neck and scorches my face. The bathroom door is half-open, and I don't want him to pass by and see me like this. I don't want him to see that I'm dying inside.

I move slowly as the throbbing in between my legs increases. The door slams closed, and it's not enough. I want to scream.

I'm standing staring at the door, waiting for it to open and for Shay to ask me if I'm okay. No one comes. He doesn't come.

The water is warm. It runs along my flesh and washes Shay off me. It's not enough. I'm waiting for an explosion of tears, but they don't come. The flesh in-between my legs feels raw. I touch the ache and look at my hand, expecting to see blood, but I don't. Most virgins bleed.

I soap up a cloth and continue to scrub the tender flesh—like I can remove Shay's semen from me—like I might be able to remove the act.

He had made me feel dirty when he stepped out of the bathroom. I clench my teeth together as confusion assaults my body and has it vibrating with a want for a release that I don't know how to give it.

I had wanted him. I wanted all of him inside me. It had been painful, but the pleasure had overridden everything else. To have his flesh on mine had been exhilarating until he had stepped away from me like I had done a dirty deed.

I had gone down on him twice, and he hadn't just left me then. This was different. I had given him my virginity. I was now used goods. No matter what happened, no one else would want me.

I hated myself as I got out of the shower and started to dry. I hated that I didn't want anyone else to want me. I wanted Shay to want me.

I dry quickly and remember I have no clothes. Opening a large door, a row of towels faces me. Below them is a row of hanging dressing gowns. They all look brand new. Why would one person need, I count quickly, seven dressing gowns?

The innocence in me says for each day of the week. In reality, I'm sure Shay has had more women than I'd care to know stay here. Did he fuck them in the bathroom too? I can't look at the counter. Wrapping myself in a dressing gown, I dry my hair quickly and leave it down. I don't see any slippers, so I leave the bathroom barefoot. A billow of steam follows me. My feet move me deeper into the large apartment, and I hate that I'm searching for him. I stop and count.

I was more than this. Turning around, I go back to a room that I had already been in. The bar; It's empty. I close the door behind me and consider putting a chair under it, but if he wanted to get in, he would break down the door.

The excited part of me is taking in the extraordinary décor and the fact that I'm here. The thought of how high up Shay is should terrify me.

I don't face the elephant in the room. I can't face the fact that my dad and Shay are already tied together. I can't allow my mind to go there. My earlier glass still sits on the snooker table, and I pick it up and drink all the liquid down. It burns, but it's a good burn, one I want to increase.

I take the glass to the bar and refill it to the top. I start with sipping it as I step out from behind the polished bar.

"Who are you?" I ask the room. Shay is a mystery, and maybe that's what's drawing me to him. I shouldn't be attracted to him. I should be repulsed, so why am I not?

Maybe his losing Frankie and my losing my mom has created a connection in my mind. Maybe seeing the softness in him toward his mom makes me believe there is hope for us. After giving him a part of me in the bathroom, and the way he dismissed me—my throat and nose burn, and I drink deeper. I drink until the glass is empty, and I refill it again.

The room is warm, and I'm surprised by how tired I feel. Taking the glass and my depressing thoughts, I sit on the couch and take another drink, spilling some on my nightgown.

My knife. I left my knife in the bathroom. I take another drink as my eyelids grow heavy. He took your knife, I remind myself, remembering the moment in the hall that I don't want to remember. Tears burn my eyes without my permission.

Wet droplets touch my cheeks as I continue to drink from the glass, and my body grows heavier.

The thud on the floor feels distant. I know it's the glass as my hand feels empty now. But I don't care. I want to go where my body is pulling me into a sleep that will scare away all the thoughts I don't want to face.

I sleep for a while. The smell of his cologne wraps around me, and at first, I want it to vanish. It's making me remember, and I don't want to remember.

"Shhh." His breath brushes my face, that's resting against his bare chest. His heart drums away under my ear.

"I don't…" my lips feel dry, and I lick them.

We are moving, and my eyelids flutter open. He's focused ahead as he carries me through the hall. I push against him, but nothing happens.

My eyelids flutter closed, and the loss of control sends panic fluttering through my body.

"Bastard." I manage to squeeze out.

The rumble in his chest has me opening my eyes again.

"Are you laughing?" I'm waking up, the walls spin, and I quickly close my eyes again.

The rumble leaves his chest, and his heart resumes its normal beat.

"I can hear your heartbeat," I speak with my eyes closed. "I didn't think you had one."

I'm lowered, and my eyes snap open. Where am I? I'm looking around at the darkened room. The sheets under me are silk.

"I'm not having sex with you." I'm trying to get off the bed. His arm circled my waist as he drags me back towards the pillows. My head sinks into them.

"I don't have sex where I sleep." He shifts beside me.

"So what, you bring women here just to sleep?" I sneer and glance at him, hating him for looking like a god or a king beside me.

"I don't bring anyone here."

My chest tightens. "Do you really think I'm that gullible?"

He pulls the silken sheets over me. I smell him. It's all him that surrounds me. Shay sinks down on the pillows too.

"Go to sleep." His command has me opening my eyes, and I face him.

My stomach squirms; I shouldn't face him. He had no right to look like this after what he did to me.

"Was it bad?" I ask, sounding like a pitiful creature. I close my eyes tightly. "Don't answer that." My cheeks burn, and I want another drink.

My lids snap open when his large hand touches my cheek. His dark eyes roam across my face, sending my heart into a frantic rhythm.

"I'm a bastard." He removes his hand, and I seek the warmth immediately.

"Yeah, you are." Tears blur my vision.

"You're too good for me."

"Yeah, I am." I blink, and Shay's face comes back into focus. A grin on his lips has me tightening my legs together. I'm naked under the robe, and my body is so aware of his closeness.

"Go to sleep now."

"No," I say, even as my eyelids grow heavy with the command. "I hate you," I mumble as my mind fogs over.

"Hold on to that hate." His stupid words are the last thing I hear as I fall asleep.

I wake up for the first time feeling rested. As I stretch, the pain in my head and in-between my legs come to life, and I stop as I'm assaulted with everything that happened since I arrived here.

I sit up and look to my left. I'm alone. Of course, I am. I allow my head to fall into my hands. I shouldn't have stayed here last night. I should have fought him.

The bedroom door opens, and I look up. Shay's still topless, wearing only black pajama bottoms.

"Where is my knife?" The moment I ask it, I glance at his hand that's wrapped in a bandage.

"In the bedside table." He answers while carrying a tray towards the bed.

I ignore him and scurry across the large bed until I reach the bedside table. I open the drawer and am surprised to see my knife there.

"You don't need the knife, Emma." Shay sounds exasperated. I take it out and sit back as he places the tray at the foot of the bed.

I don't release the knife as he flicks on some lights. The room is lit up, and I see him even more clearly now. I wince as the pain in my head throbs. I pull the robe closer to my body.

"These will help."

Shay is standing at the side of the bed, holding a glass of water and some white tablets.

"Are you trying to kill me?" I ask, but I know I'm being stupid. I take the painkillers and the glass of water.

Shay moves away, and I can't stop staring at his wide back. His shoulder blades move up and down as he moves to the tray.

"I don't cook," he states, and I swear I hear something vulnerable in his words. "It's just toast and egg."

The tray is lowered, and I recognize the toast. But the egg is almost black and lumpy. I pick up the fork and poke at it.

"Are you sure it's dead?"

I glance up at Shay. His serious expression has me thinking he's pissed over my statement.

"I have to go out for a few hours."

My stomach hollows.

"There's a gym and other rooms you can go check out." I'm still holding the fork in one hand and the glass of water in the other. My knife rests in my lap.

I don't want him to leave. "Where are you going?"

"A lead I need to check up on." He turns away from me.

"Is it about your brother or something else?" I ask.

Shay drags a white t-shirt on, covering all his tanned skin. He doesn't answer me. I place the water on the bedside table and the fork on the tray.

I watch as he gets dressed. Once he's fully clothed, he faces me. "Don't leave the apartment."

I pick up a slice of toast and take a bite once he leaves. I listen to the steady drum of my heart until the door closes. He's gone.

I chew the toast slowly, but I don't attempt the egg.

Shay is gone for ages, and I get dressed in one of his t-shirts and my jeans. The gym is impressive; it must be the same size as the drawing-room. I exhale loudly as I just stare around the room. I couldn't relax here. I couldn't relax anywhere with Shay. I've searched the apartment twice looking for a phone, but there isn't one or a laptop or any device that would allow me to connect with the outside world. The TVs all work, and I flick through the endless stream of channels. A distant knock has me turning off the

TV and throwing the remote on the couch. Was he back? I leave the sitting room as another knock comes from the front door.

I take two steps toward it and pause. Shay had said not to leave the apartment. He never mentioned not answering the door.

"Hello." The voice that comes through sends my heart rate skyrocketing, and I'm moving to the door.

I open it, tempted to greet Lucian as Chief Commandant or Mr. Sheahan. Either seems odd, but I don't have to say anything as he speaks first.

"Emma." My name sounds funny on his lips, and I wonder why it should until I remember why, I'm Emily. Not Emma.

"Emily," I correct, but give a slight bow of my head, so he knows I don't mean any disrespect.

His gaze narrows intentionally, and a grin plays on his lips. He is wearing a gray suit, and his hands are held behind his back. He looks regal, like someone who belonged to a time of kings and queens.

"No, I had it correct the first time. Emma."

My stomach plummets into my shoes. He knows who I am.

CHAPTER NINETEEN

O'REAGAN
AN CHLANN
EMMA

"Mr. Sheahan..." I start, and he steps into Shay's apartment.

"It appears we both know the other." His hands are placed behind his back, and once he moves across the threshold, I see the other two men standing outside, both dressed in black, both mean-looking.

"I'm Emily," I say it stronger and turn to Lucian. "I'm sorry for the confusion." The smile on my lips trembles and dissolves as Lucian keeps walking down the hall.

"Emma Murphy. The daughter of Red Murphy."

I'm following him while glancing over my shoulder at the

open door. The two men haven't entered, but their gazes follow me as I chase after Lucian. He stops outside the bedroom, and my heart leaps into my throat as he picks up my knife off the unmade bed. He turns and gives me a soft smile before placing the knife in his pocket.

"You came with nothing else?"

His question I answer with a shake of my head.

"Where are the clothes you wore yesterday?"

My throat tightens, and I'm listening for footsteps behind me over the roar of blood in my ears. "In the bathroom."

Lucian moves past me. "Gather them up."

It was a command. I might not be part of the RA, but to break a command wasn't acceptable.

"Mr. Sheahan…"

He pauses and turns to me. He doesn't say anything.

"If you know who I am. What are you going to do with me?" I bite my bottom lip to stop the tremble that has entered it.

"Get your clothes."

My heart pounds, and I know if I do, I'll never see the light of day again. Had Shay sent him to get rid of me? After last night he had enough of me. Why show me kindness, why carry me into his bed? Why make me breakfast?

Tears choke me. "I can disappear." I blink, and they spill.

Lucian walks away from me, and I know if I don't get my stuff, the other men are there to do it for him. As I walk to the bathroom, a pain starts in my belly. It's overriding everything else as I enter the bathroom and gather my clothes.

Shay set me up. He left, knowing that they would come for me. I brush tears away as I hug my clothes to my chest. I'm staring at myself in the mirror; I'm staring at the counter where I gave him a piece of my soul. A piece of me that I can never get back. Dropping my clothes, I pick up the soap dispenser and pitch it at the mirror. The image of me fractures, and I see a hundred green eyes stare back at me, mocking me.

My legs grow weak, and I hear them coming. Panic claws at my insides, and I'm scrambling along the floor, opening the cupboard to find something. I needed to fight. I needed to survive this.

The two men barrel in. Anything I touch in the cupboard, I throw at them. Aftershave smashes along the floor and pollutes the space. I grab bottles of shampoo and conditioner and throw them, but it doesn't stop one brute from reaching me. His hand digs into my mass of hair, and I scream as I'm dragged from the ground to my feet. My scalp burns and protests at the assault. My nails sink into the man's hand, and I rake them down to his fingers. He drags me from the bathroom. I'm working with him now, keeping my head close to his hand to try and stop the intense burn to my scalp. I'm released in the hallway and fall to my knees. Teeth rattle and clunk in my mouth. The second man passes me with my clothes in his hand.

"I can disappear." I plead on my knees.

The front door is still open, and Lucian stands outside with his back to me.

"You're making this harder than it needs to be." The man who holds my clothes slows down.

Panic swells and grows inside me, but I don't know what to do with it. I'm rising; I'm moving barefoot. I don't want to die.

Lucian walks, and the man loosens his hold on my hair and grips my arm. The tightness feels like a blood pressure band that's out of control. I yank my arm back, but his hold is as steel. I stumble over my feet. The elevator doors open, and my mind is trying to remember seeing one before, but I hadn't.

Lucian is already inside. I'm released once the other two men are in and the door closes.

The air is thin, and a whimper claws up my throat. I swallow it, fearing if it spills over that this will make the situation more real.

"Chief Commandant. I swear to you. I'll disappear." I use the correct title, and hope blossoms as Lucian's blue gaze land on me. He's going to take me seriously.

"Sometimes we cut the stems of flowers when getting rid of weeds."

"Cut stems?" Bile claws up my throat. "I'm going to die, aren't I?"

The ding of the doors and the breeze on my back is a sound that has me hunching my shoulders. The railing in the elevator becomes a rope, a beacon. It's hope, and I cling to it.

Arms wrap around my waist and drag me, but I hold on even as my legs leave the floor. I scream like a sinking ship. I scream like I might shatter this moment and be back in the room.

Another arm slams down on my outstretched forearms. The pain roars up my arms, and I'm moving away from the railing with outstretched arms.

"Silence her." Lucian follows us.

A hand clamps over my mouth, and I bite until I taste blood. I'm tumbling to the ground but grabbed like a rag doll. The other large guy drags me to him. Lucian steps up to me.

Hate—I hate him. I spit the blood across his face. There is a moment like there isn't air, and I'm waiting to shatter.

I curl in on myself as a hand strikes my face, my teeth clamp down on my cheek, and my blood mingles with the blood that already stains the inside of my mouth.

Lucian cleans my bloody spit from his face while the other man gets ready to hit me again. I curl in on myself, getting ready for the blow. But nothing could prepare me for the sting across my face. A cry of shock and pain spills from my lips, and we are moving again, moving towards a large steel door. I'm trying to turn and look at Lucian, who trails behind us. He's on his phone.

"Please don't do this!" My screams leave the hall, and I stumble into the outside world. The wind whips my hair across my face, and I stay in the cocoon of red for a brief second, hoping it will last longer, so I don't have to return to the cold reality of what's happening.

My hair moves away from my eyes, and a white van starts up. I'm trying to back away; my bare feet tear across the asphalt. Their burn fueling my panic.

"Please!"

Lucian finally looks away from his phone and places it in his pocket. I'm aware of the sliding door opening on the side of the van.

"I'll disappear," I beg one final time.

"Yes, you will." His words turn my panic feral, and I'm bucking and screaming as I'm dragged and lifted into the van. Lucian stays where he is as I jolt forward, trying to get out of the van. The door slides closed, cutting off Lucian and my view of the outside world. The darkness I'm plunged into has me thrashing my weight against the door.

"Let me out!"

I roll back on the carpeted floor as the van lurches forward, and bile crawls its way up my throat as my window of getting out of here grows smaller by the second.

Sheer hysteria clutches every part of me. My fists slam against the door, my throat protests at the assault on it as I scream until it's like I run out of screams, and my throat cuts me off. My hands relent as pain races up my arms.

Sobs that rock my body take over as I curl into a ball on the carpeted floor. It smells of bleach. Bleach, I know what that's used for. To cover up the smell of blood, bones, and decay.

I swallow another sob that lodges itself in my throat and chokes me. I'm coughing on the fumes of my terror that I'm trying to control.

Everything is out of my control. The van moves faster under us.

"It's okay," I tell myself and choke on another sob. It's not okay.

I take a calmer approach to my surroundings and feel around for a light switch that is usually placed above the sliding door. I find what feels like a rectangular light, but the switch isn't there.

Another sob rocks me, and I lick the tears off the top of my lip. My hands run along the door for a handle. I feel bolts and edges where the handle should be. Sweat makes a path down my back as I move to the back of the van, but it's the same. Someone removed the handles.

A screech rips from my throat as I start to beat the door again, but stop as I feel the indent of where the window should be. I touch it, and the material doesn't feel like it is steel. Running my fingers blindly around it, I'm picturing black covers over the glass, but I can't find an edge.

Lying on my back, I shuffle closer to the door, and with both legs, kick out to where I think the windows are. The vibrations roll up my legs and rattle my teeth. I don't stop. I don't stop until my body cries out.

Sweat soaks my face. My hair clings to my cheek, making it itchy. I'm frozen, lying on the ground as tears leak from my eyes. The van continues to sway, and I feel each bump. It's a reminder that right at this moment, I'm alive.

Closing my eyes, I enter a new kind of darkness. One that's familiar to me, unlike the van's darkness. I'm smiling through my tears as I picture Lady racing through the fields. I'm on her back again. The wind cools my burning skin. I've opted to ride her without a saddle. My thighs clench around the beast under me as I encourage her to go faster.

Noel's large black stallion races beside me, and I meet my brother's gaze. He grins as he shoots ahead. I want to call him out on cheating. He's all saddled up. I nudge Lady, and she unleashes her true power, racing after Noel. It's my turn to grin at him. My laughter floats behind me and through the clear blue sky.

The van under me jolts, and my eyes snap open. The memory disappears until only wisps of the freedom I once experienced lingers. I want it to cling to me like smoke, but it doesn't, and I can't breathe in the back of the dark van.

I'm up and crawling to the front. My aching hands work along the paneling. There's always a way to get into the front. I'm pulling and prodding. A stream of light, the size of a pin-prick, floats in, and I pause, blink, wondering if that is a mirage in the desert. The sounds of a radio playing snap me out of my state, and the stream of light disappears as I push my finger through and hook it before dragging it back. The heavy plastic cuts into my finger, but I don't stop. The panel cracks, and I finally pull back my finger. The hole is slightly bigger. Lying on my belly, I press my mouth to the hole and scream at the top of my lungs: the van jolts, and a man curses. I'm fired backward as the van stops abruptly.

"Shut the fuck up." A voice has hope blossoming inside me.

I'm crawling to the hole. "Please let me go. No one has to know. I'm begging you."

Something heavy hits the divide before we start to move again. I don't scream again, but I work on the hole, cutting each finger, but I don't stop; it's freedom. It's keeping my mind occupied. The hole widens until I'm able to get two fingers in.

The van stops again, and I brace myself against the paneling. Light pours in and burns my eyes as I face it. A different man, this one wearing a rainbow-colored beanie hat, fires a cigarette to his left before climbing in toward me.

I kick out and scream. He's stronger than his thin frame suggests as he drags me from the van.

"Would you shut her up?" The driver moves into my line of sight with a raised hand—a reminder of how good his backhand is. I shrivel up, and the slap doesn't come. The doors of the van slam shut, and I'm moving across an empty lot.

My feet burn but are cushioned by long stems of grass. I'm trying to look around, I'm trying to take it in, but my mind is jumping and clinging to silly things, like the bike that's lying on the grass. It looks new. It looks like it belongs to a kid.

The smell of cigarette smoke from the guy wearing the beanie hat gives me comfort. My stomach twists as I think of Shay. Why would he do this to me?

It shouldn't hurt this badly, but his betrayal distracts every part of me as I'm entering a room with no memory of the building.

The flooring under me is a soft gray carpet; a half-circle reception desk with a silver chrome on the front hides a woman. The top of her head is the only thing I can see. She looks up and smiles at the guy holding me; the smile falters as her gaze dances to me.

She's standing now, large loopy earrings moving as she comes from behind the desk.

"Could you not have brought her in the back door?" She's wearing a dark red top with the shoulders cut out. Diamonds stitched into the edges.

"Help me." I swallow the bit of saliva that I have left. My voice is low. I don't think she heard me.

"This is the back door." Beanie guy releases me.

"The other back door." The woman approaches me and grips my shoulders. "She looks strong." She pats my arms and gives me a little shake. Her dark eyes roam across my body.

"They're getting skinnier, but I can work with that."

"She's not here for that."

The woman shrugs and returns to the desk.

I'm paralyzed as I watch her sit back down, her head disappearing.

"Help me," I say louder, and she looks up. For the first time, her face displays some sympathy.

The two men who had taken me from Shay's apartment arrive. One of them doesn't slow as his hand grips mine, and I'm hustled along.

The hallway reminds me of a hotel. Red carpet and endless doors sprawl out before me. Groans erupt from one of the doors we pass, and something beyond fear takes root. I'm turning. I'm running. I'm panicking.

I don't see beanie guy as I run straight into his waiting arm that impacts my throat. The ground sucks me up and extracts all the air as the space around me grows dark. I almost welcome the darkness. I can't face my worst thoughts.

I'm in a brothel, and I'm going to be raped.

CHAPTER TWENTY

O'REAGAN
AN CHLANN
SHAY

"Where is she?"

The room is filled with men turning to me as I walk toward Lucian. He's sitting at the head of the table. Documents spread out in front of him. He doesn't look up at me as he moves papers around with his index finger.

"I'm in the middle of a meeting, Mr. O'Reagan."

All eyes are on me, and I honestly don't give two fucks. "Just tell me where Emma is."

I've garnered Lucian's attention as we stare at each other

for a beat. I'm ready to drag him across the fucking table. Self-preservation has me stuffing my hands in my pockets.

"Give us a moment." Every man rises at the command, and it's a brief reminder of my place here. But no one else had the power or access to Emma, only Lucian. If he disrespected me, then I would disrespect him.

Each man that passes in their suits and well-polished shoes glances at me. Most with curled-up noses that are begging to be smashed in. They didn't grow up like me. None of these men are like me. They come from education; they are respected members of the community. If people really saw under the masks and suits, most of them would be locked up.

The double doors close behind us. Lucian has returned to moving sheets of paper on the table. "First, you should knock." He glances at me, but I'm in no fucking mood.

"You had no right going near her." I cut in.

Lucian sits back in his chair. "You forget your place here, Shay."

"I want her back."

"Still, you forget your place." Lucian stands, and I pick a spot on the wall, so I don't attack him.

"You came here only yesterday requesting to have power over the square." Lucian walks toward me. "I told you I'd look into it. Yet, you went and sought out Amanda."

I remove my hands from my pockets. If they swing, I hope they swing fast and hard. "You are keeping tabs on me?" I grin.

"It's necessary when it comes to you, Shay." Lucian steps

closer, and sometimes I forget that we are the same age. He acts older, more put together than I am, but in a fight, I'd win.

"Chief Commandant, where is Emma?" I use his title. I use her name. Since she is missing, he must know who she is.

Lucian steps away from me. "I don't know." The lies pour from his mouth, and I'm moving. The gun in the back of my trousers is cold against my flesh.

"Shay, think before you act." His voice is low but has an effect on me. I pause and leave the gun where it is. If I did anything to him, I wouldn't get out of this room alive, and even if I managed to, I would never get the answers I seek.

Lucian sits back down. "Now, on your way out, you can tell the men to come back in."

I clench my jaw, knowing it would take something drastic to make him talk, and I can't afford to do that.

His eyes slowly rise to me. "Now, Shay."

He wields his power like a fucking burning sword. One day I would take the fucker down and shove the sword up his ass. Today isn't that day. I give him a nod. "Yes, Chief Commandant."

His jaw tightens at my mocking tone as I leave the wanker to his papers. Opening the double doors, I don't tell his men to go back into him. They fall silent as I approach and move over for me as I make my way back to my apartment.

The bathroom sends fear skittering up my back. I kneel down and examine the contents on the ground. I have no idea what I'm looking for, but nothing makes sense. Her clothes are gone; even the knife that she threatened me with is gone. Yet, she didn't leave voluntarily. The bathroom looks like there was a struggle. But why struggle and take your belongings? I get back up and check the hallway before returning to the bedroom where I had watched her sleep. I had craved her peace as she had slept soundlessly beside me last night. She was a beauty that I didn't want to let go of. Last night, I worried about the damage that I could bring to her, and now that fear has taken its rightful place in my reality.

I thought I had left her in the safest place. Clearly, I was wrong.

I do a walk-through one more time before leaving the apartment and going outside. I walk the perimeter. I think the small markings of blood on the asphalt are fresh, but it's hard to tell. I light a cigarette as I stare down at the markings. Voices from the side of the building have me straightening and following the sound. Two security guards are out smoking. When they see me, they crush their cigarettes and look ready to bolt.

"Don't panic, lads, I won't tell the boss." I grin as I approach them. They hesitate but don't leave.

"Either of you see a red-headed girl around?"

Both shake their heads. "No, can't say we did, Mr. O'Reagan."

I let a laugh splutter from my lips. "Call me, Shay."

I slap the nearest one on the back; he's built like the hulk, and my mind races through names. "Edward?"

His gaze shifts to the left. "Yeah."

Scratching his neck, his hand is pretty torn up—my gut twists. Nail marks, and they are fresh.

"What happened to your hand?"

The dumb cunt is shaking his head as he pushes his hands into his dark leather jacket. He doesn't answer.

"Your hands are all clawed," I say before putting the cigarette out on the ground.

"I'd better go back in." The other security man grips the door, and I don't stop him.

"A cat." Edward coughs up.

I jut out my chin at the departing security.

Edward shifts like he's getting ready to leave.

"You should get a tetanus shot for that." I pick up the cigarette off the ground and pocket it.

Edward watches me.

I straighten. "Save the planet," I explain the cigarette.

He nods.

"I think you should get your hand seen, too."

"I'm fine."

"Edward, I fucking insist. I'll take you." I start to walk away, not wanting to force him. The building is surrounded by cameras. Cameras that happened to glitch when I went to see what happened to Emma. No doubt they weren't glitching now.

"Really, Mr. O'Reagan."

I glance at him over my shoulder. "I told you to call me Shay. I'm not asking, Edward."

He looks back at the door, and I will shoot him in the fucking back if he dares to run. He turns to me and starts to walk.

"I honestly feel fine." He rambles on like I give two fucks about how he feels. He can drop dead once I get my information out of him.

I unlock the car and climb in. He hesitates for a second before getting in, too. The car dips with his weight, and I start the engine and pull away from the parking lot. I keep looking in the rearview mirror to see if we are being followed.

"It doesn't even hurt."

"Did you hurt her?" I ask, and I can't look at him. "Don't lie to me." I divide my attention between the road in front of me and the rearview mirror.

"No."

My gut twists painfully. So he was involved in taking her. If I look at him, I'll tear his fucking head off.

"Where is she now?"

"I don't know."

I slam my foot on the brake and turn to Edward. Color drains from his face, and I don't hesitate as my fist collides with his flat nose. Blood gives me satisfaction as it pours down his face. He howls, holding his face, and I have to restrain myself from continuing.

"Where is she?"

"Brothel. Ludlew Street. With Tracy." Each word is said through his pain.

I continue driving while everything inside feels hollow. They took her to a brothel.

"Who gave the order?"

Edward half cries, and I keep driving while I swing my fist into his side. The car swerves, but I pull it back onto my side of the road.

"Lucian."

"Why?"

Edward whimpers. "I swear, I don't know."

He's not lying, but that doesn't stop me from striking him again.

"I swear!" He's getting fucking blood all over my car. Tracy's isn't far away, and I make it there in record time.

When I get out, Edward doesn't move. He's pissing me off as I walk around to his door and pull it open.

"Get the fuck out!"

"He'll kill me." Is his pathetic answer.

I withdraw my gun. "I'll kill you."

Edward gets out, and I keep the gun at the ready as I walk to the building that houses one of the biggest brothels in Belfast. I've used it myself. The moment Tracy sees me walk through the door, she's standing and smiling. Her smile falters as Edward walks in behind me.

"The red-headed girl, where is she?" I don't point the gun at Tracy, this is her job, but that doesn't mean I won't get the answers I want.

"Calm down, Shay." She's stepping around the counter with her hands half in the air.

I don't like Edward behind me, so I turn to him. "Get on your knees, you cunt." He does, folding his large frame, and I keep the gun pointed at him.

"I'm not fucking around, Tracy. Where is she?" I keep my gaze on Edward.

"They brought her in a few hours ago. Said she wasn't for the brothel, they took her down the hall, that's the last I saw of her."

I take a look at Tracy. "If you fucking lie to me..."

She lowers her hands, her confidence growing. "I wouldn't fucking lie to you."

"You stay here; if you move, I'll hunt you down." I threaten Edward before leaving and entering the hall.

All the doors are closed. I know exactly what goes on behind them. My chest tightens when I think of Emma stuck behind one of these doors, sucking some fat guy's cock.

My foot connects with the first door; it gives way on the first kick. A girl screams and climbs off the man she was fucking. Her dark hair has me moving onto the next door.

Two kicks, and the door bounces open. More screams. This time the man gets up off the bed and glares at me. I raise the gun, and he sits his ass back down on the bed.

The third door, I'm ready to kick in.

"Jesus, Shay." Tracy's voice rings behind me as my foot slams into the third door. Three girls scatter to different sides of the room: all blonde, all naked.

"I can do this all day," I say to Tracy as I move to the next door.

She curses and leaves. People are starting to come into the halls, men half-dressed, women scurrying around looking for Tracy, I'm sure. The fifth room is empty. The further I go, the more my worry grows. I don't want her to be behind one of these doors, but if she isn't here, then what the fuck have they done with her?

The door I kick in doesn't stop the brunette from sucking the guy's cock. He looks at me alarmed but doesn't move as he continues to half enjoy getting his cock sucked.

"Shay."

The gun in my hand feels heavy as I turn to my da, who stands at the end of the hall.

"Could you close the door?" I turn back to the brunette who wipes spit from the side of her face.

I point the gun at her. "Suck his cock," I command, wanting to hurt someone.

My da was here. My da was in on this. I couldn't process that right now.

"Suck his cock." I raise my voice and step into the room. She wraps her lips around the head of the guy's cock while looking at me.

"Shay." My da's voice has me clenching the gun.

"Keep sucking it, you tramp."

The brunette does as I tell her, but I'm sure the guy is soft in her mouth.

"Shay."

I step out of the room and face my da. "What are you doing here?" I know it's not for women. My ma is his world, so that leaves one thing—Emma.

I don't want it to be Emma, but logic tells me it is. I haven't put the gun away. I keep it at my side.

"Where is she?"

Tracy ushers all the women and complaining punters back into their rooms. Most go, but one guy wants a fucking refund.

"Where is she?" I ask my da, who steps closer to me as the punter continues to whine behind me.

I spin, my temper flaring, and push the gun to his head. More screams fill the halls. "You want a fucking refund, you fat bastard? She should be paid to allow your fat ass on top of her."

"Shay, it's fine." Tracy tries to push herself closer to me. "You'll get your refund, now get in the room." Tracy pushes him, but he doesn't look away from me or the gun as he backs into the room.

"Ma had said you were at a meeting yesterday. Was it with Lucian?" Was it about Emma?

I face my da, and he turns, walking back towards the double doors he had come through. I follow fast on his heels. "Where is she?" My voice rises. The moment we pass through the doors, I'm slammed against the wall. My da's temper flaring.

"Hit me," I taunt, wanting something from him.

"You are forgetting who you are, boy. You can't come in here kicking in doors and waving a gun. That's not how Kings act."

I push my da's arm away from my neck. "Taking my bride-to-be away from a King is not how other Kings act."

"Is this how you spoke to Lucian?" My da's question has me ready to explode.

"Are you ringing each other and telling tales? I just want Emma, and I'm gone." It takes the unthinkable to make me see what I had. I've always been this way. I can't help it. But I know Emma doesn't deserve this fate. I don't deserve her, but I want her.

She was given to me, and she is mine.

"I can't allow that, son. I tried to dissuade you before. You can't marry her."

The gun still hangs along my side. I'm aware of its weight.

I put the gun away before I use it and live in regret. "So what now?"

My da relaxes like I'm giving in. "All I know is that this wedding can't go ahead. Liam O' Reagan can't have any power in the North. No matter the cost."

I nod like I'm weighing in on it. "The cost is Emma?"

"The cost is you or her. I won't lose another son."

CHAPTER TWENTY-ONE

O'REAGAN
AN CHLANN
SHAY

"She has to disappear." My da keeps his voice low as he speaks to me.

"She's innocent."

My da tilts his head; his gaze diverts away from me as he runs his hand across his face. I know what's going through his mind—that I never minded killing innocent people before.

"The bombing..." I start gaining my da's attention. He exhales and touches the belt on his trousers. It's a reflex he does when he's worried. "I won't allow that to happen again, Da."

"Your words are dangerous." He's closer to me, making me think we aren't alone.

"My actions are dangerous. I'm trying to make things right. That girl doesn't deserve to die."

"The decision has already been made."

Fire flares up inside me. "Where is she?" My voice rises and bounces down the hall. I want to grab him and make him tell me, but years of discipline have my hands remaining fisted at my side. "I won't fucking stop. I won't let this go. I won't have her blood on my hands."

A door behind me creaks, I'm aware of it, but I'm not fast enough. Pain pulsates through the back of my skull as something heavy smashes into my head. My knees give way, and I hit the ground hard. My vision blurs as I roll onto my back while gripping my head. There must be an open crater in the back of it. Pain pours through me, and I try to see through the swirl of colors. Two people move above me. My da's voice breaks through the buzz of pain.

"I had it under control." My da's words fade as I lose more than my vision.

"Cunt." I manage to mumble before pain consumes me, along with the darkness.

I'm moving. Hand's grip my arms and legs. My back bounces off the floor, and all I want to do is cradle my head that roars for protection. I'm trying to stay awake and keep my head up slightly. Each rough movement sends pain slashing at my neck. What the fuck did someone hit me with? A hammer?

"Da." I'm not sure if he hears me, but I need him to put me down.

"We are nearly there, son." He sounds breathless; I'm not light. He must be taking me to a hospital. I need to get Emma.

My legs hit the floor, and a wave of sickness has me swallowing. My arms are still gripped tightly. Large hands wrap around my legs, and we are moving again.

Sickness chokes me, but through it all, I hear a soft female whimper.

I'm released onto the ground and try to open my eyes. Pain explodes across the back of my skull, and I roll.

"What did you do to him?"

Emma.

Her voice is close. Small, soft hands touch my face. "Shay." Her voice breaks. "What did they do to you?"

It's not that bad. I want to say, but my voice doesn't work. Instead, I let the smell of vanilla and the soft touch of Emma's hands drag me deeper away from the pain.

I blink several times. My head is cushioned, the heat is nice, and I grip a thigh. I know it is Emma before I see her legs that my head is resting on. Her hands move in a rhythm across my cheek. I turn but pause as pain bounces around my skull.

Her hand stops, and I want her touch again. "Shay." Red hair fills my view, and through it all, a set of emerald green eyes that are filled with worry make me smile.

"Are you okay?" My voice works, but each word causes more pain. What the fuck did they hit me with?

A half-laugh falls from her chewed-up lips. "You should see yourself."

"Nah, I know I look good." I force myself off her legs while I keep my eyes closed. I sway, and my stomach rebels, but I hold still leaning against a solid cold wall behind me. I want to return to the warmth of Emma and have her drag those hands through my hair, but we need to get the fuck out of Dodge.

"How long have I been out?"

I open one eye and look at Emma. She's on her knees facing me.

"A few hours." Her puffy red eyes and chewed-up lips make me think of all the stuff she could have suffered.

I'm not ready to accept any of it. "Okay." I try to get up and fall back on my arse. Emma's hands grip my arm.

"Jesus, Shay. You need to rest."

I can't look at her now without thinking about what must have happened. I focus on the room while shrugging off her hands that fall away immediately. The room is large but empty. No light shines in from the window over our heads, telling me a lot of time has passed.

"We need to get out of here." I try to stand again and manage to keep upright. Emma rises with me.

"I thought you sent them to get rid of me." Her voice is tiny, so fucking tiny, but I hear her. I just can't answer her.

"I thought you made them bring me here."

I want her to stop.

"I thought I was going to die." A sob chokes her words.

Her head is hanging, her arms dangling at her side, and

something in me breaks. I reach for Emma, and she immediately walks into my arms. Her small frame shakes and rattles, and I hold her tighter.

"Let it all out, love." I run my hands up and down her back, just like she ran them across my cheek. "I've got you." I bend my aching head and press a kiss against the crown of her head. She still smells like herself. My brain is searching for the smell of a man.

I take my nose out of her hair. "We need to leave."

She sniffles. "You're in no condition. Please sit down and rest for a few minutes."

I give in to her demand, but only because my legs won't hold me up any longer. Standing causes my head to spin. The moment I sit down, I feel a bit more stable. Emma sits beside me and curls into my side. I wrap an arm around her; her head rests on my chest.

"Tell me something about you."

I want a smoke. "I don't know, Emma. You know pretty much all of it."

She buries her head deeper into my chest. "Tell me about Frankie."

In the darkened room, with my senses not fully intact, I talk about Frankie. "He was gay, but not like a fucking girl gay. He was a man who liked men. You wouldn't know, really. My ma knew. I think all ma's know." I smile when I remember them in the kitchen together. He always made her smile.

"He could be a little prick at times, stealing my aftershave." What I wouldn't give to have him steal it now.

"My shirts."

"You were the same age?" Emma's words make me aware that she's listening to me.

"He was younger." He was better than me. So much better.

I don't want to talk anymore. I let my hand sink into the mass of red curly hair that's untamed and wild, just the way I like it.

"My mom wasn't exactly motherly. I got a lovely warm feeling off yours. My mom wasn't like that."

I deepen my hands into Emma's hair and let my fingers circle along her skull. She arches into me.

"But, she still took care of us. Her boys were her world. She favored Noel."

Emma isn't jealous. I can hear the smile in her voice. "It made sense that she favored Noel; he never did anything wrong. He took care of us all." Her voice wavers.

"At the end, there was nothing left of her. Cancer ate right through her flesh and mind. I remember watching Breda wash my mom's body down. It was skin and bones; hollow, empty, and I remember thinking if that happens to me, I want someone to put a bullet in my head."

"I'll remember that," I say as I press a kiss to her head. She was so fucking brave. Braver than most I knew. Right now, I was too weak to even ask her what happened when I wasn't here. I'm terrified in case something happened that I can't take back.

I'm not brave enough to ask.

"That's if we get out of here." Her words have my hands pausing. I remove my hand and tilt her chin up, so she's looking at me.

"I'm Shay O'Reagan. I'm a fucking King. I'm going to get us out of this."

Her emerald gaze roams my face, and she nods.

Her tongue flicks out and licks her red ruby lips.

"Okay." Her one word of confidence in me makes me a little bit braver.

I lean down and press my lips gently to hers. "I'm sorry, Emma," I say and deepen the kiss, not wanting her to tell me, but I want her to know I'm sorry she was stuck here in this room. In this place.

She's staring up into my eyes like I mean something to her—my gut twists.

"I had it all so wrong. I had been raised to believe that all Northerners were evil." Her lips drag down along the edges. "Northerners aren't evil, Shay. Men are."

I close my eyes against the pain her words ignite in me. We need to get out of here. I want to know what happened while she was alone. My bravery grows. I can kill a man or command a room. I can stand naked in front of the world for all I care. But to find out if anyone touched Emma is weakening me by the second.

"We need to find a way out," I say as I glance around the room.

"I've tried everything." Emma moves out of my arms.

I take a step toward the door and manage to stay upright.

"The door is locked. The windows are sealed. The vent is too small for even me to fit through."

I spin in a circle, understanding that those three ways are the only ways that might be considered as an out.

The door rattles, and I'm moving back. "Get behind me."

I'm reaching for a gun that my mind has already decided isn't there. It isn't. My da would have made sure I was checked.

"What if they hurt you again?" Emma speaks beside me, and I reach around and push her behind me.

It's my da who steps into the room first. I see the silver suit outside the door. Lucian. He's on the phone, but he turns and meets my gaze.

"I'll speak to you later." He ends the call and steps into the room with my da. I keep a hand on Emma, who stays behind me. Her warmth gives me the strength not to attack them. We stand and stare at each other.

"You made a deal that you had no right making." Lucian breaks the silence as he kicks the door closed behind him.

I grin. That was fucking stupid. He must have a gun or two on him to feel secure in a room with me. My da was here to try to get me out of trouble. I was still pissed at him, but Lucian was stupid to think if this went south that my da was on his side. Between us, he wouldn't leave this room alive.

"Liam O'Reagan will never have any control over the North. It can't be allowed."

I grin. "Why didn't you just say that, Lucian? You didn't have to do all this." I grit my teeth, hoping to stay as calm as I can, but already I just want to hurt him.

"You are a King, you have power, and you can make those types of deals." My da steps closer and pauses when I flash him a warning. What he has done to me is a betrayal I'm not sure I can forgive.

"Clearly, I can't," I speak to Lucian. He's the one in charge here. Kings or no Kings, he has the manpower. He has the contacts that we don't have.

"Liam O'Reagan is a poison that won't be allowed in the North. Have you ever wondered why no one has ever tried to join forces before?"

I had. My assumption was that greed played a big part in all this. I wanted to stop the violence. They wanted to keep it going.

"Not even his father was allowed any control in the North."

My da shifts. That's the way I tell how uncomfortable he gets when his family is spoken about. He had a different da than the rest. It was his da who controlled the North until he was killed.

My hand still rests on Emma's side. She is still behind me. "So, why bring Emma here?"

"You can't marry her. She is what ties this deal together, a deal that won't go ahead."

"So just ask me to call off the wedding."

My da takes another step towards me. "Would you have? Did I not already ask you that?"

He had.

"If I walk away from this, we don't have a seat in the South."

Lucian lets his long fingers flutter through the air. "Another time, it might present itself in a better package."

We would never get this chance again. I would never get this chance again.

"If I refuse?" Once again, I address Lucian.

"I'd advise you not to."

"I'm not looking for fucking advice."

"Shay." My da speaks up; the warning in his gaze doesn't stop the heat that burns my insides as it seeks for a release.

"It's fine, Connor." Lucian smiles at me. It's a you-little-shit-listen-up kind of smile. "Okay. Emma will disappear." I know what that means, and that's not going to happen.

"You will be stripped of your title as King of the North, and you will be remembered for your betrayal to your country. The penalty for that alone, Shay, is death."

Emma moves, and I try to push her back, but she won't.

"I'll leave. I'll call off the wedding."

"Emma," I warn her and push her back. "What if there's a way that I can still rule in the South and not give Liam any power over the North?"

Lucian laughs.

"You find that fucking funny."

Lucian's laughter stops, and my da shifts in his stance but doesn't come any closer.

"Yes, I do. What you are saying isn't possible. Liam wouldn't just hand someone like you that kind of power."

Someone like me. Lucian's disdain for me was really showing.

I had something I could use, a card I didn't intend to play at all, but I wasn't losing the chance to join the North with the South. I couldn't walk away from it. I had to make something right.

"I know something that will sway him."

Curiosity widens Lucian's eyes. "What is it?"

I grin. Fucking Cunt.

"If I can make the deal, you let me live my life. You leave Emma alone."

Lucian rubs his jaw and turns his back on me. My da's gaze holds a look of betrayal. That whatever I am sitting on, I should have shared with him. But right now, I'm glad I didn't.

"So you get to rule alongside Jack and Liam O'Reagan in the South, and only you rule in the North?"

"There will be another member in the South; I'm not sure who Liam is selecting. But yes, only I will rule in the North."

It was a title, but it clearly didn't give me much power.

"I'd like to think if you can pull this off that you would consider the advice from us in the future."

Like fuck I would. "Of course."

"Then you have a deal." Lucian reaches out his hand. "A deal I still don't know how you are going to pull off."

"Me, neither." My da's words are growled.

"Emma will be left alone?" I squeeze Lucian's hand, but he doesn't flinch.

"Yes, once you hold up your end."

This had to work. If it didn't, I was fucked.

CHAPTER TWENTY-TWO

O'REAGAN
AN CHLANN
EMMA

"Are you sure coming back here is wise?" I don't think Shay is thinking clearly. He had driven back to his apartment. I'm not entirely sure how much of the drive he will even remember. He was hunched over the steering wheel with a pair of sunglasses on his face. I offered to drive, but I knew even as I said it that he would say no.

I couldn't drive, but that didn't stop me from offering.

"It's the safest place right now." His words would make me laugh; only there was nothing funny about the situation.

The car stops, and Shay groans as he turns off the engine and pulls out the keys. I'm reaching for the door handle when he stops me, his hand circling my wrist. His touch burns me in such a good way, like heat after the cold. It shocks me, and I want to push him away but also bring him closer. His touch has such an odd effect on me.

"What?" I ask. I can't see his eyes behind the shades, but his head is turned towards me. He releases me.

"Let's go."

Whatever he had wanted to say, he clearly wasn't going to. I'm walking across the parking lot to the run-down building, thinking that this was the perfect opportunity to run. Shay was injured; I could easily get away. I turn in a full circle. No one is in sight. My heart starts to race with the possibility of getting away.

"Emma."

Shay has dragged the glasses off his face, and my stomach twists almost painfully.

I shouldn't feel guilty for my thoughts, but he risked so much to come and save me, he had to give up so much to keep me alive, and here I am thinking of bailing on him.

He slips back on his glasses and continues his walk to the side of the building. He's not displaying his confident walk that tells you he owned the world. He was wounded.

I half jog to catch up with him. Shay holds the door open for me, and once again, I know this is a significant moment. I'm following him because I want to. Not because he's forcing me. We don't speak as we make our way back to Shay's apartment. Being aware of my surroundings, I can see the portion that hides the entry to the elevator. I also notice far more security men. Each large man clad in black sends my heart racing, but each face is a stranger. These aren't the men who took me, but they would on a single command.

Shay removes the glasses once we are in his apartment. Fear freezes me, and I don't want to go any further.

"I won't stay if you leave me again. I can't be on my own." I can't relive someone taking me. That fear is still riding pretty high in my system. Shay staggers and leans against the wall like his body can't go much further. His eyes are closed. "I won't ever leave you again."

I want to believe him so badly, but I still can't move—his dark gaze swings to me. There is so much strain on his face. Blood has caked into the back of his neck. He needs stitches.

"I promise."

I didn't think Shay would make a promise lightly, so I take a step of faith filled with unease towards him. The moment I reach him, I take an arm and wrap it around my shoulder to support his weight as we make our way to his bed. He falls into it and groans.

Going into the bathroom has fear skittering up my spine. The moment I thought Shay had betrayed me was terrifying. I step around the mess and try not to look at the smashed mirror as I wet a towel and bring it back to the bedroom.

"Don't come near me with that." Shay's eyes are closed as he speaks. I ignore him and sit on the bed. His wound isn't bleeding any more. I don't think so anyway. I start to dab at it, and Shay doesn't move at all, so I keep going. I keep going with the belief he has fallen asleep.

"Do you sing?" His question has me pausing. Most of the blood is cleaned off; the wound isn't as deep as I thought it would be. It was still nasty and must hurt like hell.

"They said you played the tin whistle."

I start to clean the blood off his tanned neck. I have to pull his top away to get the cloth all the way down his neck. It's awkward. "You want me to play the tin whistle?" I ask. I didn't have one, but the idea of playing for him sends a thrill through my system.

Shay moves and sits up; his lids tighten in pain. "You need to rest." I'm ready to push him back down when he opens the buttons of his shirt. "Fuck no, I don't want you to play the tin whistle."

It wasn't a piano or guitar. I got that it wasn't to everyone's likings, but coming from Shay, his words deflate me. Shay struggles with taking off his shirt, and I don't help him. Instead, I allow myself to take in how perfect his body is. His eyes are closed so I can look all I want.

"My head is aching, so a tin whistle would really drive it mad." He explains, and I feel petty that I was allowing him to struggle because I felt offended.

"Let me help." I tug on the sleeve and get his arm out of the shirt. Once it's off, he lies back down on his side. Blood has dried past his shoulder. He lost a lot of blood. I return to cleaning it while humming a Christy Moore song that makes my gut tighten and my heart ache with the pain in the words. I don't know why I picked this song, maybe it's everything that has happened, and a part of me wants to share that pain with Shay without me using words.

I only stop humming until long after the blood is cleaned

away. I lie down beside Shay and let my fingers flitter across his back. At my first touch, his muscles bunch together, and the movements fascinate me enough that I keep going. I keep going until he finally relaxes under my touch, until I can sense the rhythm that he falls into as he sleeps.

I don't sleep. I don't leave him. I find a sort of peace in lying beside a sleeping giant. His skin is so warm as I trail my fingers across it. The right thing to do would be to pull the blankets up over him and let him sleep undisturbed, but I don't want to stop touching him.

He came for me.

He saved me. What would have happened if he hadn't found me? They would have killed me or put me to work. That thought was more terrifying than death itself.

"What happened at the brothel?"

I swallow a scream. "I thought you were asleep." I cover my heart with my hand and roll onto my back to try to calm it.

"I was, but I can't rest." Shay turns and groans.

"Don't lie on that side." I sit up, getting ready to move to the opposite side of him so he doesn't lie on his wound, but he grips my wrist softly.

"I need to know, Emma."

My heart bounces around in my chest. "Lucian told the men to take me there. So they did. Once I arrived, I thought I would be raped."

Shay doesn't blink; his hand doesn't leave my wrist either.

"But they put me in that room, and I stayed in there until you came."

He blinks, his fingers release my wrists.

"But while I was in there, I kept waiting for the moment that the door would open, and they would drag me out into another room. I couldn't stop picturing a man raping me." I blink as the tear rolls down my face. I know it didn't happen, but the anticipation was worse.

"I wouldn't have gotten away." My lip trembles. Shay sits up. His hand tightening on my arm, his grip pulls me closer to him. "You would have."

I shake my head. "I might act like I'm tough, Shay, but that? That would …" destroy me, break me. Both.

Shay drags me closer and plants a kiss on my forehead before releasing me and getting up. I'm watching him as he opens the bedside table and takes out a black gun. It looks larger than a gun should look.

Shay climbs back onto the bed and holds out the gun. I don't take it. "What are you doing?"

"Have you ever fired a gun?"

I shake my head.

Shay takes my hands and wraps them around the cold metal. "Feel the weight, Emma." He releases it, and my hands drop slightly before I adjust them to the weight of the gun.

"Don't pull the trigger." Shay grins as he speaks.

"It's loaded?"

"There's another gun in the wardrobe, another in the bathroom under the floorboard in the cupboard, and two in the kitchen. Every gun is loaded."

Shay leans over and flicks a small lever near the top. "That's the safety off."

"Put it back on." I'm ready to hand him the gun back.

He does as I say. "The safety is on them all. But just knock it off." He moves behind me and covers my hands with his. The warmth of his chest penetrates my clothes and flesh.

"Aim." He brings my hands up to the level of a man. His mouth moves closer to my ear. "And pull the trigger. Don't ever hesitate, Emma."

My finger is over the trigger, and I'm wondering if I could really pull it—if I could take a life.

"If you hesitate, you die. If those men came back, what would you do?"

Fear skyrockets, and I'm ready to turn to look at Shay. I hate that he would even say such a thing, but he keeps his arms clamped around me, his hands still over mine. His chest pushed against my back.

"What will you do? Will you let them take you again?"

"I had no choice."

"Now you do. So what is it? Go with them or pull the trigger?" His words are angry and harsh in my ear.

My finger presses down, and my stomach flips at the click of the gun.

A kiss is pressed to the side of my face. "Good girl."

Shay doesn't release me, and the longer he is pressed against me, the more I become aware of his growing arousal.

"You deserve more than an arranged marriage."

My heart palpitates. "Are you giving me an out?" I'm half smiling at the door.

"No. I wish I could." He takes his hands off mine, and I'm ready for the loss of his warmth, but he doesn't move. His hands run down along my arms, skimming my stomach before they dip into the waistband of my jeans.

"I'm marrying you, Emma."

His fingers run along the top of my panties, and I suck in my stomach, hoping to give him more room to move his fingers deeper.

"For your seat in the South?" I ask, still holding the gun while his fingers dip a little deeper. I don't want to let go of the cold metal against my palm.

"Yes."

I know what we had wasn't love, but I could see how easily I could fall in love with Shay; I just wasn't sure if he could love me. Yet, he had come for me and saved me. His worry over what happened to me in the brothel was genuine; that had to count for something.

His hands move back up, and I can't stop the whimper of disappointment that's short-lived as he unbuttons my jeans and pushes them down my hips to my knees.

This time there is nothing blocking his hands. I gasp as his large fingers enter me. My wetness immediately allows him to easily fill me. My hands wrap around the gun tighter as he pushes two fingers in. The fullness of my breasts weighs down my bra, and I'm so aware of how heavy they feel right now. I have a yearning for Shay's large hands to touch them. His fingers pull back out, and he runs them along my clitoris. The click of the gun in my hand has my eyes springing open.

"I think I should take that gun from you." Shay's words don't sound worried; he sounds as turned on as I feel. I want to turn and see him, kiss him, but he plunges his fingers back inside me, and I'm losing myself in the arousal that this man ignites in me. The bulge pushes against my ass, and I remember how it felt inside me. My core tightens around his fingers before he pulls them back out and drags them back up to my clitoris, where he circles it slowly with his wet fingers.

When his other hand slowly moves up my stomach towards my breasts, I'm almost vibrating with anticipation. His hand cups my breast, pulling it out of the bra before he allows it to slide down and squeeze my nipple. I'm nearly ready to tell him to stop before I come all over his fingers.

CHAPTER TWENTY-THREE

O'REAGAN
AN CHLANN
EMMA

"Are you going to give me the gun?"

I turn my head to see Shay, my cheeks heat, my heart races faster. He's teasing, but I sense something more in his words, and they send a thrill through me.

"No."

His smile tells me I've given the right answer. Was this roleplay? I had no idea. Shay releases me, and I turn to him, holding the gun.

"Let's unload it first." The grin is still there as he holds out his hands. I know this isn't part of roleplay, so I hand him the gun. He removes the cartridge and ejects the bullet that sits in the chamber. My core throbs as his dark gaze travel all the way back up to my face. He leans over and places the bullet and clip on the bedside table. When he hands me back the gun, I take it.

"What do I do?" I feel unsure, inexperienced.

"You like the feel of it in your hands?" He shuffles closer.

I nod as I wrap my fingers tighter around the gun.

"Point it at me." He sits back and spreads his arms wide.

"No." I'm shaking my head, a sinking feeling entering my stomach. 'The devil puts a bullet in a gun every ten years.' It's an old folks tale, but one I remember.

"Point it at me." Shay's hands wrap around mine, and he raises the gun so it's pointed at his chest.

"I don't want to do this." I try to draw my hands away, but Shay holds them steady.

"Do you trust me?" His question I want to answer with a huge No. But, I do trust him. He came back for me.

"Yes."

His gaze lights up, and he takes his hands off mine. "Then pull the trigger."

My heart hammers hard and fast in my chest.

"Come on, Emma. You pull that trigger…"

I don't let him finish. I press down, and the click has my body going rigid.

His smile is instant as he moves closer and pushes red curls out of my face. "That's a good girl."

I don't feel very good. In fact, I feel the furthest thing from good.

My lips crash down on his, and he tastes like everything

that is bad but oh so good. I know Shay isn't someone you took to meet your mother. Maybe I was lucky I didn't have mine around anymore.

My top is yanked up, and I switch the gun from one hand to the other. We break the kiss for a brief moment as Shay throws it onto the ground. He removes my bra too easily, and I can't stop my mind from going somewhere darker, but it's dragged right back as Shay lowers my hands until the gun is pressed against my core.

"Lie back," His command is said without even flinching.

I lie back with the gun sitting over my pelvic bone.

Biting my jaw stops me from moving as Shay takes off my trousers and panties. His large hands move up my legs. "Touch yourself."

I crane my neck to look at him. He doesn't waver as he bends his head and places a kiss on the inside of my thigh before spreading my legs further. I've never felt more exposed and vulnerable. The gun is cold against me, and I move it along my clitoris. It's powerful and wrong, but nothing feels more powerful than the force of Shay's kisses moving up my thighs. Each kiss drives my heart higher, my want for him further, and my body is wanting this sweet torture to end.

His tongue drags along my pussy, close to the gun, and I move it for him, so the cold metal rests along my leg. I still don't want to let it go.

A half scream is dragged from my lips as Shay's tongue dips inside me. I arch my back, raising myself so he can go deeper.

He eats me like I'm something delicious. Drinking up my juices like they are sweet nectar that he can't seem to get enough of.

His large hand wraps around mine that holds the gun, and as he sits up, he places the gun on my wet pussy. I move it up and down, but I'm already yearning for him.

I crane my neck as he pushes down his trousers and boxers. His cock is huge. Pre-cum coats it, and I want to taste him again, but he's moving in-between my legs. The large swollen head of his cock sits at my entrance.

His hands are huge on my hips as he tightens his hold and drags my body into his cock. He fills me, and pain laces itself with a heightened pleasure that floods my veins. When I close my eyes, I'm spinning like I'm drunk. Opening my eyes, I raise my hands above my head, still holding the gun, as Shay pulls out of me before thrusting his powerful body back into me.

His gaze never leaves me, and each thrust is like a stitch to the damage he had done. Each thrust, I feel so deeply, yet it's not enough.

The pain fully dispels as he moves faster into me. Muscles on his chest clench, and I want all of Shay. I'm craving every single part of this man.

He pumps harder, his hands sink painfully into my sides as he raises me, giving himself full access to my pussy, that tightens around his cock. The pleasure grows, and when he growls, it undoes me. I get no warning that I'm going to come; having Shay this deep inside me sends me over the edge. I scream out his name as I cum, and his powerful strides grow faster and harder. His breaths are heavier, and I watch him as he climbs harder and faster until he explodes inside me.

My body continues to tremble from the aftershocks that I've never felt before. Shay moves over me but doesn't remove himself.

His breaths are harsh and fast, and they mingle with mine.

"You're a little minx." His grin has me clenching the walls of my core around him.

"Is this normal?" I ask and finally release the gun to reach up and touch his face.

"What?" His gaze drags across my face.

"To want to do it again?"

His grin turns into a full smile. "I'm game." His lips press against mine, and the hunger in me starts to grow faster than before.

After two more times, I still can't get enough of Shay. I'm sitting against the headboard naked as he gets out of bed and lights up a cigarette. His body is perfect, and I drink it in. He puffs smoke as he walks to the bedside table where I left the gun and reloads it. It's a stark reminder of the situation we are in.

The cigarette dangles out of the corner of his mouth as he holds the gun and points it at the wall.

"How many times have you pulled the trigger?"

Stupid question, I know. But I want every single detail about him. I don't want to miss a thing, no matter how bad it is.

"I don't keep count." He places the gun on the bedside table and removes the cigarette from his mouth.

"When it comes to it, you pull that trigger." It's like he's scolding me.

My stomach twists, and I clench my legs together. He isn't saying if; he's saying when. I nod my head. The chance of someone coming in here and taking me again would make me pull the trigger.

"I hope you won't have to. I won't leave you again." He isn't looking at me as he speaks. He walks into the bathroom, and runs the water. He returns without the cigarette and sits down on the bed. I'm struggling to keep my gaze on his eyes. I feel like a pervert. He's here trying to have a conversation, and all I can think about is his body, his cock, and the fact that he had said no one had ever had sex in his bed before.

"I'm going to marry you, Emma."

I bite the inside of my jaw, so I don't smile like a foolish girl. I know this isn't a whirlwind romance like I thought it would be, yet with Shay, this feels so right.

"So what, you want to keep your wife with you?" I sound young, naïve. I can't hide the delight his words make me feel.

Shay doesn't smile. "I want to keep my wife alive."

My heart beats too fast in my chest. "If this wasn't arranged?"

Shay gets up off the bed, and I know I've stepped into dangerous territory. "Emma, I'd let you go if I hadn't already made the deal."

My stomach drops into my feet. "Thanks, Shay." I pull the sheets higher up on me and tuck them under my arms. I knew this wasn't love, well, not on his part; I could see myself falling harder and faster for Shay, but he didn't have to be so fucking blunt.

He sits back down. "Emma…"

"Don't. I get it." I wasn't his type.

"What do you get?"

"That I wouldn't have been your type."

"I'm not a nice guy, Emma. You deserve a nice guy."

I push down the blanket; heat roars across my cheeks as I climb out. "I don't want a nice guy." I want you.

I march to the bathroom and turn on the shower. I don't expect Shay to follow. He isn't the chasing type, so when he enters the bathroom, I turn to him.

"Well, you got me." That grin undoes me. It's not self-assurance. It's a matter of fact. It's a this-is-what-the-universe-has-decided type of grin.

I hold my hand under the water, and when it feels right, I step in without looking away from Shay. He makes me feel bold, like I've never felt before.

"And you got me." I smile for the first time, and when a quick laugh bubbles from his lips, I inhale sharply.

I'm doomed.

Shay steps into the shower, towering over me. I want him again, and from his growing cock, he wants me too. I turn my back on him and retrieve shower gel from the stand. Handing it back over my shoulder, I can't stop the smile.

"Wash me." My heart beats wildly as the bottle leaves my hands. I wait as he opens the bottle. The gel is cold, but his large hands move across my back, and I close my eyes while rising on the tip of my toes at the sensation.

"You're hard to keep satisfied, love."

I want to dip my head into my shoulder as his breath brushes my neck. I open my eyes, loving how he says, love.

"I don't think I'll ever get my fill of you." I turn and face him. Heat scorches my face, but it doesn't stop me from being open. "I don't think anyone could."

His dark gaze swirls, and he looks angry or like someone who's ready to bolt. I bend down and pick up the shower gel. My nipples are hard as I pass his cock, but I squirt the gel on my hands before dropping the bottle and start to wash Shay. He moans slightly, and his jaw relaxes, and it's everything.

"You said you never had sex in your bed before?"

His eyes open.

"Is that true?"

He nods as I continue to wash his chest, moving further down. "Yes."

One word has me smiling, and I take his large cock in my hand. "Why now?" I stroke, and he groans, throwing his head back.

"You will be my wife." His answer is breathy, and as I stroke him, I let my fingers trail down in between my legs. I touch myself and moan.

I continue to stroke him and touch myself at the same time. This time it doesn't take much for me to cum. I move faster and stop stroking Shay. His hand takes over, and I focus on myself as I cum again.

Leaning against his hard chest, the beat of his heart has me looking up at him. He's watching me, and his gaze gives me a power I never knew I had.

The swell of his cock grows as he speeds up until his seed splashes across my thigh. How many times had we done it, four?

Between my legs throbs, but it's a nice kind of throb. It's a nice kind of pain. We finish washing and re-enter the bedroom.

"I need clothes," I say, looking at the same top and jeans. I can re-wear the bra, but I wasn't putting back on the same panties.

"We'll go now and get you some things." Shay pulls on a clean pair of jeans, and I envy him as I push my legs through my dark ones.

The black shirt he drags across his wide shoulders has me hunting for my bra; I want him again. How was that possible? To hide the burn of my face, I focus on putting on my bra and top.

"Emma." I'm sitting on the bed, pulling on a pair of Shay's socks when he sits beside me, fully dressed. His hair is still damp, and all I want to do is run my hands through it.

"When we get you some clothes, I need to visit someone."

"Okay." I know there is more.

"It's someone I'm going to hurt."

Now he has my full attention. "What did they do?" I don't expect an answer.

"She paid a man to kill my brother."

I'm stuck on the word she. He was going to hurt a woman. Should that make a difference? "You want me to fight her?" I ask, but I don't think I can.

He doesn't laugh. "I'm going to kill her."

I try to allow his words to sink in, but they don't. "You're telling me this because I'm going to witness it?" I'm not sure if I'm asking or summarizing what he's saying.

"I can't leave you behind. I just want you to know my intentions when I find Amanda."

"Kill her, like torture her or shoot her or…." Did it matter? He was admitting that we were going clothes shopping and then taking a woman's life called Amanda. The air grows thin.

Shay stands. "I haven't figured that part out yet. But no matter what, she has to die."

Bile claws its way up my throat, and I swallow it. I should stay here. I shouldn't know these things. But being alone was scary as hell, too. Was someone else planning to come here and kill me? What if this woman, Amanda, was innocent? Even if she wasn't, did she deserve to die? My mind spins. "How do you know she paid someone?" I ask.

"Because I found the person she paid."

I'm nodding, my whole body moving. "Found him?"

"He's dead, Emma." Shay's voice holds no remorse. This is the part of him I barely knew. This man right now who's standing in front of me looking like a model but with the words of a monster.

"Maybe you should reconsider the killing part?"

This time Shay moves, turning his wide back on me.

"I'm leaving in five minutes." He steps out of the room but stalls at the threshold. "I wish things could be different."

"You don't have to wish, Shay. Things can be different."

My words have him leaving me with swirling thoughts and a sinking feeling in my stomach.

CHAPTER TWENTY-FOUR

O'REAGAN
AN CHLANN
SHAY

She barely looked at any of the clothes she picked. The back of the car is filled with bags of everything imaginable, yet she's sitting in the front seat staring out the window. Twice I've noticed her chewing her nails, something I've never seen her do before. If I could leave her somewhere safe—I would—but she's the safest with me.

The underground fight club is approaching fast. Emma's words about me not killing Amanda are irritating. This bitch took my brother from me, and I want to know why and also take pleasure in killing her.

I won't torture her, and that's only because Emma is with

me. I pull up slowly to the curb and remove my gun from the glove compartment.

"This feels wrong." Emma's voice cracks.

"Emma, love." I place the gun in my waistband and face the red-headed beauty. "I know this is shit. But, I have to do this."

I don't want to argue with her about it. Her large green eyes glaze over, and I get out of the car. She follows, and once she reaches my side, I take her small hand in mine.

We walk down the sidewalk, and I wonder if we look like a regular couple out for a stroll. When I glance at Emma, she's pale, and I want to walk back to the car, deal with this another time, but I can't leave the North without finding out why Frankie died. I need redemption for my brother. Maybe then I will have a chance at building a life with Emma. That is if my blackmailing Liam O' Reagan doesn't tip the scales in his favor.

As we enter, a few people mill around, but the moment they see Emma and me, they give me a nod of respect. How many of them know? None, really. They were nobodies. They wouldn't know that Frankie's death wasn't just an average fight. It was murder.

"We're closed." Amanda makes me smile as she focuses on counting money. When she looks up, I love the fear that fills her face. It dissolves slightly when she sees me holding Emma's hand.

Good.

"No fights?" I ask and walk right up to her. She rises, her gaze darts everywhere.

"I'd like a word in private." She looks over my shoulder, but I don't care if there is an army behind me. All I want is her.

She keeps looking at Emma, and I'm tempted to pull Emma behind my back, but I don't. Her seeing me holding Emma's hand is giving her a false sense of safety.

"Peps, will you hold the fort? I'll be back in five," Amanda calls to whoever Peps is. I don't turn to see who she's talking to. Amanda takes us into the back office. It's a shell, just like the fight club.

"Aren't you going to ask me what I want?" I release Emma's hand, and I swear she sways slightly.

"I know what you want, Shay." Amanda turns her back on me and opens a cupboard. My hand moves to my gun and rests there until she turns back around with a bottle of scotch and a glass.

"They always said the territory would never be sold." She uncaps the bottle and pours herself a full glass.

"Your da was winning all their money. Every fight he won, punters wanted the underdog to win. But against your da..." Amanda drinks the full glass of scotch. "They had no chance."

I keep my hand on the handle of the gun and the other on Emma. I want to empty it into Amanda's chest, but I also need a name first.

"They wanted a way to stop him." She laughs. "They suggested that you be taken out in the cages." She refills her glass. I release Emma's hand and pick up the scotch.

"Did you suggest Frankie?" I drink the glass down as I keep an eye on Amanda.

"Yes. He was the easier option." She admits it.

I place the glass on the table. "Refill it," I tell her.

Amanda does. "It was the only way to get rid of your da." Amanda's hand shakes for the first time. Once she has the glass filled, she reaches for it, but I take it.

"You couldn't just ask him? Tell him that the territory was under new management?"

I turn to Emma, who's looking far too fucking white, and hand her the scotch. She blinks a few times like she's just waking up but takes the glass from my outstretched fingers.

She takes a sip. "Drink it all." I nod.

"We did, Shay. He laughed at us, and no one would touch him."

My da had been warned. Something close to shock ripples down through my system, but it doesn't matter. They still killed Frankie to get rid of him.

"Tell me who controls the cages now."

The pulse in Amanda's neck is flickering wildly, the only sign that she's afraid. She won't answer.

I take the chair that's at the front of her desk and place it in the corner facing the wall.

"Emma, go sit down." Emma's like a zombie as she carries her drink and sits on the chair. She's facing the wall. I don't want to do this in front of her, but I don't trust anyone outside this room. If I don't kill Amanda before I leave, she will warn the people who put the hit on Frankie's head, and all this will be for nothing.

I remove the gun from the back of my jeans. Her gaze snaps to it, and she shakes her head.

"Shay."

I fire a shot to the left of her head. Her scream is accompanied by the smashing of glass. I glance at Emma, who's still sitting on the chair. Her shoulders are hunched, and the glass is shattered at her feet.

I turn back to Amanda. "You know that the timer's set. You tell me now, or I'll take you from this room and kill you slowly."

"I swear to God, Shay. I never met them."

I step up to the desk and push the gun against her forehead. "Don't fucking lie to me. Someone told you something."

"Yes. Someone I met once gave me instructions to have you killed. I suggested Frankie as he would be easier. That was it. I got paid."

"How much?" I tap the gun against her forehead.

"Ten G's."

"And what, you gave three to Michael?"

Amanda's gaze pleads with me. "You're telling me you have no idea who took over this area?"

Sweat trickles down the side of her face. "I swear to God, Shay. Please."

She isn't lying.

"I have footage." She swallows her panic. "I have footage of the guy who gave the order."

I take the gun away from her forehead and grin. "Get it."

She's moving from behind the desk and bends down to another cupboard. I keep the gun aimed at her head.

She's taking her sweet time.

"Amanda," I warn as she rises. She's quick, but I'm quicker as I pull the trigger a millisecond before she does. She slams into the wall—the bullet tears past my head and into the office door.

Blood oozes from the bullet hole in her head.

Emma's sobs have me moving towards the cupboard that Amanda had been at. I push aside more bottles of alcohol and open several files for all accounts and fights that took place here. I throw them aside until I see a small black cassette tape at the back. Picking it up, I slip it into my pocket.

I cross the room and catch Emma, who stumbles from the chair. I keep her facing forward and take her out of the office. I close the door behind me, so she doesn't look back. No one is in the cage area. Either the bullets made them scatter, or I'm going to step into an ambush.

"You stay behind me." I move Emma, so she's shielded by my body and keep my gun at the ready as I move quickly across the concrete floor. The moment I reach the door, I slow my pace down. I turn to Emma. "No matter what happens, stay behind me."

She nods, her red lips chewed down to the open flesh. I don't have time to comfort her. I move, and she stays right behind me as we enter the small hallway.

No one is in sight, and that worries me even more. I move slowly. I don't want to linger this long. If no one is here, they must have reported the gunshots they heard, and us delaying isn't wise. But walking into an ambush isn't something I want either.

I open the door and lean out into the stairwell. I don't hear or see anything and move through. Emma grips the back of my jacket, and I start to climb, keeping my focus on what's above us and below us.

I push Emma to the wall as a bullet bounces off the railing, just missing my fucking hand. I return two rounds and hear footsteps racing.

I grab Emma's hand and start to climb fast. I stop when we are close to the top and lean out, firing one shot ahead of us. No one moves; there is nothing at all.

"Let's go." I grip Emma's hand and clear the rest of the stairs. I open the door slightly and fire off a shot. Nothing is returned, and I walk out slowly. The area is clear. Whoever fired is gone.

I keep the gun at my side and take Emma's hand in mine as we walk up the ramp and out onto the road. I keep the gun in my hand but push it into my jacket as we jog across the road. I'm watching from every corner, waiting for someone to come at us. No one does. I unlock the car and release Emma's hand. She scurries around and jumps in. The moment I pull away from the curb, I glance at the building, but I don't see anyone.

I don't relax until we are a few miles away. Emma hasn't spoken a word, and I don't need to ask her if she's okay. Her face is too fucking pale. I know she's alive from the rise and fall of her chest.

Leaving the North would be wise after what I did. Whoever owned the territory would find Amanda dead and know they had been compromised.

I could only pray that whatever footage was on the tape led me right to them before they found me.

I drive back to my apartment. It's a stark reminder that I'm not safe anywhere, and neither is Emma.

"I'll get someone to bring the bags up," I say.

She blinks at me before getting out.

"Emma. Say something" I hate how frightened she looks.

"She shot at you?" She asks, and I don't want to have this conversation outside.

"Yes."

I could see how she was trying to justify what I did. But Emma wasn't stupid; she had to know that even if Amanda hadn't fired at me, I was still going to kill her.

"Self-defense," Emma mumbles.

I take her hand and continue back to the apartment.

Two security people meet us on the first floor.

"I've bags in the car; bring them up." These aren't my men, but when I fire my keys at one, he grabs them and leaves.

"You had no choice." Emma rambles on as we take the stairs the rest of the way. We could always take the elevator, but I didn't want any chance of bumping into Lucian.

Once we enter the apartment, I lock the door, and Emma stops walking and looks up at me.

"You would have killed her, anyway." It's a statement. I could tell her that it was self-defense, that otherwise, I wouldn't have really killed Amanda. I could allow her to believe that I was the good guy with morals who didn't shoot a woman in the head.

But that wasn't me. "Yes."

Emma scratches her neck, leaving a trail of marks behind. Her tongue is pressed against her teeth as she continues to scratch. I hate seeing her in such turmoil. I walk to her and take her hand in mine, stopping her from ripping her skin.

"Emma, love."

She pulls away from me. "You had a choice." Her words are loud, but the knock on the door is louder.

I don't answer her and remove my gun from my jeans before opening the door. I open it fully and allow the security man into the hallway. "Leave them there." He does and leaves.

I relock the door before turning to Emma, who is no longer in the hall. I don't want to chase her and comfort her. My words won't help, so instead, I take all her shopping bags to the bedroom and leave them on the bed.

I strip off my jacket and make my way to the main living space.

I pause when Emma spins; her eyes are red from crying. "I don't think I can be with someone who takes a life so easily."

I continue my advance on the bar and pour out a drink. "It's a bit late for that, Emma."

She's stomping towards me, and I can see the anger in her eyes. I place the drink on the bar as she rounds it. Her hand connects with my face. The sting is instant.

I wait for a second slap that doesn't come. So I pick up my drink and empty its contents.

"You want to take another one?" I ask her through gritted teeth.

I don't expect it, but she slaps me on the same cheek. The third time, I stop her. Her wrist in my hand would be so easy to crush. "That's enough."

"Not even close." Her anger seems to grow, and I'm tempted to lock her in her room, but I remember how that turned out the last time.

I release her hand and refill my drink before leaving the bar area.

The tape in my pocket feels heavy, and I want to be alone to watch it. I want to see the man who destroyed my family. I want time to think and ponder on how I will track him down and take his life slowly and painfully.

CHAPTER TWENTY-FIVE

O'REAGAN
AN CHLANN
SHAY

Amand is sitting behind her desk. Head bent. I've been watching it the past few minutes, and so far, nothing has transpired apart from her writing in a ledger. I fast-forward it and hit play when the door opens. I can't see the man's face as he steps in. He's tall, and Amanda rises. Words are exchanged, and he slides something across the desk towards her.

Amanda's face tightens, and she glances up at the man. More words pass, and I curse the position of the camera. If I could see his face, I might be able to read his lips.

I'm zoned in on Amanda's mouth, trying to see if she says Frankie, me, or my da's name, but it's hard to tell what's being said. The man turns, and I'm sitting closer, hoping this is it, that I'll get to see his face, but he bends his head, hiding his face from the camera, and leaves.

Amanda is standing behind the desk, and whatever was said has left her shaken. She goes to the cupboard and takes out a bottle of scotch. I sit and watch her drink three glasses before the tape rolls into static. The flickering black and white illuminate the living space, and I'm ready to get up and turn it off when a new image flickers to life. It's outside the club. The streets are empty. Rain is visible as it blows sideways under the lamp-post. A dark-haired man leaves the building, and by his height and build, I recognize him from Amanda's office. He keeps his head down like he knows he's being watched.

"Look up, you fucker." I don't blink as he walks closer to the camera.

It's in the last second, like he heard me, that he looks up.

My heart jumps in my chest, and I hit pause and stand up, staring at the man I don't recognize. I've never seen him before. I return to the bar and pour another drink before returning to the TV. I stare at him, every detail about him, I allow it to sink deep into my brain. The small tear-drop tattoo on his cheek, dark ink rises along his neck, but I can't make the tattoo out. His hair is shoulder length. His face I will never forget. I finish my drink and salute his image.

I will find him.

"Who's that?" I pick up the remote and turn the TV off before turning to Emma. She looks different. She's showered and changed into a pair of light jeans and a white blouse. With her hair tied up, she looks stunning. Her creamy skin looks fresh against the white blouse. Small red curls fall around her face, and her cheeks heat the longer I stare at her.

"You look good."

Her hands are clasped behind her back, and when she brings them forward, she looks at the purple and white paper bag in her hand.

"I picked something up for you when we were shopping."

I don't move. I had left her for a few moments, but I had no clue she had bought anything.

"How did you pay for it?"

Her grin is quick as she steps into the room. "I didn't." She bites her red ruby lip, and guilt churns in my stomach. She looks so pure and innocent. She shouldn't be subjected to this life. Emma deserved someone to take care of her and give her everything she wanted.

I take the bag from her hand and open it. I take out the silver drinking flask. "Are you trying to tell me to drink more?"

She's fighting a smile; her eyes still hold the weariness that she's displayed since Amanda. "I notice you keep picking up cigarette butts and putting them in your pocket, so I thought you could seal them in the flask." She shrugs like what she said is stupid.

My fingers tighten around the flask. I can't remember the last time anyone bought me a gift.

"Thank you."

She steps deeper into the room. Each step is unsure. She

looks at the TV over my shoulder. It's off, but even when I look, I can still picture the man's face who paid to have Frankie killed.

"Who was he?" Emma steps up beside me.

She's so small. Breakable.

"Another one of your victims?"

I grin at her words. She's still angry at me.

I sit down on the couch, still holding the silver flask and the paper it was wrapped in.

"He's the one who paid to have Frankie killed." I turn back on the TV, and his face slowly reappears.

Emma blocks my view as she passes me and sits down.

I glance at her. She places her hands in-between her thighs. "So Michael, Amanda, and now this guy will die too."

"Yes."

"What if he isn't the end? What if someone else paid him?"

I look at Emma, and she holds my gaze. "Then I will find him or her and kill them too."

"So one life equals how many, Shay?"

She didn't understand. I came from a world where if you didn't bite, you would be bitten.

"As many as it takes."

"What about yours?" She's moved sideways, so she's really looking at me.

"What about it?" The flask is heavy in my hands, and I want to give it back. I don't want to accept her gift. I leave it on the coffee table.

"You think every life you take doesn't take some kind of toll on you?"

I laugh and get up. "This is it, Emma. This is the world I was born into."

I go back to the bar and pour myself another drink. If killing took a toll on us, then we were all pretty much fucked.

Once I have the drink filled, I take a sip. Emma hasn't looked away from me. I point at the TV with my glass. "They have cameras on the street and inside the fight club. That means they will be looking for us, and now they know what we look like."

Emma's skin pales. "What do we do?" Fear clogs her throat, and I don't leave the bar as I watch her worry grow and weigh down heavily on her shoulders.

"Come on." I take my drink with me as I go into my bathroom. I don't use the main one that Emma had been attacked in. I had closed the door, and she seems fine with not using it, either. All the bags are no longer on the bed. I don't see her clothes, so I can assume she has put them away. I should have told her we weren't staying long.

I enter the bathroom and take out my electric razor. Emma leans against the counter with a raised brow. "Are you cutting off your beard?"

"Yes. This will be the biggest transformation of all time." I grin at her as I put the blade to my beard. Her small hand rests on my forearm.

"Are you sure?" Color has re-entered her face.

"Why? Are you worried what I look like under all this?"

Emma smiles and folds her arms across her chest. "Yes. It's like a woman washing away all her makeup. I mean, you could have a face like the back of a bus."

I laugh at her wording. "You have quite the mouth on you." My gaze travels to her red ruby lips, and all I want is to kiss them or have her wrap her lips around my cock.

"You're not the first man to tell me that."

My humor fades faster than ice melting in a desert. My hand tightens around the blade in my hand.

I want the fucker's name.

Emma's lids flutter closed, and she's half-smiling. "My brother says my mouth will get me into trouble one day." Her gaze flickers back up at me, and I remember to breathe.

Her brother.

"He isn't wrong." I exhale and return to the mirror, afraid to look too closely at the anger that swells in me.

"He also says I'm as thick as a donkey going backward."

I start up the razor. "I think your brother and I would get on well."

"I think so, too." Emma's voice is low. "Noel would like you."

I run the blade along my beard and watch the sink fill up with black facial hair.

"You don't sound convinced that he would like me." I continue to shave.

"It's just we aren't big on Northerners in our household. But if he gives you a chance, I think he'll like you."

I take a peek at the hopeful look on Emma's face. "Am I starting to get ugly?" I ask as half of my beard is gone.

"No." Her word is breathy.

I shave it all off. It's an odd feeling as I run my hand across my face. I see my father stare back at me and look away from the mirror.

Turning on the tap, I let all the hair run down the drain.

"Your turn," I say to Emma once I'm finished.

She's staring at me, and I raise both brows. "It can't be that bad."

She shakes her head. "It's not." She licks her lips. "So what are we doing to me? I don't have a beard."

I grin at her and step closer. She cranes her neck back to look at me as I reach into her hair and take out the bobbie that holds the mass of curls up. "I can cut it if you want."

Her green eyes are wide as she stares up at me. She nods. "Okay."

I retrieve a pair of scissors and place Emma in front of the mirror. I hadn't cut anyone's hair before, but it couldn't be that hard. The curls fall down the middle of her back. I never give much notice to women's hair, but now touching Emma's, it doesn't feel right to cut it. "Maybe you could just color it?"

Emma reaches her hand back. "Give me the scissors."

I don't. "I'll do it." I hesitate again, and Emma rolls her eyes in the mirror. "I wish you gave this much thought to other things."

Her face grows hard, and I can imagine what those other things are.

I snip and watch the curls fall onto the bathroom floor.

"Happy now?" I don't know what was making me angrier, the fact that I didn't want to cut her hair or the fact that she was still looking at me like I'm a monster.

"Ecstatic." I meet her gaze in the mirror.

Her eyes soften.

I look away and continue cutting. When I'm done, the floor is covered in red curls. The shoulder-length hair seems like it's tripled in size.

"You're going to stand out even more," I say.

Emma blows a curl out of her eye.

I keep my hand firmly on the scissors, so I don't turn her around and fuck her against the counter.

"I could color it." She pulls a curl, and it bounces back.

My cock continues to grow at how innocent but beautiful she looks. I step away from her.

"What color?" I ask like I give a shit.

"Blonde?" She turns to me now. "Do you think it would suit me?"

I place the scissors on the counter and step up to her. I take a curl and run it through my index and thumb. "You're a red-headed beauty."

Her eyes widen before they fill with a want that I would do anything to fill. "You're a dark King." She whispers back; she doesn't smile or make a joke of her words.

"Dark? Because of my hair?" I ask as I keep my gaze on her lips. Her small tongue flicks out and licks them. My cock twitches.

"Your hair, yes, and other things."

She has my attention. I'm waiting for her to continue.

"Your soul is a little bit dark." She rises up on the tip of her toes and presses a kiss to my lips. Her hand touches my bare cheek, and it feels strange to be able to feel her touch so clearly.

"I'm a whole lot of dark, Emma." I take another kiss more forcefully.

Her hands leave my face and rest on my chest, she pushes me slightly, and I stop.

"I know, Shay." Her humor has fled, and now I see the anger and confusion seep back in.

I step away from her, my own mind going to Amanda and the scumbag whose face was on my TV screen.

"I need to get some pictures developed."

Emma folds her arms across her chest and nods, the curls bouncing with the movement. "Family holiday?"

I don't answer her and leave the bathroom. She follows me but doesn't fire any more questions my way.

I enter the living room and take the small videotape out of the player before pocketing it. The flask on the coffee table catches the light, and I pick it up too and place it in my chest pocket before putting on my coat.

Emma is staring at me. "Go get your coat."

She shifts for a second before doing as I ask.

Emma keeps quiet the whole way to the pharmacy, where I get them to freeze the frame on the tape and print out the image of the guy. She's put on a white fluffy hat that covers some of her hair, but a lot still sticks out.

She's twirling the sunglasses stand, trying some on.

"You want a pair?" I ask from the counter.

"No." She puts them back and marches away.

The assistant smiles at me. "In the bad books?"

I smile. "Always."

Her laugh is loud, and Emma reappears at my side. "What's taking so long?"

"It's nearly ready." The assistant moves away from the desk and climbs the three steps to where the photos are being printed.

I lean against the counter and glance down at Emma.

"You're like a badly behaved dog."

She tenses, and her face flames. I'm fighting a smile. She was too easy to rile. "Did your brother ever tell you that?"

"No. He wouldn't compare me to a dog." She's ready to march away.

"Only a donkey going backward," I mumble and know she hears me. I swear I see a smile as she disappears down an aisle just as the assistant returns with my photos. I pay her and find Emma checking out makeup. It's something I've never seen her wear. She doesn't have to.

"You want some?" I ask.

She shakes her head. "Are we ready to go?"

Her mood has changed again, and I'm not about to ask her what's wrong.

I don't have far to go before I pull up into Fairview Estate, where John lives. He's a retired investigator who can find anyone.

I leave the engine running. "Stay in the car. I won't be a minute."

Emma doesn't answer me.

"Emma." I force a warning into my voice, and she glares at me. "What's wrong?" I give in and ask.

"I just want to be normal for once. I want to be like other girls." I have no idea where this was coming from.

"You aren't like other girls."

"Yeah, they don't have to sit in the corner of a room while someone is shot. Or lie on the floor of a vehicle to dodge bullets. Or watch their future husband go crazy in a cage fight. Or …"

I cover her mouth. "What do you want me to do?" It's a growl. "I can't fucking change any of that. This is it."

Her eyes glaze over, and I remove my hand. "I just want to do something normal."

What the fuck was normal?

"Let me just make this quick stop, and how about we go for food?" Because we aren't running for our lives.

"I'd like that." Emma doesn't sound happy at all, but I don't have time to baby her anymore.

I can't stop looking back at Emma in the car. She's watching me, and it feels weird not to have her at my side as I knock on John's door.

I'm thinking the worst. What if some car speeds into the estate and shoots up the car, or she decides that she wants out and jumps into the driver's side? That second thought feels far more plausible and has me making things quick as I knock again.

John opens the door, and I hesitate, looking back at the car, but I need to find this man. I step across the threshold and leave Emma in the car, hoping she doesn't run.

CHAPTER TWENTY-SIX

O'REAGAN
AN CHLANN
EMMA

I feel stupid. Stupid for wanting something like makeup and flowers. The moment I had seen the makeup in the pharmacy, it made me think about all the parties I had dreamed of hosting while getting my makeup and hair done. I just snapped.

I glance at the house that Shay had gone into. My stomach keeps tightening. I hate not having him beside me. I lean across and lock his door, just in case someone comes along and jumps in. Being in the pharmacy and in the normal world with Shay had been so nice for one second. When the assistant had laughed at whatever Shay had said, my blood had boiled, and all I wanted to do was attach myself to Shay, so she would know he was taken.

I glance at the house again. I don't see any movement. It's only been a minute, but it's a minute too long.

The thought of going for food with him had excitement bubbling in my stomach. Movement at the house he had gone into has me turning, and I bite my jaw to stop the smile of relief that fills me as Shay half runs toward the car. He ducks his head to take a good look at me, and my stomach twists for a completely different reason. He's even more breathtaking without the beard. I didn't think that would be possible, but he makes it impossible for me to think straight. He could have been a model, and he would be filthy rich.

He pulls the door handle, and when the door doesn't open, he glares at me. "Emma." The warning has me staring at him. He thinks I've locked him out.

I grin.

He doesn't smile back, and I lean across and unlock his door. His smell circles me the moment he gets in the car. The car still hums under us, but Shay doesn't drive.

I'm ready to ask what's wrong when he pulls away from the curb and we are moving. It feels stupid now to go for food when we were targets. I steal several glances at Shay, but he doesn't look at me. His jaw is tight; he's aware I keep looking at him.

My skin is tight and itchy, and I want to break the silence that is growing and emptying out all the oxygen from the car.

"This place serves nice food."

It's like a balloon pops, and the oxygen pours back into the car as he speaks. I duck down to see the small one-story building that's been plopped in the middle of nowhere. The thatch roof resembles buildings that are sprinkled across the Galways landscape. I didn't think we would find this kind of structure up north.

"I like it." I like the cottage look, from the white walls to the red window sills that support flower boxes.

"Not many eat here." Shay continues as he drives around the back. He's right. Only three cars are in the large car park. He doesn't linger; the minute he parks and kills the ignition, he's out of the car.

The air is cold, and I'm glad for my hat and coat as we walk across the car park. At the back door, Shay holds it open for me—like a gentleman. I can't stop the smile that tugs at my lips. My stomach twists when I look up to find him watching me.

"Thank you."

"You're welcome."

His manners surprise me as we walk into the small restaurant. It's dark inside with its low windows and sporadic lighting, but I already like it. I tug off my hat and push curls out of my eyes as I take in the quaint restaurant.

A tall man, whose head is held high, comes through a set of swinging doors that would be better suited to a western.

His eyes light up in surprise when he sees Shay. "Mr. O'Reagan. We didn't know you would be here today."

Shay shrugs out of his jacket, and the tall man takes it from Shay. Two caterpillar-like eyebrows sit above his blue eyes, making his gaze heavy. He holds out his arm, and I realize he's waiting for my jacket. I quickly take it off and hand it to him along with my hat.

"Thank you."

He gives me a tight smile before walking to a large table in the center of the restaurant. I sit down when he pulls out a chair for me.

"The usual?" The waiter asks Shay.

"You can make that for two, Leo."

The waiter leaves. "I'm not sure how I feel that you ordered for me, too." I take another peek around the restaurant. No one else is here. The cars must belong to the staff. That isn't exactly a good sign about the quality of the food.

"You'll like it."

I return my focus to Shay. He appears relaxed in a way I haven't seen him before.

I lean in closer, not wanting to be rude. "The fact the place is empty doesn't give me much hope for nice food."

Shay grins. He doesn't get to respond as a woman in her forties, early fifties, bustles up to the table. She doesn't speak, just pulls Shay into a half hug. He gets out of his seat, and his smile is lighting up the room. I feel like I'm intruding on a very private moment, but I can't look away.

"Marta. Leo looks great. You're feeding him well."

Marta's giggle is odd; it's like a teenage girl. "You look good without the beard. Leo said you had female company." She releases Shay, and Marta's attention swings to me. "I didn't believe him, so I had to come right out here and see for myself."

Shay doesn't seem put out by Marta's words but sits back down.

Marta smiles at me. "You're a beauty. Are you treating him good?"

Fear shoots through me. I don't know why. What the fuck had he said? I glance at Shay, not hiding my horror.

Shay's laughter is so unexpected. My face blazes.

Marta's laughter joins Shay's. "I'm only jesting, love. You must be a good catch. You're the first female that Shay has brought here."

"Okay, Marta." Shay's tone is still playful, but Marta gives his shoulder one more squeeze and leaves us.

"Are you a weekly visitor here or something? Or is this another safe house?"

I can't decipher the look that Shay is giving me. "It's my restaurant."

"Oh." That explained their friendly approach to him.

"Do other people come here?" I ask.

"Not many. Marta and Leo have run it for years, and I always loved coming here with Frankie. So when the recession hit, they were going to close."

Frankie again. His brother's death had played an enormous role in his life. My heart hurts just thinking about the loss of Frankie.

"So I bought the place with the promise they would work here. Marta makes the best food."

Emotions swell up inside me, and I can't hold Shay's dark stare. The heat has me pulling at my blouse. "Thank you." I start before I refocus on him.

"Thank you for sharing this place with me."

He doesn't respond, and once again, Marta's timing

is impeccable, almost questionably so. Two large plates of shepherd's pie are placed in front of us, and the smell has my stomach grumbling.

"Okay, I see why you bought the place." I tease when my plate is cleared.

Shay looks satisfied, too, as he sits back in his chair.

Leo arrives, and I thank him as he removes our plates. Two pints of Guinness are sent to the table.

"Thanks, Paddy," Shay says, and I'm staring at the huge pint.

"It's not very ladylike for a woman to drink from a pint."

"I think it's sexy," Shay responds.

I pick up the pint, and he grins as I take a sip. It's a strong taste, but I've always liked Guinness chocolates. So the taste, I know.

I'm watching Shay, wondering what kind of life he would have led if Frankie hadn't died. Would he still have joined the Irish Mafia? Would he have carved a different life for himself?

I'm lost in thought when he gets up and walks over to a jukebox.

I smile as the song '*Lady in Red*' fills the space. Shay holds out a hand. "Dance with me."

I'm getting up. "You dance?"

"I have rhythm." I take his hand, and he spins me in towards him.

"Good choice of music."

"It was more the title that caught my attention. I'm not exactly a Chris de Burgh fan."

Shay twirls me again and spins me back into his chest. I rest my head there as we sway, and it's another moment. I realize I'm gathering a lot of moments with Shay O'Reagan.

"Is this normal enough for you?" Shay asks after a brief silence.

I look up into his handsome face. "It's not even close to normal." I touch his bare cheek. "It's perfect." A lump forms in my throat again as I look up into his face. "You're a good man." A good man who made a lot of bad decisions that were driven by grief. I don't voice everything I want to voice. I didn't want to change the mood that was set here.

Shay runs his hand into my hair and places my head back on his chest. His way of not knowing how to deal with a compliment. I lie there swaying as the music changes from one slow song to the next. When I look over, I see Marta leaving the jukebox. She's been the one playing the music. I can't stop the smile.

"Long song."

The laughter rumbles through Shay's chest. "It's like someone keeps putting on new songs."

"Odd, isn't it?" I lean out so I can see Shay. My heart hammers as he lowers his head and captures my mouth with his.

This kiss is different from all our other kisses. It's gentle; it's slow; it's perfect. It's a moment.

Shay breaks the kiss and places one on the crown of my head before he resumes dancing.

"Marta, you could make yourself busy and get me some of your pie."

I look over to see Marta at the jukebox again. Shay's voice carries the love he has for Marta, the love he has for this place.

She isn't sheepish about being caught but winks at me before entering the kitchen.

The music ends this time, and we return to our seats. I drink some more Guinness and watch Shay drink his.

"What did you want to be when you were growing up?" I ask.

Marta brings out the pies and gives Shay a kiss on the cheek before she leaves.

"Women really love you."

"I hadn't noticed." Shay smiles into his pie before his gaze darts up to me. "Are you including yourself in that bracket?" It's a joke, I know, but when I think about him, I'm not sure I can be excluded from that bracket.

Fear. That's what I see fill Shay's eyes. He stops eating. "Jesus, Emma." He sounds horrified, and my face blazes.

"No, I'm not in that bracket, so you can lose the look of pure horror from your face, Shay." I bark too loudly, and it spoils the moment. I hate the way he's looking at me.

"What would it matter if I was?" I fire and drop my spoon. "Why, is that so bad?" My heart pounds rapidly in my chest, with my own fear of coming to terms with something like that and also with humiliation with how he's looking at me like I'm stupid.

"It would matter a lot." His tone is cold, and I see the old ruthless Shay reappearing. I want to reach across and touch him as if it might stop this horrible transformation.

"Well, I don't."

"Good." He nods and picks up his drink.

Marta arrives again. She must have heard us. I don't look up. I can't let her see my burning face.

"Excuse me. I need to use the bathroom." I rise.

"The door on the left at the entrance, love."

I can't look at Marta as I leave the table with humiliation heavy on my heels. What was wrong with me? I reach the bathroom and stop at the mirrors. The moment I meet my eye, I blink, and the tears spill.

I really look at myself. There was nothing wrong with me. It was him. This was his issue, not mine. It doesn't stop the burn at the back of my throat. I splash some water on my face before I relieve myself and return to the table. Marta is no longer there, and Shay has a face on him that would have a flock of sheep scattering for safety. At times he really looked like the big bad wolf. That's what he wanted the world to see. I sit down and keep my head high. It didn't matter what he said, I had seen the real Shay O'Reagan, and no matter what happened, he'd have to get over it.

I'm ready to confront him. I'm ready to lay it all out on the table when his phone rings. He gets it out quickly like he's on Who-Wants-To-Be-a-Millionaire, and this is a lifeline.

"John, I didn't expect to hear from you so soon."

John speaks, but I can't hear what he says.

Shay's face transforms, and when he looks up at me, trepidation drips slowly down my back.

CHAPTER TWENTY-SEVEN

O'REAGAN
AN CHLANN
SHAY

"The south?" I'm aware of how Emma is watching me as I rise from the table. I found him. Marik Ales. That's the man from the footage, the one who paid to have my brother killed—all for money.

"Send me the address," I say and hang up. Marta walks out of the kitchen; her steps become faster. As she reaches the table, she keeps a smile on her face. "Everything okay? Can I get you anything else?"

She isn't asking about the food. I stand up and pull her into an embrace that she doesn't expect but returns. I have no idea how this will all end, but her presence here has always made me feel closer to Frankie.

I kiss her head before I release her. Worry shows in her eyes.

"What can we do?" Her smile wobbled.

"Just do what you always do."

She gives a half-laugh before her attention turns to Emma. "It was lovely meeting you."

I don't linger on my goodbyes as I leave the restaurant.

"Do you want to tell me what's happened?" Emma's half jogging to keep up with me, and I know with her I have a choice to make. The way she looked at me earlier made me realize that I wanted her to look at me like that, yet having someone else to care for is dangerous in this world. Her falling in love with a man like me isn't wise.

I need to create distance between us.

I force a grin as I unlock the car. "It's good news, Emma. Don't look so worried." I climb in, and when she's in her seat, she faces me.

"We are going back to Meath." I start the car.

"Why?"

"You don't sound very happy." I shift into reverse, a welcome excuse for doing anything else but looking at her.

"I am." She stutters and drags on her seatbelt. "It's just you didn't look happy. I thought there was something wrong."

"No, everything is fine."

"I know when you're lying to me."

Her words have me tightening my jaw, but I laugh. "Emma, love. You wouldn't be able to tell the difference."

Emma falls silent and stares out the window, but from the set of her shoulders, I can tell it won't last long. She's festering and ready to explode, and I don't want to have this conversation with her.

"I don't like leaving my ma. Going down south isn't where I want to be, but it's where I need to go."

Like magic, the weight falls off Emma's shoulders. As she faces me, her features soften. "Why do we need to go now? Why not spend some time with your mom then?"

"We are going there now to say goodbye."

"It's still not adding up, Shay." Emma continues, and I'm wondering how much more she needs to be fed. She has seen and heard too much already.

"You got the man's location. The one you are going to kill." Her words swell and sound bruised like she knows I'm going to lie to her.

I tighten my hands on the steering wheel as I drive to my ma's. Emma stops asking questions. The moment I pull up outside the house, I wait to see if anyone comes out; no one does. I should just leave and go back down south, but the last time I left on such bad terms, it didn't sit right with me. I turn off the car.

"Are you sure I should come in?" Emma's voice carries a high level of uncertainty. She's thinking of my da, no doubt.

"No one will hurt you." I reach for the door handle. Emma's small fingers touch my arm, stopping me from getting out.

"Is it what I said about the whole love thing? Because I don't love you."

I detect the lie, so I give her a moment before I look at her.

"There is nothing wrong. You're overanalyzing everything. I don't blame you. A lot has happened, so every decision you need to look at closely, but this time, we are just going back south. You can plan the wedding, live your life. I really thought you would be happier."

Emma's fingers leave my arm. "Okay." She looks away from me as she speaks. I get out, and Emma follows. The front door opens, and I smile, a real smile as my ma smiles at me.

The moment I'm in reach, she hugs me. "I've been worried." She whispers in my ear while her hands run through my hair like they did when I was just a boy. It was her way of making sure I was alright after a fall or argument with my da. To think she's still doing it has me stepping out of her embrace but taking her hands in mine.

"Stop worrying about me. Da and I always fix things."

She tightens her lips together, her eyes glaze over, and she nods her head. I kiss her cheek and release her hands.

All her emotions dissolve, and she relaxes and smiles at Emma. "I'm surprised you haven't run a mile." She hugs Emma. "I'm glad you haven't."

"My dad and brother are always at loggerheads." Emma smiles at my ma, and I hate how much it fucks with my head. How much I want this for both of them, but I can't give them what they want.

"But I know Noel's really my dad's favorite."

My ma laughs and closes the door as we all go into the kitchen. "Connor adores Shay. They are just too much alike."

My ma walks up to me and touches my bare cheek. "Since you shaved, it's like looking at a younger version of your da. Brings back memories."

Noise on the stairs has me sitting at the kitchen table. Emma must have heard the noise, too, as she sits down beside me, pulling her chair closer to me. All I want to do is put distance between us, but right now, I don't want to see the fear on her face. I throw my arm along the back of her chair, and she leans into me until she's almost resting on my shoulder. I tilt my body, so I'm facing her as my da enters the room.

His gaze hardens on Emma, but he doesn't say anything about her being here. His limp from the shooting is still visible as he sits down at the table.

"Your da went by your place earlier." My ma sounds nervous as she puts on the kettle. I want to tell her we won't be staying long, but it keeps her busy as I stare at my da.

"I took Emma out for food." Emma sinks closer to me as my da's gaze lands on her, and I'm surprised at the level of protection I feel. "What did you want? To apologize?" I grin at him, knowing like fuck he did.

"Yeah, your ma was upset, and I didn't want that."

What a backhanded apology. I often wondered what my ma would think if she knew the things he did? What would she do if she knew the things I did?

"I don't want that either," I speak the truth.

Ma places a pot of tea on the table and pauses.

"We are heading back to Meath, but we just wanted to put all this behind us."

My ma smiles. "Of course."

"You're going back already?" My da is asking if I'm going to fix things with Liam.

"Yeah, Emma is eager to finish planning the wedding." Emma looks up into my face, and all the lies crash and burn. She looks at me with so much hope. Her eyes dance as she looks into mine, and my gut tightens. She was too good. I lean in, not thinking, and place a kiss on her red ruby lips. The tenderness she brings out in me has me feeling itchy. I look up to find my ma beaming at me like I'm the best thing ever. Her happiness pours out of her eyes and her smiles, and I tell myself that's why I just kissed Emma. To make my story stick. I would marry Emma, I needed to in order to be King of the South, but afterward, I would let her go. I would set her free with divorce papers.

My gut twists again, and I refocus on my da. "Uncle Liam has some work for me," I say.

"Give me the date." My ma sits down at the table, still swimming in her happiness.

"Two weeks from today," I say quickly, and this time when Emma looks up at me, I don't look down at her.

"I can't wait."

I refocus on my da. He nods his head. "We'll be there."

I have a cup of tea as my ma and Emma talk about the wedding. My da sips his while watching me. I want to tell him what I found out about Frankie, but maybe it's time to let them bury it. Maybe it's time to cut the cord.

My ma is smiling as she talks to Emma, and for now, she deserves her happiness.

"Can I have a word?" I say to my da as I stand and take my cigarettes out of my pocket.

"Just going out for a smoke," I say to Emma like I need to explain myself, but she's looking like someone pulled the chair out from under her. She composes herself quickly, and I head out the back where I light up a cigarette.

The minute my da steps out, I offer him a cigarette, and he takes one.

"I found out what happened to Frankie." I blow the smoke into the air. "Amanda didn't like losing money on the fights. So she decided by killing Frankie, it would keep us away."

I don't blame just him; I put myself in that bracket.

Turning to him, I see the pain along with the guilt that flashes across his face.

He doesn't speak for a moment. "She had asked me to stop fighting. But I laughed at her."

"You didn't think she would kill Frankie, Da."

My da faces me. "Is she dead?"

I nod and throw the cigarette on the ground. "Yeah, I shot her in the head after her confession."

My da grips my shoulder and squeezes it with his head bent. "It's over, Da. Frankie can rest."

"Thanks to you."

I pick up the cigarette butt and take out the silver flask that Emma got me. My father watches as I place the butt in the flask and reseal it.

"I'll fix things with Liam," I say as I place the flask back in my shirt pocket.

"What are you going to blackmail him with?"

"Something Jack did. I know something that could get Jack killed." It isn't true. Jack covered it up, and so did I. It was something his girlfriend, Maeve did, and that I would use to get out of this mess.

"Blackmailing Liam isn't wise."

I nod. I know my da is right. The last time I did it, he tricked me.

"I won't allow Emma to die."

My da is really looking at me. "She means that much to you?"

She did, but I can't tell him that truth either.

"I refuse to watch another innocent person die, Da."

My da grips my shoulder again. He's looking at me from under his brow. "Frankie wasn't your fault, son. Amanda took him, and now she's dead. I want you to find peace."

My da wasn't sentimental, and I'm tempted to laugh, but his face remains serious.

Peace is reserved for people like Emma, not for people like me.

"We'd better go," I say.

My da releases me. "Be safe."

We say our goodbyes, and some scared part of me doesn't want to leave the warmth of my parents' kitchen and their protection. I often feel like a boy again, one whom my da would protect.

But now it's my time to protect them. I'm no longer the boy who looked up to his da. I'm a man.

I don't see Lucian as I return to the apartment and pack. Emma packs all the clothes she got, and we leave. All the way back, I know I have to put as much distance as possible between Emma and me. Right now, she's asleep; her features are so soft. Each time I look at her, I can't stop the smile that spreads across my face; each time, I have to remove a curl that's fallen into her face.

I drive until the sky darkens. Emma stirs when we are nearly home. She sits up and rubs her eyes.

"There's a sandwich and drink in the bag." I point at her feet. I had stopped an hour ago and got us some food.

Emma takes out the water and drinks deeply. "Where are we?"

"We just entered Navan. We should be there in thirty minutes." I can't say home. It doesn't feel like home. Home is North.

Emma nibbles on the sandwich. "I can't believe I slept for so long."

"You were tired." I keep my words short.

Emma focuses on her food, and the silence stretches as we near the house. I slow down along the back road. Her clothes that had been thrown across the drive are no longer there. Lights are on in the house. I keep driving up the drive while opening the glove compartment and taking out a gun.

"What is it?" Emma's words are low. "Is someone there?"

I pull up close to the front door. "I don't know."

The minute we stop, the front door opens, and a man I've never seen before comes out. I keep the gun on my lap and roll down the window.

"Mr. O'Reagan?"

"That would be me," I say with a smile as I take the safety off the gun.

"I'm William, your new butler. We have been awaiting your return."

I don't put the gun away as he moves down the steps.

"Your father rang ahead to say you were coming."

That was my next question. I put the safety back on the gun.

"The bags are in the trunk." I hit the button on the dash, and the trunk opens. William calls over his shoulder, and a young version of him comes out, gives me a quick nod before helping William.

"I think you can put the gun away." Emma's hand touches my leg, and I glance down at it before looking back up at her.

She removes her hand. I slip the gun into the band of my trousers and turn off the car. Inside, three security men are waiting for us.

They are all new faces, and each one of them will be fired in the morning, including William and his son. I would pick my own staff, not snitches from Liam.

"We don't need anything tonight. You can all go home." I say as the last bag is placed in the hall.

No one moves.

"Now." I open the door and smile at them. They file out, one at a time. Once they are gone, I almost regret it as I know I'm alone with Emma, who's standing behind me.

"You didn't have to be so rude to them."

"Tomorrow, you can pick your own staff. All of them were selected by Liam." I explain without looking at her. "Now, get some rest. I've some work to do." I move past Emma and move down the hall. I'm sure I saw an office here somewhere. I find it.

The laptop on the desk, I'm sure, is being tracked, but I need to find out where Malik Ales lives. I can't wait much longer. I want answers tonight. Being back in the south, I know Emma isn't in danger. I am. So, I'm not wasting any time. I need to find the man who had Frankie killed. Once that is done, I will make the deal with Liam, marry Emma, and then let her go.

CHAPTER TWENTY-EIGHT

O'REAGAN
AN CHLANN
SHAY

We've been back in the south for nearly two weeks now. I've barely seen Emma. I try to keep out of the house during the day, and when I'm there, I hide out in the office. At night I sleep on the couch or in a different room. The distance between us should make me want her less, but it has the opposite effect on me. Between that and coming to a dead end with Malik Ales, my frustration keeps growing.

Some old security personnel that I've worked with before are stationed around the house. I expected a call from Liam asking why all the staff was changed, but I haven't heard from him.

He would know I'm back, yet he hasn't made a move yet.

A knock at the office door startles me. "Come in."

It's Emma. I don't know what has prompted her to come find me. She has kept her distance as much as I have.

"Yes, Emma?"

She shrugs; the uncertainty has her staying at the door. She's kept busy the last two weeks with the wedding and redecorating the house. Each time I come home, something else has changed. She couldn't be bored already.

"I just wanted to say hi." She steps in, her gaze travels across the space. "What color would you like to paint the room?"

I sit back in the chair. "I like it as it is," I answer.

Emma glances at me. "Why don't you stay with me at night?"

Her words have me sitting up. "I do. I just have work to do, so it's late nights."

"No, you don't. I'd know if you were beside me."

I don't answer her.

"Is this how a marriage to you is going to be?"

No. Because you will be free. "Right now, I'm just busy, Emma."

"Anything I can help with?" Her eyes grow bright with hope as she steps up to the desk. I close the file that has all the addresses that Malik Ales lived at. Each one was a dead end. Each one had me hurting someone to get answers that were useless.

"No."

"What do you want me to do?"

"I want you to leave me alone, so I can work."

Emma's brows pinch together like she's in pain. I hate

hurting her. "What did I do?" She isn't like other girls. She doesn't back down; instead, she moves closer. Her voice rises. "How can I fix this?"

I get up, not wanting anything to get back to Liam. I close the office door and turn on Emma, who's flushed with anger, and all I want to do is take her.

"There is nothing to fix. So keep your voice down." I take a step toward her.

She crosses her arms over her chest. "So now you are worried about what the staff thinks? You should focus more on your future wife."

I'd smile, I'd kiss her and take her if things could work between us, but they can't. I remind myself of that and go back to my desk. "You're acting like a child."

Emma's face grows redder. "Because you keep lying to me." Another knock at the door has me wondering what the fuck is happening today. Two weeks and not one fucker comes near me, now all of a sudden I'm a wanted man.

"Come in." The door opens, and I get up.

"Shay. I heard you got back." Liam steps into the office, and I hate everything about him, from the smug look on his face to his sharp gaze that takes it all in.

"I've been back two weeks now. I thought you would have come by sooner."

"I had business to attend to."

When he looks at Emma, it's enough to make me get out of the seat. "Emma, can you give us a moment?"

Emma snaps out of her daze and smiles at me. "Of course." I hear her mumble hello to Liam. He waits until she leaves before he speaks.

"Your father was rather insistent that I come over and speak to you."

"How's Jack?" I ask as I sit on the desk and light a cigarette.

"What do you want, Shay?" There is no pretense in Liam's voice, so I drop mine, too.

"You can't have a seat in the North."

Liam opens his suit jacket and places his hands in his trousers pockets. "Is that so? Are you walking away from our deal? That's a shame."

"Not quite. You can't have a seat in the North. But I still want a seat in the South."

Liam doesn't react, and I'm watching for any sign of how he's reacting to this. He's impossible to read.

"That wasn't the deal."

"It is now." I stand up.

Liam shows the first signs of irritation. "You offered a seat in the North for one in the South. What am I missing?"

"I offered to marry Emma to secure a seat in the South. That part I will keep to. The North is off the table."

I take a final puff of my cigarette before I stub it out in the crystal ashtray. My fingers are itchy to pick it up and place the butt in my flask, but I don't.

Liam doesn't say anything, waiting for me to explain my confidence. He's a clever man.

"The day Cian died, I was there."

"I know that, Shay." Liam removes his hands from his pockets and re-buttons his suit jacket.

"I shot him in the head," I admit. I still feel no remorse for what I did. His neck was broken. He was my way into the South, and I took it.

Liam's eyes light up in surprise. It's the first time I've caught him off guard, and I keep going, hoping to drive home my point.

"His neck was broken from the fall he took off the balcony when Maeve pushed him."

The surprise leaves Liam's eyes, and my gut tightens. He knows this already.

"Jack covered it up. I helped."

"Why are you telling me this?"

"You don't get your seat in the North, and the truth about Cian will be buried."

"I'm sure you told Jack that it was buried when he convinced me of this deal in the first place."

I step up to Liam. "This is the last time I'll mention it. If it comes out, I'm fucked too."

Liam doesn't move a muscle, and once again, I have no idea how well this is going until he speaks.

"Fine."

Too easy.

"You keep your seat in the South, as long as this knowledge is buried right now."

Now it's my turn to wait and hear what the catch is.

"Do we have a deal?" Liam holds out his hand, and I don't take it. Not having any resistance honestly frightens me.

"If anything happens to me, this knowledge will end up in Shane's lap."

Liam smiles. "I didn't think it would go any other way with you, Shay." He keeps his hand held out.

"Nothing happens to Emma," I add before placing my hand in Liam's.

We shake on it. "This is over, Shay. My son's name will never be associated with Cian's again." Liam tightens his hold on my hand, crushing my fingers.

"Yes." I agree.

He releases me. "Well, if that's all."

I don't feel settled, but I don't know what else to say. I nod.

Liam pauses at the door, and a part of me is relieved. I want the other shoe to drop now so I can deal with the fallout.

"Good news." He turns to me while still holding the handle of the door. "You don't have to marry Emma."

"Why?" I try not to sound so shocked, but I can't hide it.

"Her brother wants her back."

"And you agreed to that?"

Liam smiles, and it chills me to the bone. "I'm not an unreasonable man, Shay."

Like fuck. He pulls the door closed behind him, and I'm left fucking stumped. I stay in the office for a while, retracing over our conversation. It had gone exactly how I had wanted, but I'm not happy. I'm not happy with how easily it went, and I'm not happy with his final comment about Emma.

I sit back down behind the desk and place the cigarette butt in my flask.

I'm not sure how long I sit there when another knock sounds. I'm not in the mood to see anyone else.

It's Emma. She steps in and looks around. "He's gone?" She asks.

"Yeah." I'm looking at her now, and I should tell her that she's free.

She closes the door and pulls the cream jumper down over her knuckles. Red silky curls bounce around her face. Her green eyes focus on me, and I can tell she's nervous.

"What did he want?" She asks and bites her lip.

I get up from behind the desk and walk to Emma. Her eyes dart around the room but settle on me when we are toe-to-toe.

She's beautiful. I can let her go. I can tell her now that she doesn't have to marry me.

"To welcome us back." I lie and take her face in my hands.

I'm taking in the gold flecks that swirl in her emerald eyes, her thick lashes, and down to the spray of freckles across her nose. I let my thumbs run back and forth over her creamy skin.

Her red lips part, showing a flash of white teeth. She's fucking perfect.

I have to let her go.

I press a kiss to her lips. It's meant to be a goodbye kiss, so for the first time with Emma; I don't hold back. I kiss the woman I've fallen in love with. The knowledge has me breaking the kiss and looking into her eyes. I hadn't seen it, but now that I'm losing her, I do. I love everything about her.

She reaches up and recaptures my lips, and I can't resist. She's light as I lift her up, and her legs instantly wrap around my waist. She feels perfect in my hands as I carry her to the desk and sit her on the edge. Her hands move fast, trailing across my chest before she rubs the bulge in my jeans. I groan into the kiss, and I know I should stop this and tell her.

I do break the kiss, but only to quickly peel out of my clothes. She does the same, and each layer of fabric that falls to the ground has my cock growing harder and harder.

I step back up to her naked, and she leans back, spreading her legs. I want to fuck her hard. I want to fill her tight pussy with my cum. Pulling her body into me with my cock at her entrance, I place a soft kiss on her lips. One which I mean. The gentleness she returns, and I slowly let the tip of my cock enter her. She gasps with each inch, and once I fill her, I pull out slowly and look my girl in the eyes.

I can't tell her how I feel, but from the widening of her eyes, I think she feels it, deep down in her soul. Her hands grip my shoulders, and she doesn't look away from me as I push into her body again before pulling out. Her lips part, and her breaths grow heavy and fast. All I can hear is both of us breathing heavily as I allow myself to be free with Emma.

"Shay," She calls out my name, and it sounds so fucking perfect.

I can't hold back and pump faster. Her breasts bounce from the force, and her heavy breathing turns to squeals that make me go faster, burying myself as deep as I can inside this beauty.

Her eyes widen before they close, and she throws her head back and let her juices pour all over my cock.

"Emma," I call out her name as I pour my seed inside her.

She clings to me as I empty myself, and when I give the final drive into her body, I hold her while pressing kisses to her temple.

She's trying to catch her breath. "I missed you." Her words have my gut tightening.

I give her another kiss and press a few more kisses to her temple. "I missed you, too."

I don't let her see me as I drag her to my chest. I should tell her now. I should come clean about what Liam said.

I don't.

Most brides don't see the groom on the night before the wedding, but this is different. I've contemplated letting her see her family, but I'm afraid that they will tell her that she doesn't have to marry me. It's fucking selfish, but I want Emma. I've decided that I'm not giving her up. She's mine.

We stay in separate rooms, keeping some tradition alive.

It's the morning of the wedding, and I'm nervous. I've ordered James, one of our security guards, to stay with her every second until she's at the venue. I've also told them to keep an eye out for her brother. I don't want him to get to her before she walks up that aisle. I want Emma.

I'm dressed and ready to go when a knock on my bedroom door has me pausing. "It's me." My da's voice makes me nervous. I didn't expect him to be here.

"Come in." I turn away from the mirror to face my da. He looks proud as he steps into the room.

"You look good," I say. He's in a suit, and he fills it. I haven't seen him dressed up in such a long time.

"You too, son." He joins me near the mirror, and I can't deny how much we look alike.

"What are you doing here, Da?" I'm afraid Liam told him that I didn't have to marry Emma, and he was here to question why I was.

My da looks me in the eye. "Frankie should have been here with you."

"I'm proud of you, Shay." My da squeezes my shoulder before stepping away. "Your ma hasn't slept because she's so excited."

That makes me smile. I'm ready to leave when the light hits my flask that's on my bedside table. I turn back and pick it up, placing it inside the breast pocket of my suit jacket.

"Are you ready?" My da asks.

I smile at him. "Yeah." I am.

CHAPTER TWENTY-NINE

O'REAGAN
AN CHLANN
EMMA

"You are stunning."

I spin on my heels and face Breda, who is standing in the doorway. I blink like she might disappear. She doesn't. She's really here.

"Mr. O'Reagan told me where to find you."

Getting down off the podium, I walk quickly to her, dragging my dress with me. The moment I'm close enough, she opens her arms, and I step into them. I didn't expect to see anyone. I wasn't sure how these things worked, but I assumed I would speak to everyone after the wedding. "I'm so glad you're here."

She tightens her arms around me. "You look breathtaking,

but I knew you would be." Breda stands back, and I step out of her embrace. I'm looking behind her to see if anyone else has come to see me.

"They are all out front. Your dad is ready at the aisle to give you away."

My heart jumps at the idea of my family waiting out front for me. This is the moment I have waited for, and now I would marry the man I loved.

I force a smile. "Noel?" He's the one I'm thinking of the most. I want to see him and tell him that I love Shay. That it's okay, he doesn't need to stop the wedding and rescue me.

Breda's eyes dampen. She shakes her head. "I'm sure he will be here soon."

"You're telling me he isn't here?" Disappointment courses through me, and I try not to show it, but I can't hide the truth from Breda as she steps closer and takes my hands in hers.

"It's Noel. He will be here." The conviction in her eyes has me nodding.

Breda releases me and glances at James, who stands in the corner of the room. He doesn't speak, and Breda doesn't ask why he's there. He hasn't left my side for one second. He has been with me since I left the house this morning and was brought to Slane Castle.

"You look so grown up." Breda smiles at me again, and I turn to the full-length mirror. The dress is everything I could have wished for with its heart-shaped neckline. It's been handcrafted just for me, and the lace workmanship is stunning. The train runs down to the ground and a meter onto the floor. My hair has been pinned back, some curls manage to escape, but it's perfect. I do look older, maybe even a bit wiser.

Breda steps up beside me. "Are you okay?" She half whispers.

I nod as emotions clog my throat. "I love him." I turn to Breda as I speak.

Her smile widens, and she tuts. "He is a fine-looking man."

I laugh, and James glances at us, but I don't care. "You saw him?"

"He's the one who told me to make sure you were okay. He's at the altar waiting for you. He's very handsome. I'm happy for you, Emma."

I take a moment and drag in a sharp breath.

"Your mother would be very proud."

I look at myself in the mirror again and try to see some of her in me, but I don't.

"I can take you to your father now." Breda holds out her hand, and I take one final look in the mirror before I take her arm.

Today we own the castle; no other guests, only the wedding guests, will be allowed on the property. The castle is huge, and the tour I got a few days ago had brought my childhood dreams to life. The hallways are arched and wide, the sound of my shoes and Breda's echo and bounce back to us.

James trails behind us until we pass a pair of solid oak doors that are opened from the inside. The wedding venue is everything I could have imagined.

Snow-white drapes hang on either side of the room, and

they billow ever so slightly. The candlelight casts shadows over everyone. It feels magical, and when the music starts and everyone turns, the air catches in my lungs again.

My dad is there, and it's like a dream as he smiles at me. Everyone is smiling, looking at me, and I'm searching for Noel, but I don't see him. My heart starts to hammer. He should be here. I want him here. My heart continues to pound until my gaze lands on the King at the front of the room.

My breath halts in my chest as my gaze clashes with Shay's. My throat tightens as I take a step towards my future husband.

"Easy girl." My dad takes my arm, and we begin to walk to the altar. I had almost forgotten about him.

I blush at my eagerness, but Shay is like a God, and everything around me dissolves: all I see is Shay. His lip tugs up, and he smiles at me. It nearly brings me to my knees because of what I see in his eyes. I see something that I had thought I had seen the other night—love. That's what shines in Shay's eyes. I can't stop smiling as I reach him. My dad presses a kiss to my cheek as he hands me over. Flashes blink somewhere in the distance as I look up into Shay's face.

"Wow." His one word nearly undoes me. He leans in and steals a kiss.

"We aren't at that part yet." The priest has Shay leaning away, and I can't stop the smile. A few people close by chuckle, and I meet Shay's mother's watery gaze. She dabs her face as she smiles, and my face aches from smiling so wide. I feel like someone has cast a spell on me.

The music ends, and the priest steps up to us. "Welcome, everyone." He opens his arms wide. The altar behind him is dressed in a white cloth. A large gold cross with red rubies embedded in it catches my eye. The man before me recaptures it as the priest begins.

"Today, Emma Murphy." He looks at me, and I nod my head. "And Shay O'Reagan." Shay doesn't look at the priest; his dark gaze never leaves me. Shay holds his head high. His dark gaze swirls with pride and love.

I want to tell him I love him, but I will have my moment if he can't see it already in how I'm looking at him.

"Will join in matrimony. Everyone here will be a witness to this union." This time I don't look at the priest either. I can't look away from Shay.

From the corner of my eye, I see one of the solid oak doors open. I don't turn away from Shay, but chatter starts drawing everyone's attention. The chatter spreads before it turns to panicked movements as three armed men enter the wedding venue.

The ground shifts under me, and I sway as I meet my brother's gaze. "Noel," I say his name in disbelief.

"I made you a promise, sister."

No. My gaze travels to the gun in his hand. He isn't looking at me any longer. He's glaring at Shay.

"You planned this?" The hurt in Shay's voice knocks me out of my shock just as shots are fired and panic tears through the room.

Shay doesn't move as bullets fly around the room. People scream and crawl across each other. Bullets tear up the altar, the cup of red wine splashes across my dress, and I scream as I watch the wine soak in like blood.

"Stop!" My roar is no match for the panic in the room. But I see Noel with his gun raised. I'm shaking my head. I'm running towards him, holding out both hands. "No!" But it doesn't matter how loudly I scream. He's focused on one person.

Shay.

"Noel, no!" I'm being pushed back as panicked people try to scramble for exits. More shots are fired, but I'm screaming at Noel.

"Nooooo!"

It's like he can't see me anymore. My brother raises his arm, and with a look devoid of everything but pure hate, he pulls the trigger.

I'm spinning and turning as Shay's hands clutch over his heart where he was just shot. I'm screaming as I watch him fall, and the moment he hits the ground, I know he's dead. I'm screaming as more shots are fired. One rips past my head, and I'm being shoved by the crowd. My heart is shattering as I try to fight my way back to Shay. A woman grabs my arm, and I'm being dragged out a side door and into a corridor.

"You need to run." She releases me as she takes her own advice. I'm half running and trip several times over my feet. Clinging to a wall, I cringe as another shot is fired. The wall is cold under my palms, but I'm dragged away again—only this time by a man.

I break free of his grasp. I can't see where I'm going through the tears that pour down my face. My legs wobble, and I stumble out of the crowd and into a room. I can't breathe as I slam the door and stare at it.

The air is too thin. I can't breathe. It's like a swollen storm that's all caught up inside me—rose-red blossoms on my once-white wedding dress. My fingers play along the destructive substance as I drag air painfully into my lungs. The dress had been designed just for me. All of the trim was done in lace, each stitch done by hand. It was truly a masterpiece that was smashed to pieces.

The room tilts, and I dig my hands deeper into the soft fabric to keep myself on a small, navy stool. I focus on the white piano in front of me, the cover open, the white stool at an angle, like it's waiting to be used.

My vision blurs, and I close my eyes as I drag another breath in. It hitches on a sob that I can't hold in any longer.

It's their screams and panic that still pierces my mind. Hundreds of people were fighting to get over each other, love flew out the window, protection didn't exist at that moment, as each person fought for their own safety.

Yet, all the while, he had stood at the altar staring at me, knowing who was behind this.

It's the look of absolute betrayal in Shay's eyes that I will never forget.

Bending my head, I seal my lips together so the scream doesn't spill from me. He hadn't run like everyone else. He hadn't dived to the ground. Instead, he had stood before me in his dark suit looking like a King that had just climbed off his horse, only to find out that there was nothing at all here for him to rule.

Footsteps pound along the wooden corridor, and I tuck my head deeper into my chest. *Keep running, check other rooms. I'm not here.*

Brown eyes widening before narrowing flood my memory as guns released countless rounds of ammunition. Hysteria reached its peak as everyone scrambled across church benches. Large golden candle holders collided with marble stone, the impact rattling the ground.

Another sob has me slipping from the stool, and my hands touch the dark wooden floor. My polished nails drag along it as my mind grows more frantic. I replay the pain in Shay's eyes as I realize he is no longer a God with a shield around him. No. He became a man, made of flesh and bones. The moment he hit the ground, I knew the game was over.

My nails sink a little deeper until they bend and threaten to snap.

Right now, as I sob on the floor, the thought that races through my mind is, what have you done, Noel?

What have I done?

I should have found a way to tell him that I was happy. He had sworn on mom's grave, and I knew that meant that no matter what, he would keep to his word. I just didn't think he would open fire at the wedding.

More pain rips through me. I shouldn't have left Shay's body down there. Tears blur my vision, and panic builds inside of me until I'm ready to get sick.

The door bangs, and fear tightens its bony hands around my throat. They are going to kill me. This is my fault. I stand up, my legs barely keeping me upright.

More tears pour down my face, and I know I don't want to die. I can't hold back the sobs that steal the air from me. The doors rattle loudly before they smash in, and it's Noel.

"Emma." He's still holding the gun. Racing towards me. He looks all wrong holding the gun. This isn't my brother. I never saw him hold a gun, never mind fire a weapon. I'm staring into the face of a stranger. "We need to go." His hand tightens around my wrist, but I can't move.

"How could you?" I'm asking a useless question; I know that. I told him to get me out of this marriage. I made him promise.

"Are you hurt?" He's staring at the red wine that's splashed over my dress.

"How many are dead?" Pain laces across my heart and soul.

"Are you hurt?"

I jump at his roar. This isn't Noel. This isn't my brother. "No. How many are dead?" I ask again.

"I don't know, but we need to leave right now." He's pulling me towards the door where some guests still scurry past. He's dragging me out the door, and I can't think straight.

The image of Shay hitting the ground has me tightening my eyes. "Shay," I say his name as I'm clutched by pain that has me stopping in my tracks.

Noel tightens his hold on my arm and drags me down the hall. "He's dead. I shot him directly in the heart. You have nothing to worry about. But we need to leave now."

This isn't right. I can't leave Shay. My Shay. Dead.

"Why did you kill him?" The words tumble from my mouth, and I pull myself back from Noel.

He stops walking, his strong jaw clenched with irritation. "He took you away from us, up North. I couldn't get to you. I'm sorry it took me so long." He grabs my arm. "Emma, this place will be swarming with his men. We need to leave right now."

"I loved him," I say, but I don't think Noel hears me as he grabs me, and I'm airborne as he slings me across his shoulder. The world is upside down as he jogs through rooms. When he halts, I nearly fall from his arms, but he slowly puts me down, and I don't understand what I'm looking at.

My mind can't take anymore as I look down the barrel of a gun.

CHAPTER THIRTY

O'REAGAN
AN CHLANN
EMMA

"How? I watched you get shot?" I take a step towards Shay, who still has the gun pointed at me.

"Don't sound so disappointed." Shay's words are growled as he reaches into his suit jacket pocket and extracts the flask that I had bought him. "You didn't rob a cheap one." His grin is for show; I can see the pain behind his eyes. The bullet is still lodged in the flask that he holds. His gaze snaps to Noel.

"Drop your gun, or I'll drop your sister where she stands."

Noel does as Shay commands, and fear chokes me as the gun is pointed at Noel now.

"Shay!" I race towards him, and the gun swings back to me. I'm fine with that—anything to have the gun away from Noel.

"Please." I keep my hands up. His jaw clenches, and he's looking at me with so much pain that I nearly fold in two. "I didn't mean for this to happen."

"Remember the other day when Liam visited me in my office?"

My mind scrambles, and I find that piece of information amongst my sheer panic. "Yes, yes, I do."

"He told me I didn't have to marry you to keep my seat in the South."

Confusion floods me, and I slowly drop my hands even as Shay keeps the gun pointed at me. "I don't understand."

Shay takes a step closer. The anger has darkened his inky eyes. Pools of hate and anger burn so brightly, I can almost feel the flames lick my skin.

I want to scream at him that I didn't betray him, but I don't speak.

"You came into the office then. I was going to tell you that you were free…" He sneers, and it's like a slap. "I was so fucking stupid. I see that now."

Noel shifts beside me, and a shot is fired. I scream and turn to Noel, who's still standing and glaring at Shay.

"That was a warning shot. The next one will be in between your fucking eyes if you move again." Shay's words are growled.

"Shay." I'm walking on eggshells. He's too close to snapping. I've seen it before. The time he grabbed me by the neck, the time he lost control in the cage. I can't allow him to take Noel from me. I just can't.

His gaze swings back to me. "I wanted to marry you." His words are low, and he shakes his head the moment he says the words. His laughter chills me to the bone. "I fell fucking hard for you, love." The endearment squeezes my heart.

Tears spill from my eyes and enter my mouth. "I asked Noel to make me a promise, that he would come and take me away, that I wouldn't have to marry you. I made him swear on our mom's grave."

More pain flashes behind Shay's eyes. "How did you contact him?"

"I didn't. This was before I was taken away from my home."

Shay lowers the gun slightly, but not enough to make me comfortable.

Footsteps pound down the hall towards us. "Shay, you can't let anyone hurt Noel." My vision blurs, and he takes another step towards me. "He fucking shot me in the heart!"

Shay steps towards Noel. "Five people are dead, you cunt!"

"Please, Shay!"

Liam, Shay's father, and Jack stepped into the room. All enemies to Noel now. I can't breathe. Noel pales; he knows his actions are going to cost him his life. I just can't watch my brother die.

"That was quite the spectacle." Liam leads the pack of wolves.

My heart is out of control in my chest. I turn back to Shay, who's watching me. "Please!"

"My sister shouldn't have been forced into this marriage."

"There was no force. Your father signed the contracts." Liam steps up to Noel and kicks his gun away. A gun I keep my eye on. I sense someone watching me and glance up to find Shay's dad glaring at me.

Shay's movement catches my eye as he puts the flask away.

"Your ma was convinced you got shot."

Shay shakes his head. "Nah. I was quicker than the bullet." He sounds so self-assured, and my heart cracks.

Jack is the only person in the room who looks uncomfortable with this situation.

"You gave me your word that she would be returned once I gave up my seat." Noel continues, and he doesn't exude the fear that everyone else seems to have for Liam. I'm not sure if this makes my brother extremely brave or stupid.

"I did pass on the word."

Noel doesn't move, but he looks away from Liam. "Your word has no value. Passing on the word and keeping your word isn't the same thing."

"I'm the one who told him to stop the wedding. I made him promise me that he would." I speak up, and Noel narrows his eyes at me.

"Be quiet, Emma!" His bark surprises me.

Liam turns, and I'm not sure what to do when he pins me with his soulless eyes. "So you reneged on a contract you signed, too? His punishment could be yours." Liam's words freeze the blood in my veins.

"She will be kept out of this." Shay moves and steps in between me and Liam so Liam can't see me anymore. "She won't be touched." His fierce words make my knees wobble. I was faced with so much, but right now, all I can think about is that he still cares. He doesn't want me dead. A sob catches in my throat.

"My sister is to be allowed to walk away from this." Noel continues with his demands. Once again, I'm floored at his demands. He knows who these people are.

Shay's dad appears; he walks past Shay and me. "You're as brazen as your father."

I'm ready to move, gathering up my wedding dress off the floor, so it doesn't slow me down. Shay's fingers clasp around my wrist, and my gaze snaps up to his. He shakes his head. I don't move but look back at Noel and Shay's dad.

Noel grins, and I want to kick him. "What's a man got to do when he's faced with death?"

Another sob lodges itself in my throat.

"He should beg." Shay's dad steps up to Noel, and Liam joins him. I try to move, and Shay's grip tightens on my arm.

"I'll beg." Noel looks from one man to the other. "But my sister is let go right now."

"Noel, I'm not leaving you." I yank on Shay's hand, but his steel grip doesn't falter.

"I'll escort her out." Shay starts to pull me away, and I know if I leave this room, I'll never see Noel again. I'll never see that cheeky smile or hear his playful insults. I'll never feel the safety that he offered me my whole life.

"NO!!!"

I pull against Shay, and he drags me to his chest. "Stop it."

"I won't leave him." My vision wavers as I plead with Shay. He picks me up and ignores my words. "Shay, please!" Hysteria claws at me as I look over Shay's shoulders. Noel is still standing, and he smiles at me like he knows he's going to die, but it's okay because he kept his stupid promise. His name spills from my lips over and over again, and it's filled with the torture and pain that's consuming me. We are still moving, and it's Shay's dad who takes out a gun.

Noel and I race on the horses, and we are neck-and-neck. His laughter tickles my ear as he takes the lead, and I know I can't let him win. Just like right now. I know I can't let him die.

Everything in me snaps at once. I'm clawing and screaming at Shay, but he keeps carrying me from the room. "Please, no. I'm begging you. Don't leave him. I can't leave him!"

Shay tightens his hold on me as I fight like it's my own life on the line. I need him to understand what Noel is to me. He's the sleeping giant under my bed. He's the blanket that cushions me when I fall. He's all the goodness I've ever known. "He's my Frankie!" I scream at the top of my lungs, and Shay's steps falter. I'm gasping with adrenaline, fear, and hope. "He's my Frankie!" I shout again, and I look up to find Shay's dad staring at me.

"He's my Frankie. I can't let him die." Tears spill, and I'm pushing against Shay's chest like I can carve each pain-filled word into his chest. "I love you, but if you make me leave this room, I will never forgive you. Save him." I feel twisted too tightly, like at any second, I'm going to break.

The moment Shay puts me down, I'm ready to run back to

Noel. But Shay grips me by the shoulders. "You stay here." He shakes me. "Don't you dare move."

I'm swallowing tears and air as Shay turns to his dad.

"Wait." Shay holds up his hands, and I'm nodding like if I stop, this situation will reverse. Each nod is like a push behind Shay towards my brother.

"Shay." His dad looks past him at me like I'm something vile. I don't care how he sees me. I just want my brother to live.

Vi Carter

CHAPTER THIRTY-ONE

O'REAGAN
AN CHLANN
SHAY

She loves me. Her words are still reeling through my system, and I'm staring at Noel. I want to rip his fucking heart out. *'He's my Frankie.'* Her screams tore through my anger and pierced through the veil of blood lust.

"Shay." My Da warns me again, but I keep a hand raised.

I take a quick peek back at Emma. She's stiff, her eyes wide, she doesn't blink, and I don't think she's even breathing as she waits for her brother's fate.

"He lives," I say while looking at her. A sob pours from her lips, and Emma sinks to the floor, surrounded in white material from her wedding gown. She sobs into her hands with relief.

"You think you have the power to make such a call?" It's Liam who asks. He doesn't sound pissed off. Frankly, he sounds entertained by my confidence that they will do as I say.

"Yes, I do." I'm still looking at Emma. I want to walk to her and scoop my broken bride off the floor, but securing Noel's safety has me walking to my Da, Liam, Jack, and Noel.

"He shot me in the heart." I remove the flask from my pocket, the bullet embedded in the steel. My gut tightens at how close I had come to dying. What would have happened to Emma? My ma and da would have snapped. The loss of two sons would be too much. I push the dark thoughts aside. "The two other men with him are responsible for everyone else. Noel only shot me, and I'm willing to forgive him since I'm still standing." I take a pack of cigarettes out of my pocket and light one up.

"You think I will let this stand?" It's my da who pipes up.

I take a long drag. "You will respect my wishes as a King of the North and South." I stand straight and come face to face with my da. I'm asking for the respect that he should give me. I'm a King and his son.

He isn't happy, but he says no more.

"You have every right, since he only shot at you," Liam speaks up, and before I look away from my da, I see the warning in his eyes. The warning to be very careful of Liam.

Jack hasn't said a word, and he stands at his da's right shoulder, looking out of place. He has more of his ma in him than Liam, which he should be grateful for.

"You get to keep your life today, Noel. You are a very lucky man." Liam speaks up. I'm keeping an eye on Liam. Noel doesn't look like he believes us. I don't blame him. He should be fucking dead. I glance back at Emma. She's standing again, her eyes red and raw. She looks like she might crumble at any minute.

"But your seat is now gone." Liam's voice heightens, and there is a note in it that makes us all pay attention. "I have someone who will take your seat."

"Shouldn't we all get a vote on it?" I ask.

"I'm respecting your wishes, Shay. I'm allowing a man to walk away who should die for attacking a member of the O'Reagan family."

I sneer. Like he gave two fucks about me.

"So I am merely asking for the same respect." Liam opens a button on his suit jacket. It's a movement I have noticed him doing a few times while in his presence. Why he does it, I'm not too sure, but I'm making a note of anything he repeats, so one day, I just might find a kink in his armor.

I take another drag of my cigarette and wait like everyone else to hear whom he has selected. This is all premeditated, which makes my stomach curl.

Had we all played right into Liam's hand?

"Richard is coming home."

"Richard?" Jack repeats his brother's name like a fucking parrot.

"He is going to take a seat with us."

"Father, Richard wouldn't want this." Jack sounds so fucking confused, and I don't blame him with the lies his head has been filled with about Richard. He's been told Richard is off exploring his mother's country with a group of friends. How naïve Jack is almost makes me laugh.

"So, he will fill the fourth seat," Liam says, ignoring Jack.

"It seems unfair." My da steps closer to me.

"We are all O'Reagan's. The same blood pumps through our veins. So it shouldn't be tit for tat, brother." Liam's words have my da stepping closer. I shift, eradicating the distance between me and my da. His neck looks stretched, and that's normally when my da is ready to unleash hell on someone. That someone can't be Liam.

"You're right. An O'Reagan is an O'Reagan," I say.

Liam smiles, "See, your son knows exactly what I mean."

I stop my da by resting a hand on his arm. Liam is very aware that he's riling my da up.

"But, we should still get to vote."

"Cast your vote, Shay." Liam buttons his suit jacket back up.

"I vote no." I know my vote is useless, but I need to make them aware that I don't approve of Richard.

"Jack?" Liam doesn't even look at his son as he asks him to vote.

Jack looks from me to his da, and I know he won't cross him, but I can always hope.

"I vote for Richard," Jack says.

Liam smiles in victory. "He gets his seat."

Of course, he does.

"When is Richard arriving?" I grin as I put out my cigarette.

"In three weeks."

"Seems like everything fell into place nicely for you," I say as I pick up the cigarette.

"It does seem that way, Shay."

"Does Mother know?" Jack is still looking fucking stumped beside his da. I'd love to tell him why Richard was sent away to another country. I'd love to tell him how ruthless and fucked up his brother really is, but he will just have to learn the hard way. I'll be prepared for Richard's arrival and what that will mean for the Irish Mafia. To have Liam and Richard have equal power makes everything uncertain.

The idea that they would have had their hands in the North makes me understand my da's fear. Could he have known about Richard? I didn't think so, as he looks as shocked as I am.

"Of course." Liam steps away from his son and towards Noel. Emma is moving closer, and I stop her from going any further when she reaches me. I don't trust Liam around her.

"You are free to go," Liam says to Noel, who barely moved a muscle through this whole exchange.

Noel nods his head. His gaze jumps from me to his sister, where it rests and softens. "Let's go." He's walking towards Emma like he can just take her.

"She's not going anywhere," I inform him. "I might have let you live, but that doesn't mean you have any say over Emma."

"She's my sister," He speaks through gritted teeth.

"Noel, stop." Emma steps around me, and I hold my hands at my side so I don't reach out and drag her away from Noel.

"I don't want to leave Shay. I love him." Emma's words are low like she can keep everyone in the room from hearing her words. But they all do. Liam gives me a nod before turning to Jack.

"Let's go, son." Jack follows his father out of the room. His head is bent with confusion, but when they leave the room, some weight is lifted off my shoulders.

"We should go, too." My da is looking out the door that Liam had gone through. He's right. This place will be swarming with Gardai soon.

"It's called Stockholm Syndrome," Noel's petty words make me laugh.

"Don't be such a cunt." I take Emma's hand, and she glares at me with irritation.

"We need to leave now, love. This place will be swarming with Gardai soon."

"Come with us." She tells Noel.

I can't help but be a vindictive fucker and grin at him. I won, so now he can fuck off, but he agrees with his sister.

"What about Ma?" I ask as we start for the door.

I knew my da would have had an escape plan, especially at an O'Reagan wedding. The death of his brother's wife had left them all over the top about functions and security. I didn't have my guests searched. In hindsight, I should have.

"I've already got her safely outside, and she's waiting for us."

We leave the room, and I hold Emma's hand tightly as we move through passageways that have been mapped out for us.

We emerge close to the river that flows at the back of the

castle, and my ma stands near the edge, her hair billowing around her from the wind. She pushes it back as we walk toward her. The relief is instant when she sees both my da and I. She's running, and when she bypasses my da, I drop Emma's hand to catch her as she bursts into tears.

"I thought…." She cries into my neck. "My baby." Her sobs continue as Da walks to the river's edge with Noel and Emma.

"I'm fine, Ma," I tell her and unwrap her from my neck.

"I thought you were shot."

I grin at her. "Nah. Come on, we better go."

My da disappears, and as I lead my ma to the edge of the river, my da is waiting with outstretched arms and takes her from me. I turn to Noel and Emma.

I'd push him into the river if I could. I hold out my hand to Emma, and she hesitates. "Noel first," she says.

"He can manage himself."

I keep my hand out, and once Noel fucking moves and gets into the waiting boat, Emma takes my hand. She pauses and looks back at the castle. I can see so much pulsate across her face.

"We will get married, love."

She turns to me with widening eyes.

"Just not today." I kiss her hand before releasing it and get into the boat to help Emma in. Once we are all aboard, my da kicks the engine into gear, and we are speeding away from the destruction of the day that should have been perfect. I pull Emma close to me and nestle her along my side, blocking as much of the wind as possible as we race towards safety.

She still trembles beside me from the cold and shock. I remove my jacket and wrap it around her shoulders. I look up to find Noel watching us. His gaze dances to where he had shot me. It aches, and I know at this second I am so lucky to be alive. I tighten my hold on Emma and press a kiss to the crown of her head.

She was safe, and I got the North back. My ma is sitting beside my da, and when they look at each other, I can see hope. Hope that it has all ended and they can live their lives.

I had given them some peace telling them that Frankie's murder was resolved. I wouldn't rest until I found out who was behind it, but I'm grateful I can give them some peace.

In the distance, I see the flashing blue lights as several Gardaí cars race down the driveway to the castle.

I face forward with more hope than I've ever had in my life.

EPILOGUE

O'REAGAN
AN CHLANN
EMMA

"Get off the horse." I place my hands on my hips to let Shay know I'm serious.

"What, love?" He tries to give me an innocent look that he can't pull off.

"You can't smoke while on a horse. So just get off if you aren't going to take this seriously."

Shay crushes the cigarette between his thumb and forefinger. "Happy?" He forces a smile.

I drop my hands from my hips and smile at my husband. "Yes. Now take Lady's reins. Gently."

Shay puts the cigarette in the flask that he places in his breast pocket. Each time I see it, it's a stark reminder of what I nearly lost. He's replaced the flask since, but each time I see a flask, it's all I can think about. He's quick putting the flask away like it plays out the same reminder for him.

"Now what?" he asks once he holds Lady's reins.

I walk around the front and rub Lady's muzzle. "You be a good girl," I whisper. "Be careful with him."

"Are you talking to the horse?"

I glance up at Shay and stand back. "Tap her gently on the side, and once she moves three steps, pull the reins."

It takes Shay a few tries before he actually gets Lady moving. It's slow, and his body catches up with the rhythm quicker than most. I don't know why, but I expected that from Shay. After a while, he takes off, and I jog beside them for as long as I can until Shay whistles softly before telling Lady to go faster. His foot digs into her side, and she obeys.

"Traitor." I'm smiling as they race across the field. The sun blinds me for a moment, and I cover my eyes as I watch Shay control Lady like he's been doing it his whole life. I didn't think I could love anyone the way I love Shay, but the longer we are together, and the more I get to know Shay, I'm falling deeper in love with him.

Two weeks ago we got married with just us and his family and mine. We kept it intimate and quiet. It was perfect.

Shay turns and starts galloping back to me. I hear a vehicle and look back up at the house as a BMW pulls around the back. It was his dad; he had the code to the gate. He didn't like me, but we were civil to each other for Shay's sake. His mom, on the other hand, I loved. She climbs out and waves at me. I give her a wave back, and I'm genuinely happy to see them here.

The hooves pounding the ground grow louder as Shay makes his way to me. I turn back to him and drop my hand from my eyes; the closer he comes, the clearer the image of him gets.

"Did I tell you my parents were coming?" Shay asks the moment he stops beside me. He climbs off Lady with ease and rubs her side. "That's a good girl."

"No, you didn't." I meet him at Lady's side. "But I'm glad they are here."

Shay stops rubbing Lady and looks at me. It's a look that I don't think I'll ever get used to.

"I'm so fucking lucky." He leans in and captures my chin, kissing me.

"Yes, you are," I respond with a smile into the kiss.

"Go on up to the house. I'll put Lady back in her stable."

Shay presses another kiss to my lips before he walks off toward his parents to greet them.

Everyone is in the kitchen when I wash up.

"Ava, thanks so much for coming." I accept the hug from Shay's mom. She's always so kind.

Once I step out of the embrace from her, I meet Shay's dads' gaze. "Mr. O'Reagan." I address him.

"Emma." My name is clipped, but he has started to acknowledge me now.

With Shay's mom, it's so easy.

"Sit down, and I'll put a salad together," I say.

She's smiling. "I love your home." She's looking around the newly furnished kitchen. I love it too. It's decorated real Irish country style, not what you would expect from the outside, but I wanted something that was warm and welcoming.

"When will the food be ready?" Shay asks while closing the fridge door. I know he drank from the orange juice carton.

"Did you drink from the carton?" I ask.

"Of course, he did." Shay's mom sits down, but her voice holds such love for Shay.

"Actually, I didn't." Shay lies, and when he grins, my heart jumps.

"Food will be ready in twenty minutes," I say and open the fridge door, forcing Shay to move back. I take out everything I need for the salad.

"Okay, we'll be back in twenty minutes." Shay leaves the kitchen with his dad, and I can't stop the nervous flutter as they leave the room. I don't think his dad is bad, but whenever they chat recently, Shay always looks troubled. When I ask him what's going on, he tells me it's nothing.

"Let me help you." Shay's mom pulls me out of my thoughts as we start to prepare the salad together. It's so easy going with her, and we fall into a rhythm talking about the house and the honeymoon that Shay and I have yet to take. I've never left Ireland, so I'm excited.

"I'm thinking of Scotland. Shay wants to stay here in Ireland."

Shay's mom laughs. "Neither of you are very adventurous."

"Where did you and Connor go?"

Shay's mom smiles and stops chopping the onions. "Africa. We went on a safari; after that, we spent a week in Paris. Connor was very romantic." Shay's mom's smile is contagious, and I can't stop the smile that covers my own face.

"Maybe Paris could be fun," I say while thinking of the city of romance.

We finish preparing the salad, but there's no sign of Shay or his dad. "I'll go get the boys," I say to Ava as she finishes setting the table. I'm not sure where they are, but I'm assuming that they would be in Shay's office. When I look in, it's empty. I can hear their voices like a low rumble. They're outside. Leaving the office, I make my way to the side door that's in the laundry room.

I reach for the door handle but stop.

"I'm worried, Shay." Shay's dad's voice is clear. The window in the room is open, and I can smell the cigarette smoke.

"You make it sound like hell is about to open its gates, Da."

"It is. You think Liam is bad. He has nothing on Richard. Richard is a younger version of Liam, but he's ruthless, son, and unpredictable."

"I can handle it." Shay sounds irritated. "You keep going on about Richard, but remember, I've met him. I know what I'm up against."

"No, you don't." Shay's dad's words are growled, and then silence falls.

I can picture them glaring at each other.

"I'll be careful."

"I'd prefer if you and Emma left for a while."

"And go where?" Shay sounds really angry.

"Come back up North. You'll be safe."

Shay's sneer doesn't sound friendly. "I'm not afraid of Richard, Da."

"You should be. When he comes to take his seat, I don't think anything will remain the same."

A chill raced up my spine.

"You saw him do something first hand?" Shay asks.

I can hear Shay's mom call me. She's probably wondering what's taking me so long.

"No, but Darragh did, and I've heard too much about him. You know why he was sent away?"

"Yes." Shay sounds shaken now.

Shay's mom's calls are closer, and as much as I want to continue listening, I don't want to get caught. I grip the handle and open the door.

"Shay?"

Both of them look at me, and I force a smile. "Food's ready."

Connor enters first, and Shay follows.

"Everything okay?" I ask.

"Everything is fine, love." Shay smiles at me, but I'm starting to get used to spotting the smiles that are reserved for moments like these. Moments he won't share with me. Shay follows me, and before we enter the kitchen, his hand tightens around my waist, and he drags me back into his chest.

"Thanks for being so good to my ma."

I turn in Shay's arms. "I really enjoy having her here." I step up on the tip of my toes.

"I don't fucking deserve you." Shay presses a kiss to my lips.

"I know," I say, and his laughter has everything in me tightening.

We enter the kitchen, and Shay's mom smiles at us. Once we sit down, we start to eat, and the talk of Richard slowly disappears as we sit, eat, and have a few drinks into the early hours of the morning.

Leaning into Shay, I feel so blessed to have a man like him at my side. When he looks down at me, I see so much love in his eyes. I honestly never thought love could fill me up so much. But it does.

THE END

I hope you enjoyed *Mafia King*.

Mafia Games is the next book in the Young Irish Rebel Series.

Read Richard and Claire's story.

Download below:

Or read on for a sneak peek:

MAFIA GAMES

O'REAGAN
AN CHLANN
CHAPTER ONE

T he tennis ball bounces back to me like it has done a million fucking times before. Staying sane in a place like this isn't easy.

At first, I screamed that I wasn't mad. When a lunatic, aka mad dog, screamed that he wasn't mad either, I knew I was rightfully fucked as they dragged me to the back of the asylum. The nurse on duty enjoyed sticking a syringe into my neck a little too much. "This area is reserved for the real fuck ups." His words were warm on my cheek, and I grinned, even as my body failed me.

The moment they dropped me into a wheelchair, my legs were strapped down. As the nurse strapped my arms to the chair, I opened my sluggish eyes and forced a steady voice. "I'll remember you." And I would. Like a sketch artist, my mind took in everything about him, down to the mole under his left eye.

He pulled back instantly, and fear latched onto him like a starving person to a hot meal. I stared at his face as long as I could before whatever the fuck was in the syringe did its job.

I tried to stay aware as they wheeled me down a half-lit corridor.

"You're as white as a sheet. Lighten up." A male voice behind me broke through my foggy state.

"He didn't tell you; he'd remember you."

"He'll be secured in a glass box for his duration here. So relax."

"He's on suicide watch?" Shock laced mole man's words, his fear erased as this knowledge settled in.

"Yep. Director said we have to keep a close watch on this one."

Light moved across my lids, and I half opened my eyes as the wheelchair was spun fully around, the nurse moving backwards through a set of double doors.

Mole man stumbles when he sees my eyes open.

"He's still awake."

The man steering my wheelchair laughs. "I put enough in the syringe to knock out an elephant."

I grinned, or I hoped I did. That's the signal I sent to my lips as I stared at the nurse.

"I'm telling you, Gerard. He's fucking smiling at me."

We stop moving, and I wished I was more alert. I relaxed

my face and let my eyes close. The squeak of shoes halted in front of me.

Gerard tuts. "This is going to be a really long shift if you keep this up."

"He was smiling at me a minute ago."

"He's out cold. So stop fucking around."

We are moving again. I am tempted to open my eyes, but the drugs that raced through my veins have taken over. My will to stay awake is no match for the shit in my veins.

The tennis ball hits the glass wall before coming back to me. Rodger, in the next room, is screaming. His mouth agape as he tears at his hair. I throw the ball again, and he goes wild, frothing at the mouth. My lip twitches as he throws himself against the glass wall that divides us. His large body that has been deprived of anything healthy has no impact on the glass. These glass boxes were built to keep us in. I know this already. I have tried every single thing to escape in the three years I have been here, but this place is tighter than a nun's gee.

My tennis ball hits the glass again, and he loses his shit. I should really stop, but this is my only entertainment. This is what I have been reduced to. Torn black hair floats to the ground as Rodger continues to have a psychotic breakdown. His room turns red from the swirling light over his door. On instinct, I glance at mine. I've only ever seen it lit up once before.

After stuffing the tennis ball down between my bed and the

only stone wall, I get up and walk to the far wall that's made of glass, too.

My glass coffin holds a single bed, a piss pot, and a small locker with no door.

Three nurses, all wearing protective clothing, line up outside Rodgers' room. They look like they are ready to enter into a violent crowd. Rodger backs away and starts pointing at me. When he glances at me, I wink at him, setting him off again. He launches himself against the wall just as the door opens. My gaze flickers to the nurses who are entering. I don't want Rodger to get sedated too quickly. What was the fun in that?

He follows my gaze and dives away from them. He's quick; I have to give the fat fucker that much. He races to his bed and stands on it; the mattress dips with his weight. They try to pull him down, but he's kicking his short fat legs and screaming. I'm grateful as I watch the madness that there's no sound. The red light stops swirling, catching my attention. When I look back, Rodger is restrained on his bed as a sedative is injected into his ass.

Shows over, folks.

I turn my head and come face to face with Lenny, the piece of shit. I salute him, and he juts out his chin while wearing a toothy smile. He holds his fist to the glass, and I mirror the action. We fist bump as if we were friends. Not in my world, but in this morons world, we are friends.

There is nothing memorable about Lenny. He looks like a regular guy. I'd even go to the extreme and say a happy regular guy. That is the furthest from the truth. Lenny is the type of man you think of when places like this are built. Some of us don't deserve to be here, but he does—every single ounce of him.

He's all my anger and hate stuffed into an overgrown body. Sometimes when I look at him, I start to drown in my hate, and I have to remind myself that my revenge will be the sweetest thing I have ever tasted.

I let my lip drag up. He nods his head as his gaze moves past me. I turn as Rodger is carried from his room. The door closes behind the three nurses as they wheel him somewhere deeper and more fucked up in this building.

My body is tight, and I don't want to turn to Lenny. I don't want him to see a snippet of my truth, so I walk away and sink to my bed. I throw my arm across my eyes. It's a do-not-disturb sign or an out-of-service sign. I lay still for a while and picture her.

She's smiling, but I can tell the emotion isn't real. Her long piano fingers shake as she lowers them to the table; it's her tic. She clutches her hands together to stop the tremble, but the tremor never really leaves her fingers, and yet he never sees it. I do. I see everything.

The buzz is subtle, but I know what it is. I don't move even as my door opens. I don't shift my body, but every cell in me is alert and awake.

"Richard, you got yourself a visitor."

Hope surges, but it's stamped into the ground by anger that I don't display as I sit up. William keeps his hand on the door. His mop of red curls obstructs his vision. He blows hair out of his eye only to have it fall back. I glance behind him to where two more nurses stand. One steps in, holding a pair of chained cuffs. I'm tempted to smile at Gerard. His gaze narrows, his stance stoic, as he steps to the left of my room.

I rise off the bed and hold my head high. At six foot four inches, I tower over most of these men. Holding out my arms in front of me, I spread my legs slightly and wait as they circle me. I want Gerard to use the cuffs he holds. His left-hand keeps touching the baton that's strapped to his side.

William takes the cuffs from Gerald's hands, much to my disappointment. The third nurse has moved to my right. A drop of sweat makes a pathway down the side of his face.

"Hold your arms still," William states as he approaches.

I don't blink as he clasps the cuffs on me.

"Aren't you going to ask who your visitor is?" He asks once I'm cuffed and deemed non-threatening.

My gut clenches, but I refuse to allow any emotions to enter my features. "Who is it?" I ask. William smirks at me with bravery that he shouldn't own. "You'll have to wait and see."

I ignore his laughter as I glance at Gerald. He's watching me. There is no laughter or amusement on his face. His fingers still rest against his baton. He knew chains wouldn't hold me back if I really wanted to hurt someone. A lesson he learned the hard way.

Right now, I didn't want to hurt anyone. They had me curious about the visitor.

We leave my glass box, and the air is different. It's poisoned by the smell of shit.

"What the fuck is that smell?" It's Gerald who asks. William clutches my chains and moves me along like I'm a dog on a leash.

"It's Derek. He covered his room with feces again to prevent us from seeing him." This tactic I had seen used before. It wasn't the smartest thing to do, considering you were stuck in a glass box with the smell of your own shit.

I know the moment we are coming to the front of the building. The floor under my feet is tiled, the walls painted and not flaky.

They steer me right, and we move down another hallway that I have been down only once before. "Is this where visitors are taken?" I ask, knowing full well they aren't. There is only one room down here.

"Yes." William's voice carries humor, and when I glance at Gerard behind me, he's watching me. I turn back around as William stops at the door and knocks.

"Come in."

William brings me in and reaches for my cuffed hands.

"Leave the cuffs on."

I should have a million feelings right now, but I have none as William steps aside and my father, Liam O'Reagan, head of the Irish Mafia, comes into view.

He's seated behind the director's desk, sipping a cup of tea.

"Sit down." He puts his cup down on the desk as he speaks to me.

It's been three years since I've seen him and not even a "how are you?" Or an explanation as to why my mother or siblings never came to see me, I keep it all in I move to the desk.

"You can leave." My father speaks as I sit down.

"Are you sure?" Gerard speaks up.

"Yes." My father still watches the men over my shoulder. It takes twelve seconds for the room to empty and the door to close.

His dark gaze swings to me. "Son. You look good."

He looks slightly older. His dark hair peppered lightly at the front. His suit sits perfectly on his straight frame. My father gives away nothing as he waits for me to speak.

"What do you want?"

Disappointment flashes in his gaze, and it pisses me off.

"You show your hand too quickly." He picks up his tea.

I slam my cuffed hands on the table. "You came all this way to teach me a lesson?"

"No. But it is a lesson you clearly haven't learned. Contain that anger, Richard, before it consumes you."

Contain. I am barely breathing because of how fast the anger is pumping through my veins.

"Why are you here?" I ask, gritting my teeth.

"I'm here to take you home."

His words should have me smiling. I've fought to get home for three years, but right now, at this second, I want to be taken back to my glass box where I plot against them all. Leaving here would put everything into motion. It would have me spilling all the blood that deserves to be spilled.

"Let's go." I raise my chained hands in the air, testing him.

"Your freedom has a price."

I control the darkness that threatens to blanket my mind. Let me introduce you to my fucking hateful father. Everything has a price, most of what he has given me has cost me way too much, and I am pretty sure this time will be no different.

Working with my father had already cost me my freedom and landed me in this madhouse.

Download below:

OTHER BOOKS BY VI CARTER

WILD IRISH SERIES
VICIOUS #1
RECKLESS #2
RUTHLESS #3
FEARLESS #4
HEARTLESS #5

THE BOYNE CLUB
DARK #1
DARKER #2
DARKEST #3
PITCH BLACK #4

THE OBSESSED DUET
A DEADLY OBSESSION #1
A CRUEL CONFESSION #2

THE BROKEN PEOPLE DUET
DECEIVE ME #1
SAVE ME #2

YOUNG IRISH REBELS
MAFIA PRINCE #1
MAFIA KING #2
MAFIA GAMES #3
MAFIA BOSS #4
MAFIA SECRETS #5

MURHPY'S MAFIA MADE MEN
SINNER'S VOW #1
SAVAGE MARRIAGE #2
SCANDALOUS PLEDGE #3

THE O'SULLIVAN'S BRIDES
WHEN KINGS RISE #1
WHEN KINGS BEND #2
WHEN KINGS FALL #3

THE CELLS OF KALASHOV
THE COLLECTOR #1
THE HANDLER #2
THE SIXTH #3

SONS OF THE MAFIA
VENGEANCE IN BLOOD #1
ENEMIES IN RUIN #2
REDEMPTION IN CRUELTY #3
MERCY IN BETRAYAL #4
VOWS IN VIOLENCE #5

ABOUT THE AUTHOR

Vi Carter - the queen of **DARK ROMANCE**, the mistress of suspense, and the high priestess of *PLOT TWISTS*!

When she's not busy crafting tales of the **MAFIA** that'll leave you on the edge of your seat, you can find her baking up a storm, exploring the gorgeous Irish countryside, or spending time with her three little girls.

Vi's Young Irish Rebels series has been praised by readers and can be found in English, Dutch, German, Audible and soon will be available in French.

And let's not forget her two greatest loves: ***coffee and chocolate***. If you ever need to bribe her, just offer up a mug of coffee and a slab of chocolate, and she'll be putty in your hands.

So, if you're ready to join Vi on a wild journey with the mafia, sign up for her newsletter and score a free book! Just be warned - her stories are so **ADDICTIVE**, you might not be able to put them down.

WHAT READERS ARE SAYING

Editorial Reviews

"Vi Carter has once again blown my mind with another outstanding story. She never fails to create a masterpiece with memorable characters that leap off the page. This book is complete perfection."- USA Today Bestselling Author Khardine Gray

Vi is one of those authors who never disappoints. She weaves **LOVE & DANGER** effortlessly. ★★★★★ stars

I definitely recommend this book. It is **SUSPENSEFUL** and exciting. I enjoy reading Vi Carter's book. ★★★★★ stars

HOW TO KEEP IN TOUCH WITH VI CARTER

Visit Vi's website: https://author-vicarter.com/.

Join the newsletter: t.ly/yZWbX

Or scan the code below:

On Facebook, Instagram, TikTok and YouTube @ darkauthorvicarter and on Twitter @authorvicarter

Or scan the code below:

ACKNOWLEDGEMENTS

I'm very lucky to have such amazing readers and Beta Readers. I want to thank the following people who worked with me on this book.

Editor: Sherry Schafer

Proofreader: Michele Rolfe

Blurb was written by: Tami Thomason

Interior Formatting: Elise Hoffman

Beta Readers

Amanda Sheridan

Lucy Korth

Tami Thomason

Laura Williams

www.ingramcontent.com/pod-product-compliance
Lightning Source LLC
LaVergne TN
LVHW040133080526
838202LV00042B/2890